THE CLEAR LIGHT OF DAY

THE CLEAR LIGHT OF DAY

a Novel

Penelope Wilcock

David C Cook®

transforming lives together

THE CLEAR LIGHT OF DAY
Published by David C. Cook
4050 Lee Vance View
Colorado Springs, CO 80918 U.S.A.

David C. Cook Distribution Canada
55 Woodslee Avenue, Paris, Ontario, Canada N3L 3E5

David C. Cook U.K., Kingsway Communications
Eastbourne, East Sussex BN23 6NT, England

David C. Cook and the graphic circle C logo
are registered trademarks of Cook Communications Ministries.

Scripture quotations are taken from the King James Version of the Bible. (Public Domain.)

LCCN 2007931290
ISBN 978-0-7814-4553-5

© 2007 Penelope Wilcock
Published in association with the literary agency of MacGregor Literary.

Cover Photo: © istockphoto
Cover Design: The DesignWorks Group, Jason Gabbert
Interior Design: Karen Athen

Printed in the United States of America
First Edition 2007

1 2 3 4 5 6 7 8 9 10
062707

Down the avenue of trees
I can see
a spot of sunlight.
I'm trying so hard to get there.
(Grey Owl)

Through the window of the train traveling north, you could see this church in a field. I want to say it was a little church, but churches aren't ever little, are they, not when you get up close to them. Only in that landscape of fields and hills, away it seemed from any village or town, it looked small. Built in the familiar yellow-grey stone, a church such as a church of any imagination would be, rugged and enduring, ancient of days, obdurate, a sharp, insistent spire pointing forever to the absent reality of heaven. I would tell you the style in which it was built—words like gothic and perpendicular, phrases like Saxon arch and barrel vaulting move in my mind like vague shapes of sheep grazing in fog at the edge of a ditch. But I don't remember them now, and I can't recall their meaning. I would tell you just where to go to find that church in the field so you could see it for yourself—I remember that I noted the place so carefully and told myself I would search for it along the lanes there someday. But I have lost it now. I don't know the place anymore, nor even if I was traveling to York or to Liverpool.

I remember only that I saw it through the window of the train hurrying north—leaned forward in my seat to see it as long as I could. A church standing in a green field with no other building nearby. A border of wall or hedging, quite high, protected the field and the church inside. I have forgotten which it was, but I remember it gave a sense of safety, hedging about that sanctuary so it should be utterly safe, a place perhaps wherein one might at last find peace.

And I know I wanted to be there more than anything; that I believed if only I could find the way there, and stay there, it would be a shelter and a resting place. I cannot remember the place from where I saw it, and I do not know the way; but in some sense what it was has lodged inside me, and is obscurely, I think, a source of hope.

ONE

Esme held this piece of paper in her hands and read what she had written so long ago. Back in the days when she wrote those words, her soul had been full of searching, of yearning—and these imply always hope. Then the church had stood for something full of quiet and mystery: heart's desire, homecoming, belonging.

Possessed in those days by a fierce hunger and hunting her miracle like the gospel story of the woman twelve years with an issue of blood, Esme had wriggled and elbowed her way through the press of life and people to find a place where she might stretch out her hand and touch the hem of the garment of Jesus; and so it might bring the restlessness of her soul to peace.

An oddity in her family, Esme had the sense of being less respected than kindly tolerated. Church attendance had been an unquestioned element of her upbringing, and her family had been established figures in the large parish church that occupied the center of the affluent village where she had grown up. Equally unquestioned had been the expectation of material success, and with a combination of personal confidence and conscientious application, Esme's brother and two sisters had solidly achieved this in their lives. The youngest child of the family, Esme had dithered, occupying herself with temporary secretarial posts on the strength of a six-month intensive course when she finished high school. She knew she was looking for something but didn't know what. Above all she hungered for a plain and authentic spirituality, sufficiently free of aesthetic pretension to pierce the conventional mold that had nurtured her. She thought she had found this when, in her early twenties, she began to attend a Methodist chapel pastored by a young and zealous minister, fresh out of college, with a fire in his belly for witness and mission and a political edge to his preaching.

Inspired, Esme involved herself in the Methodist church. She fell in love with a young man in the worship band, a budding executive in a Christian music publishing company. His lean good looks and brooding eyes appealed to her sense of romance. His sharp and fashionable style impressed her. So did his perpetual air of busyness and preoccupation, and the various electronic gadgets necessary to support the maintenance of his extensive social and business contact network. His interest in her gave her an unaccustomed sense of sophistication. He was widely regarded as quite a catch. He himself felt the importance of choosing a wife who could be relied upon not to let him down. Esme was flattered to be chosen. He went about his romance with characteristic intensity and focus, securing Esme as a bride in a matter of months. Her family, perplexed by her tendency to drift, felt relieved to see her settled. Her mother hoped she would have a baby, but Esme's new husband decided they should prioritize the acquisition of a house and a car more suitable for his professional image. Esme didn't really mind; she was happy to go along with his plans. She admired him, she enjoyed the status that marriage conferred on her, and his romantic attentions made her feel treasured and adored.

Yet something restless inside her still persisted, and she began to feel positively trapped. All her upbringing drew her toward material consolidation, but a rogue element in her soul fretted to be free, as the stars and the wind and the clear cold light of morning were free.

She burrowed further into the spiritual teachings of the Gospels. She began a daily routine of meditation and prayer. She felt drawn to a closeness with Jesus, and in her heart grew a desire to find the paths where he walked and follow his footsteps into the wilderness and the hills.

From there to the parsonage had been a long slog, not what she imagined at the beginning. Applying to become a lay preacher, training, taking exams; trial services and tutors; others weighing her in a balance hung from the safe height of their established accreditation. Then—local preacher status under her belt along with years of service to the church in

Sunday school, Girls' Brigade, coffee mornings, pastoral visiting, committees, and Ladies' Fellowship meetings—she offered herself for ordained ministry: more exams, interviews, trial services. Booklists and references and medical examinations were required, her knowledge tested and her opinions examined. Psychological screening and police checking and theological allegiances were sought. Her financial status and her relationship with her husband were inquired into. And at last acceptance, then training, then probationary ministry. Then the ordination ceremony and the reception into the Full Connexion of the Methodist church, and two more years finishing her probationary appointment.

"Formation in ministry" they called those years of testing and training; and certainly she had found them formative. It had changed her. The difference between a vocation and a career blurred confusingly. She had to polish her social and professional skills. She had to study time management and people management and develop a circumspect persona of encouraging but noncommittal affability.

Somewhere along the way, her husband, after fourteen years of marriage, had found the authority and status of her new role undermining to his sense of masculinity and deserted her for the gentler contours of a hotel receptionist's companionship. He had left her with no children (for which she felt grateful now), and a deep, unexamined wound of bereavement in the middle of her, which the passing of time flowed around and washed over but did not seem to make whole. She let their house go to him, since she had a parsonage to live in—her family expressed misgivings at this lack of prudence, but Esme couldn't bear the idea of a legal wrangle.

Her sense of herself as a desirable woman seemed to have been cauterized by this parting. She chose to throw herself with determination into her work and to ignore the helpless, frozen center of her being. The time of tears and anguish soon passed. After it came a deep sense of vulnerability. Realizing that she had nobody but herself to rely on, Esme developed a nagging anxiety about material security. She had very little in her savings account at the bank, and no home but the parsonage provided by the church for her working years. She pushed this uncomfortable feeling of vulnerability to the back of her mind and immersed herself in the myriad daily tasks of her occupation. She got used to ignoring the empty spaces in her soul and the deprivation of companionship. Her colleagues had lives as full as they could manage, and allowing her congregation to see her insecurities and her loneliness was unprofessional.

Esme turned forty. More self-possessed, easy in her production of words suitable for public occasions, more sophisticated in her religion, she had grown less trusting of other people and chronically weary. On the journey she had developed a kind of spiritual irritation, an eczema of the soul, which itched and tormented her mercilessly as she sat in the homes of the elderly members of her congregation, listening patiently to their interminable, tedious conversation, their stories of the war and the details of their surgical operations and the descriptions of their infirmities and the progress in lives of their grandchildren.

She repressed this successfully—hid it almost even from herself—so that she was approved and even loved as a pastor, and her congregation said their good-byes with tears when the time came for her to move on from her probationer appointment, extended a further three years by unanimous reinvitation.

It seemed such a very long time ago now that the call to serve the church as a minister had been the expression of Esme's desire to creep as close as she could to Jesus. Her soul indefinably bleeding inside, she had thought that if only she could get close enough, near enough to touch the hem of his robe, healing would come for that half-ignored persistent inner sense of loss. Ministry had seemed like a spiritual thing, holding out the possibility of a connection to the presence of Christ. Then.

Now, so much later, it seemed just an impossibly complicated tangle of demands and expectations. A balancing act of appeasements and accomplishments. A muddle of paperwork and meetings, crumbling properties and aging, lonely, ailing people waiting with ever-decreasing hope for her to produce what they thought any good pastor should be able to manifest—a replication of the 1950s, with fresh-faced young wives' groups laughing as they prepared huge chapel teas, and devout businessmen willing to decorate the premises and calculate the chapel accounts in their ample spare time; and cheerful youth clubs happy with campfire songs and table tennis. Only with computer literacy, sophisticated child-protection administration, and high-profile ecumenical relationships as an add-on.

She was caught in the throng and press of the crowd that stood around Jesus. It didn't look big but it knew how to jostle and shove. She'd exchanged the relative calm of the periphery for the struggle of the thick of things, apparently without getting any closer to the hem of his garment at all.

And there was something else, which no one knew but Esme, and of which she felt every day most deeply ashamed.

Back in her student days at ordination school, immersed in the Christology of St. Luke's Gospel and the anti-Semitism of St. John's; Deutero-Isaiah and demonology and doceticism; the narrative theology of the Hebrew Scripture and liberation theology of Latin America; the empowerment of inclusive language in liturgy, the dark night of the soul, and the option of God for the poor, Esme had understood one vocational reality above all else.

Her college principal, scholarly, wise, and gentle, whom she loved and admired, insisted on the pastoral centrality of prayer.

The day Esme went for her interview to the improvised

office in the converted church building housing the ordination course where she would eventually undergo her training, the principal spoke to her about prayer.

"Your people will expect many differing things of you," he said (accurately, as Esme discovered), "but one thing all of them will expect of you is that you will pray, and that you will pray for them."

Rarely a day went by that Esme did not reflect on this uncomfortable, undeniable requirement. For she had all but ceased to pray. Somehow, these days, her life was so pushed and shoved by so many people and so many tasks that the possibility of reaching out to touch the hem of his robe, for her healing or anyone else's, had receded into a distant dream.

Every few days she made herself go into the church with the book of offices, read the readings, say the psalms, remember the sick, and read the pastoral list in the context of a half hour of prayer. The rest of the time she just felt guilty. She always felt guilty. And absolutely everything mattered a bit less every day.

In her visiting, perched on the edge of an old man's hospital bed, as she looked at his unshaven face and anxious eyes, his mottled purple feet cold without socks in inadequate vinyl slippers, the inevitable stirring of compassion was outweighed by the disgust and revulsion at the contents of his sputum jar waiting on the bedside locker.

I don't love people anymore, she thought, *and I don't want to say my prayers. I'm all churched out. I just want to be left in peace.*

She couldn't face a theological book, she couldn't pray, and the people wearied her. But if ministry had taught her nothing else, it had given her the discipline of keeping up appearances. From somewhere she found the energy to keep on keeping on, and she wondered wistfully if that in itself might count as a form of prayer; or at least of faithfulness— if not with people, then maybe with God.

It never felt easy.

Now, at forty-four years old, she sat at her desk in a new parsonage, the stationing process successfully negotiated, appointed for at least the next five years to be the minister of Portland Road Chapel in the seaside town of Southarbour, with pastoral charge also of two little country chapels, one in the charming and historic village of Brockhyrst Priory, and the other in the hamlet of Wiles Green. An unexceptional appointment, but daunting enough.

In the weeks and months to come lay all the business of taking into her hands the reins of ministry among people still strangers as yet. She must win their trust and their confidence, earn their respect. Learn their names, hear their stories, discover their feuds and their power bases, their silent hatreds and alliances. She must find their hunger and feed them there, find the wounds of them and touch them gently, understand their weaknesses and call to their strength. She must seek out her ecumenical partners and discover the shape of the

Anglican deaneries and learn the social and commercial profile of one town and two country communities. She must
acquaint herself with three church buildings and all that went
on in them. She must learn the roads, the shortcuts, and the
junction approaches. She must find a dentist and a doctor, a
better baker than the one in the high street, and a cheaper
source of vegetables than the supermarket. It all lay ahead of
her, and somehow it all would get done. Except the difficult,
shameful thing: They would expect her to take time to pray
for them all. And somehow it had died in her.

This August day she had been forty-eight hours in her
new home and was still sorting through the boxes marked
"STUDY." Going through a file labeled "Worship Resources,"
she had come across any number of odds and ends that came
under no other obvious heading. And there she found again
the piece of paper she now held in her hands, that brought
back so vividly the vision of a country church, glimpsed in
the blur of passing landscape, calling to the soul of her, even
now at the memory of it.

For two minutes more Esme gazed at the words she had
written years ago, then dropped them onto the pile of papers
on the floor, destined for the recycling bin.

August was precious. The new church year began on the
first day of September. Sorting through old papers and getting her new home into some semblance of order must be
done this week or never. There was no time now for reflection. There never was.

But as (turning as she always turned from the restlessness in her soul that never quite had found peace—not in prayer, not in study, not in fellowship nor solitude) she got up impatiently from her desk and went to the kitchen to make herself a cup of coffee, Esme surprised herself by saying aloud into the empty room, "Is there no one in the world who would really listen, really hear me, really see me for who and what I am?"

Having assembled milk, her mug, the jar of coffee, and a packet of biscuits, she stood waiting for the kettle to boil. Leaning against the kitchen counter, she gazed through the window at the dark bulk of the garden shed across the yard. Because of its darkness, her image stood clearly reflected in the window; a depressing reminder that in the last six years lived in the driver's seat of a car, in the office chair behind her desk, in the chairs at hospital bedsides, and in the armchairs of housebound members' sitting rooms, she had put on thirty-five pounds. Despite which she refused to be deprived of a biscuit with her coffee.

Perhaps here, thought Esme, as she contemplated her reflection, *I should turn over a new leaf. I could build in a program of regular exercise. I could go for walks in the country when I do my visits to the villages. Maybe*—a new idea came to her—*perhaps here I could ride a bike.*

Depressed by the vision of herself in the window glass, she made her way back to the study. For a little while she sorted papers, drank her coffee, filed things, and made notes, but with less and less enthusiasm or attention. *Just this week,* she told herself, *just this week to get prepared.* But something inside her refused to pay attention and be good. She toyed with the idea of preparing ahead one or two sermon outlines, glancing through the lectionary for the Year C readings for September. But the same something inside dug in its heels and wouldn't, and in the end, she sat with her elbows on the desk, gazing out into the garden.

I want to go outside, she thought, *it's lovely outside.*

Abandoning her papers and boxes of unsorted belongings, Esme grabbed her bag, stepped purposefully out of the house, got into her car, and fished in the glove compartment for the new map book she had bought. She decided that a foray to explore Wiles Green could reasonably count as work. She had been there once only, on the day of her visit eighteen months ago to meet the stewards in each of her three chapels. Beside the grim and crumbling majesty of Portland Road Chapel in Southarbour, Wiles Green Chapel had looked like a doll's house; small and trim, set back from the road, surrounded by a flower border, sheltered by a tree, and enclosed on three sides by a yew hedge—the fourth side being open to the car park. A square gap had been neatly trained in the hedge as it grew, to accommodate the Wayside Pulpit containing a notice, that when last she had seen it had read, SEEK YE THE LORD WHILE YET HE MAY BE FOUND.

Inside as outside, Esme had been impressed to find the chapel well maintained and lovingly kept; austere and free of religious art or any embellishment, but with an indefinable sense of good cheer.

On that first day her interest had been focused entirely on the chapel. She thought it now time to explore the village. She had at least located the post office and the supermarket in Southarbour, and spent a morning wandering in the busy village of Brockhyrst Priory with its thriving family businesses, its teashops, and gift shops; but Wiles Green she remembered only as an indeterminate scattering of houses, and a pub—a place of no real consequence.

She refreshed her memory from the map as to the directions and set out to explore. She left the town and drove through the beauty of the late-summer countryside, through Brockhyrst Priory with its picturesque winding main street— you couldn't see the chapel from here, it was up behind the houses on Market Street—left at the fire station, out through fields and woodland, left at the crossroads, right at the next turning, down the hill through a lane that resembled a dry stream running between steep banks of earth fixed by the gnarled roots, green with moss, of trees that met in a canopy overhead and carpeted the road with leaf mold.

Esme remembered from her earlier visit how long the lane had seemed, tunneling through the countryside with a sense of entering depths, passing the limits of civilization. *I must drive out here at night*, she promised herself, *there will be badgers, foxes—maybe even hedgehogs and owls!* The journey had a suggestion of having mistaken the way, a profound sense of secrecy, wilderness. *I hope I'm not lost,* Esme began to think. With relief she caught sight of a rather mossy sign partly obscured by the hedge, on which she could make out most of the letters of *Wiles Green.* The road remained uncompromisingly narrow but climbed a hill past a cluster of farm buildings and cottages and then turned a corner into the hundred yards or so that made up its village street. There was the pub—*The Bull*—the ancient and delightful parish church of St. Raphaels, a dozen or so houses, mostly cottages but some more imposing residences, and a temporary-looking structure built of corrugated iron with a handmade sign over the door saying *Village Post Office & Stores.* Along the road edges the pavement came and went, and there were so many trees and hedges that the houses seemed half-buried in the undergrowth. Leaving behind these buildings, Esme came to a turning whose sign said CHAPEL LANE, and she drove along it to remind herself of her chapel's situation.

Someone had hung a new sign in the Wayside Pulpit saying THE WAGES OF SIN IS DEATH, and Esme made a mental note to order a new set of posters. She had brought the keys with her, but something in the chapel's neat appearance looked so closed and complete that she felt disinclined to go in. She could remember the interior. She would soon be preaching there. Today she could take the chance to explore places she would be less certain to see later on. She turned around in the car park and made her way back to the parish church.

There she could find no designated parking place, so she pulled off the road as well as she could and got out of her car to look in the churchyard. Roses sprawled on the old rough stones, lichened yellow, of the wall, and trees spread welcome shade over the higgledy-piggledy graves in the long grass. *Oh, but it's so pretty,* thought Esme as she ventured slowly up the path, gazing at it all, and when she reached the door and tried it, she found to her delight that it was open. She stepped inside, smelling the holy smell of cool stone and incense and beeswax candles. The sun through stained-glass windows dappled the deep golden brown of the pews with rich colors. Esme sat down in the back pew, and after a minute, pulled toward her one of the kneelers covered in hairy woolen fabric of a gentle blue. For the first time in years, she knelt down to pray, wondering fleetingly as she slid to her knees why Methodists never do.

At first she just knelt, and let the peace of the place slide into her soul, but as she did so the calloused resistance began to ease and words started to form. She whispered, "What I'd really like, please, if it can be done, is someone to be my friend. It can be so very lonely. Please." And then added, with a pang of guilt, "And help me to serve you well. And all the people."

She held the moment in silence—what was it about prayer that could so uncover the heart's surprising secrets? Surrounded every day by people, her phone ringing from breakfast time to bedtime, her diary full two months ahead and almost every hour accounted for, days off jealously guarded, she had not realized until she took this fleeting space of solitary prayer that the hunger and the restlessness had to do with loneliness; the longing to be really known and accepted and understood—not only loved and needed. *Someone to be my friend.* The thought that had come to her shone faintly with hope. Perhaps it would be. Maybe in the chapel communities she had come to serve she might find other women like herself—professional, single, with interests in common. If so, there might be a chance of some fun, projects shared, leisure outings together. A friend.

The habitual guilt began to pull at her. Here she was, kneeling in prayer—should she not seize the moment as an opportunity, commit her ministry in this area to God, intercede for her stewards, her treasurer, her pastoral visitors, her youth work, her colleagues? Probably. But here she felt somehow a necessity to take her prayer no further than honesty, to offer to God the simple truth of the desire of her heart: *someone to be my friend.*

Esme stayed where she was, looking at the sturdy stone pillars, the rood screen, and the altar beyond; the carved wooden pulpit and the polished brass-eagle lectern bearing the heavy Bible open on its spread wings. She could not quite place from where comfort came, but she was stilled by the profound serenity of the ancient place steeped in so many people's secret prayers.

After a long while she got to her feet, and slowly, communing with the living sense of the place, walked back down the aisle to the heavy door, her hand caressing the dark wooden curves of the pew ends as she passed. Before she left, she stopped and turned to look down the length of the church to its altar under the east window. "Thank you," she whispered. "Good-bye."

Out in the churchyard, the sunlight seemed dazzling. Esme lingered there a little longer, looking at the inscriptions on the graves as she wandered along the path that led back to the road, enjoying the warmth and the birdsong, watching a beetle on the grass stems and the bees visiting the flowers against the wall. With a sigh she went out through the lych-gate. There was so much still to do.

Out on the roadside, beside her car, she found a very old lady, whose clothing seemed to be composed of assorted loose layers in fabrics of a variety of hues but without the decoration of patterns or flowers, creating rather the effect of robes. Her hair, grey and disheveled, was more or less assembled in two very long plaits. On her head, she wore a multicolored African hat and some curious, primitive tribal earrings. Her right hand gripped the silver top of a walking stick. *A jazz prophet*, thought Esme. In spite of the overall impact of her appearance, undoubtedly the most arresting thing about this old lady was the unswerving gaze of her extremely dark eyes, which glittered at Esme as she emerged from the churchyard.

"Your car." It was a statement, not a question.

"Yes," Esme said. "Is there a problem?"

The old lady looked at her.

"Supposing," she said, "I was to bring out a table and chair and set it up in the middle of the road to play cards, would that be a problem?"

Esme blinked uncertainly. The old lady continued to fix her with her gaze. She didn't look cross, but something momentous regarded Esme through those bright eyes set in the wrinkled brown face.

The old lady continued, "There's something about cars that gives folks the idea that the whole world must make way for them while at the same time they have absolute right to block the way of others. 'Tisn't so. Pavements is for pedestrians. We may not have much of a pavement in Wiles Green, but such as there is, is entirely filled up by your car."

"There's nowhere else to park by the church," said Esme reasonably.

"Put it somewhere else, then," said the old lady, "and walk."

The sense of well-being Esme had found in the quietness of the church evaporated. Why was life like this? Where did they come from, these vile old ladies who made a career out of being rude and finding fault and telling people off? Did God send them to test our faith in the divine image within the human soul and the goodness of creation? Who needed a belief in a personal devil—wouldn't old ladies do just as well?

She looked down at the ground and counted to ten slowly.

"I am so sorry," she said. "I'll move it straight away."

The old lady's wrinkled face reassembled into a most mischievous grin. "There's patience!" she said, and held out her hand to Esme, "Seer Ember."

These two words meant nothing to Esme, but she shook the hand offered her, shook it politely, and said, "Pleased to meet you," climbed into the safety of her car, and left.

As she pulled away, she glanced into her mirror, chancing therefore to see the old lady, her medley of clothing bright in the afternoon sun, prodding the hedgerow moodily with her stick and pausing to spit in the road as she ambled along its verge. Esme kept her in view in amazement, until the narrowness of the road claimed her undivided attention. She had met the steward of Wiles Green Chapel. She had met this extraordinary person. She wondered who else might live in Wiles Green.

Following the lane back along its twists and turns the way she had come, Esme glanced along the unexplored ways that led off it here and there, saving them for another day. She paused at the crossroads for a very shabby and antiquated green-painted open truck to pass, otherwise meeting very little traffic until her passage through the center of Brockhyrst Priory coincided with traders and customers making their way home from the farmers' market just closing in the village hall.

When she reached the parsonage, and made the now almost familiar turn into her short driveway, Esme made a determined effort to muster the resolve necessary for tackling her desk work again as soon as she came in through the door. She began by visiting the kitchen to collect a cup of coffee and a biscuit (two biscuits—she ate the first while the kettle was boiling), which she carried along the passage to her study.

She turned on her computer and created a new file, set up the page margins, and font size and centered a heading: *Sermon Notes for Portland Street, 10:30, September 6th.* She pressed the return key and centered a subheading: *Twenty-third Sunday in Ordinary Time.* And she gazed at the empty screen, ate her biscuit, sipped her coffee, gazed at the empty screen, played a game of solitaire, and returned to the file she had begun.

The Twenty-third Sunday in Ordinary Time. "Ordinary Time."

Esme thought about all the things that happen to ordinary people in their lives in ordinary time. A baby being born to a girl of seventeen in a precarious partnership, living on welfare benefit, and housed in a basement flat. A woman of forty-eight opening a doctor's letter telling her the ominous results of her smear test. A teenager who desperately wants to be a veterinarian waiting for the results of his university application. A five-year-old clutching his mother's hand as they walk together through the infant school gates at the start of the autumn term, trying to find the courage for separation. A housewife married twenty-six years, looking across the street at young lovers locked in passionate embrace, wistful for the passing of the years and so much that slips away almost unnoticed. A young man who has tried and tried to find employment, wondering about joining the army. Ordinary time is the place where people are born and die. It is full of hopes and regrets and scored over and over with moments of deep emotion.

And *ordinary* means also that which is ordained; the paths that cross, the eyes that meet, the decisions made, and bargains struck that shape the future. She thought of how as an eight-year-old child, during the school holidays, she had tagged along with her mother going to fulfill her turn on the church-cleaning roster. While Mother rubbed the fragrant lavender wax polish onto the pews with the stiff, waxy putting-on rag and then buffed them vigorously to a beautiful deep shine with a clean duster, Esme wandered about the church, touching the cool stone and squinting through the grating set in the floor, exploring the choir stalls, and eventually, greatly daring, climbing the steps into the pulpit, like a tree house just right for a child. She stroked the faded velvet cloth on the sloping pulpit desk, peered over the edge at the rows of pews below, and wondered what it would be like to be the minister, standing here preaching the Sunday sermon. She wondered if St. Raphaels had done something to reach that child buried under the passing years. An ordinary child in ordinary time, growing into an ordinary woman with all the ordinary griefs and doubts and insecurities. Memories might open a way back to the lost self hidden by her professional persona with its collateral brittleness and weariness.

She reflected that *ordinary* means just normal and ordained; that even the casualness of every day is on purpose, meant to be. The net of heaven is wide. Not even the whisper of a thought slips through it. This imposes grave responsibility. Sometimes it brings hope as well.

Esme began to type. She had no formed ideas as yet. She was just copying the words of the Collect for the Twenty-third Sunday in Ordinary Time:

O God, you bear your people ever on your heart and mind. Watch over us in your protecting love, that, strengthened by your Spirit, we may not miss your way for us—and then the phone rang.

On the upper side of the telephone receiver, to catch her attention before she lifted it from its cradle, Esme had attached a sticker on which she had printed in bold letters, BREATHE. SMILE, and drawn a little flower. Despite this, she felt a small frown of irritation and an involuntary compression of her lips as she grabbed the thing that had scattered her train of thought and said into it, crisply, "Hello. Esme Browne."

"Um … Marcus Griffiths here."

Esme recognized already the deceptively absentminded tone of her senior steward of the chapel at Brockhyrst Priory.

"Oh, hello, Marcus." She tried to sound friendly, and then waited while he paused.

"Look—am I disturbing you? I mean, you aren't yet here, are you. Tell me if I'm intruding."

Yes, you are, leave me alone, thought Esme as she replied, "Of course not, it's lovely to hear from you. How can I help?"

"Oh, well—" he hesitated. "I mean really, feel free to say no—but really. Hilda and I thought that you might be relishing the peace, but on the other hand you might be lonely. And if you're not relishing the peace, if you'd like to—I mean, please, just say no—would you like to pop over for supper? This evening—if you'd like to? Not if you'd rather not."

He sounded so thoroughly apologetic that Esme hadn't the heart to say no. She accepted his invitation, thanked him, and went back to her sermon notes, added a few observations on the lectionary readings and on what it meant to be ordinary. She made a list of appropriate hymns and then shut down her computer and abandoned her study for a hot bath.

And so, for the second time that day, as the evening chill mingled with the amber of late sunshine, she found herself driving out to Wiles Green, where Marcus Griffiths, a retired bookseller, lived with his wife, Hilda.

Their home proved to be a comfortable family house, with pleasing proportions and low ceilings, furnished with unpretentious but lovely antique furniture (fruitwood, rural craftsmanship with an unerring aesthetic eye), armchairs, and a generous sofa occupied by a truculent-looking border terrier who watched her out of one eye. The large open fireplace was filled, in these days still hot at the end of the summer, with an arrangement of dried grasses and seed-heads. An assortment of paintings hung on the walls, striking modern oil or acrylic portraits mixing surprisingly successfully with more traditional landscapes and watercolor sketches. The ancient oak floorboards were softened with Eastern rugs whose colors glowed with the richness of silk. Taking all this in, Esme reflected that Marcus must have been a spectacularly good bookseller.

A tall, thin man, with sparse hair combed back from his brow, Marcus greeted her at the door with impeccable courtesy. A vague, indefinable abstraction hung in the air about him like the dust around an old easy chair that has had its cushions too roughly handled. His glasses provided a dual function—they focused the acute observation of his very intelligent gaze; they also served as a form of screen or hide for moments when he preferred to make himself absent. Esme thought he looked both perceptive and kind, which reinforced the impression she had received at their first meeting.

He stood aside to allow her to enter his living room ahead of him. Drawn to the view of the garden through the French windows framed in heavy linen floral curtains at the far end of the room, Esme walked across to look out at the profusion of late-summer flowers in the herbaceous borders, at the stone fountain in the lilied pond, and at the grouped shrubs, stone urns, and statuary that stood here and there, dwarfed by mature and graceful trees.

"Goodness me!" she exclaimed. "Your garden's massive!" adding quickly, "and so beautiful!"

Marcus wandered across the room to stand beside her.

"A little overblown, perhaps, at this time of year. I enjoy it at all times, but I prefer the sculptural qualities of a winter garden. So many flowers can be a little cloying at times. Rather an excess of pink, wouldn't you say? Wine?"

As he traveled across the room to fill with a generous helping of wine one of the heavy crystal glasses on the sideboard, Marcus bellowed, "Hilda!" in the direction of the door, and this was rewarded by a sense of energetic bustling that heralded his wife's arrival.

Stout and well made, a handsome woman conventionally and expensively dressed, wearing no makeup but with immaculately dressed hair, Hilda had bold, dark eyes and a determined chin that gave notice of a forceful character.

"Marcus, how remiss! I had no idea! Welcome, my dear, welcome! Won't you sit down? I didn't hear you come in—are you parked outside? It's not like me to overlook a car drawing up. I'm so glad you could come! Have you been offered—ah, yes, good—let me find a little mat for that glass. You do eat meat, my dear? I was most annoyed with Marcus—'What if she's *vegetarian?*' I said to him. 'You must check; you must always check, times have changed, these young idealistic types live on the most extraordinary things, lentils and wild rice,' but he wouldn't call you back to check, he *would not!* Not that we eat so much meat ourselves nowadays, a little savory pâté, a rasher of bacon, the odd chop. When the family was here

33

with us, it was different; of course, it was all different then! My goodness! My brood could divulge a whole bird at one sitting!"

Marcus's eyes flickered momentarily as Esme registered the strangeness of this last remark, but he said merely, "*Do you eat meat, Esme? If not, I've no doubt we can find something else.*"

Esme reassured them that she did eat meat, though like most people, less now than once; and when later they sat down to dine (at an exquisite beech-wood dining suite, the table laid with Georgian silver and damask napkins), the selection of vegetables grown in the garden accompanying tender cuts of locally raised meat with delicious gravy made her glad she had accepted this invitation to supper.

Inevitably, their conversation drifted to matters connected with the chapel, and Esme discovered that in addition to Marcus's responsibility as senior steward, he and Hilda both were key members of the finance and property committee.

"It's been a difficult year for decisions. My dear, your wine is low—Marcus! Esme's wine is low! Driving? Then some tonic water? Marcus! Very difficult. It seems not five minutes since we were raising funds for the replacing of the windows—I won't say 'replacement windows' because in a conservation area that's hardly what they are; and besides as Marcus says, it's such a quaint idea—I mean they are actually windows; but you know what I mean. But the thing is now that having made good and decorated, the awkward place with the damp has caused the emotion paint to the west corner of the chapel to lift, and I really think—more gravy? More carrots? More potato? Nonetheless, when Marcus comes to present the draft of the accounts—still to be audited of course, still to be audited, but he's rarely out—in the autumn, I think you may satisfy yourself that our heads are still above the parapet."

Marcus laid down his fork and waved his hand in vague demur. "Water," he said.

"Water? My dear, you have a full glass—Esme, too. I think sometimes you really should have your eyes checked again—try the other man this time, I'm not convinced Mr. Robinson isn't becoming questionably visionary himself!"

Marcus glanced at his wife with a kind of wondering incredulity.

"Mr. Robinson is a practical man, who could never have been described as visionary, questionably or otherwise. I am adequately supplied with beverages, and at Brockhyrst Chapel we may be considered still to have our heads above water, though, as you say, the year ahead presents its challenges."

Hilda gazed at him, baffled. "Marcus, whatever are you talking about? You're simply repeating everything I've said and adding nothing to the conversation at all—and why on earth were you asking for water if you know perfectly well you've already got some? Really, you could try the patience of a saint at times—you can see my point, Esme, I'm sure!

Heavens! Are we ready to move on to pudding, or is anyone still waiting for secs?"

"Seconds, Esme?" asked Marcus, with utter gravity, but a certain sardonic gleam behind the glasses and under the eyebrows lifted in inquiry. "I'd like you to be clear as to what you were being offered. Potato, maybe? Or meat? No? Pudding then, Hilda, I think."

Feeling most comfortably replete after an excellent meal, Esme settled herself into the cushions of an armchair as the three of them returned to the sitting room to enjoy their coffee. In their absence, the dog had moved off the sofa and now slumbered peacefully on the hearth rug, snoring slightly.

For a short while, as Hilda set off purposefully to the kitchen to fetch the tray of cups, Marcus and Esme lapsed into silence, and she wondered if she should take some conversational initiative.

"I've been thinking about getting a bike," she said, searching for something to talk about. "I spend so much time in the car, and the roads are so busy. Can you recommend a good place to go for a bike?"

Marcus considered. "How much of a cyclist are you?" he asked, at length.

"Oh well—I mean, I can manage hills and I don't fall off, but I shan't be going in for races. Just for a bit of exercise really."

"I see. Then I think Jabez Ferrall might answer your purpose. He sometimes has something to sell, and he's in any case a useful man to know. I never met anyone so resourceful. He's in Wiles Green—not far from here, fifty yards past The Bull as you come into Wiles Green from Brockhyrst Priory. Back of the Old Police House, where Pam Coleman lives, you'll find him. He could certainly advise you and maintain for you, regardless of what he may or may not have in."

Esme fished in her bag for her diary, which experience had taught her to take with her everywhere, and in the memoranda pages at the back she wrote down what Marcus had said: "Jabez Ferrall" (*Peculiar, old-fashioned name,* she thought), "Wiles Green, behind the Old Police House, fifty yards beyond the pub." "BIKES" she wrote above this memo, underlined.

Over coffee they chatted about Esme's parsonage. "Have you got all you need?" asked Marcus. "Is everything as it should be?"

"It's all in very good order." Esme hesitated. What she wanted to say sounded a little unappreciative. "Will you understand if I say that for me a difficult thing to come to terms with in ministry is that I realize a parsonage can never quite be a home? Please don't misunderstand me—the circuit stewards have worked so hard to make it lovely, the kitchen has just been completely redone, and I have not a single grumble. It's just—well—looking round at your sitting room I can see you are people who love your home, and part of what makes it home I think is that it's either the place you grew up, or the place you chose because you fell in love with it. And part of what makes it lovable is its idiosyncrasies—like a person, really. But of course the whole point about acquiring and maintaining a parsonage is to find a neutral kind of place—a sensible purchase—with as few idiosyncrasies as possible, and iron out what ones there are before ever anybody moves in. Little things, oddities, I don't know...." She was beginning to feel a bit silly and wondered if she would have been better never to begin this. Marcus and Hilda were both listening to her thoughtfully, and she could feel herself getting embarrassed and hot.

"Please don't think I'm complaining. The parsonage is really nice. There's nothing wrong with it as a parsonage, but—well, for example, here you have your fireplace, and it must be lovely in the winter to sit down by an open fire in the evening. But in Southarbour of course it's a smoke-free zone, and naturally the parsonage will be there because it's the biggest place in the section, the most convenient, and anyway parsonages never have open fires. But I do love a fire. D'you see what I mean? I can see why they don't have one—not everyone likes a fire, chimneys have to be swept, fires are hazardous, then as well they make dust and ash and so on. I can see why parsonages only have central heating...."

Marcus just watched her (and Esme wished he wouldn't), but Hilda nodded sympathetically. "I know just what you mean, dear!" she said, warmly. "It's a blessing! Central heating is a blessing. Having the circuit stewards to sort things out leaves you free to do your wonderful work. I envy you your spanking new kitchen—ours leaves a lot to be desired—the parsonage is very convenient, everything done, all mod cons—but everything has a backside."

In silence, Esme and Marcus pondered this judgment. Marcus put his coffee cup back on the tray. "Downside," he murmured, absently. Then he looked very hard at Esme.

"I know exactly what you mean," he said. "You are talking about home being somewhere that somehow recognizes one; a place where one truly belongs. Somewhere one can in the fullest and deepest sense call one's own. Well, please make this a second home. Investigate the junk shops. Find yourself a toasting fork and keep it here. You will always be welcome."

He nodded slightly to give this emphasis, and Esme felt a sudden deep gratitude for the kindness of this couple.

"Thank you," she said. "And thank you so much for a lovely evening. I won't make myself a nuisance, but certainly I'd love to come again."

Before she knew it, the remainder of August slipped away. Esme met some other members of her congregations. One or two dropped in with flowers or cards—one with an apple pie—to welcome her, and she was introduced to more people than she could remember when she stayed for coffee after worship at Portland Street and Brockhyrst Priory chapels on her remaining free Sundays. Then September came, the beginning of the Methodist year, with its flurry of committee meetings, special services, the round of preaching and visiting and leadership responsibilities, and so many things to plan and do.

Esme's diary filled up until it was back to its usual level of dense notes on every page, scarcely thinning out until two months ahead. Her day off she guarded jealously; the rest of the time was like a juggling act in a circus of bureaucracy.

She had asked God for a friend, but right now she felt grateful she didn't have any within easy reach of her—friends are a time-consuming luxury in a minister's life.

Any thoughts of exercise, of cycling, or walking in the country were shelved for the time being. She might well get to that, but for now it would have to wait.

She knew that in due course patterns would establish, and familiarity would give space in the work; beginnings are always hectic. She worried sometimes that all her energies could be absorbed by the bigger congregation at Portland Street, leaving Brockhyrst Priory a poor second and Wiles Green to fend for themselves (which is what they were used to).

As she went to bed at night, in the brief time before she fell asleep exhausted, Esme whispered to herself, "Don't panic, Es," and felt guilty that she was too tired to pray.

Two

The next eighteen months went by so swiftly for Esme. The ancient seasons of the liturgical year, with its balance of fasts and feasts resting lightly on older pagan foundations, wove in with the slightly different rhythms and observances of the Methodist calendar. In her new pastoral appointment, she went softly with the inevitable changes her personality brought.

She had been asked at her first interview with the circuit stewards: "What will you do for the young people? What will you do to involve the Sunday school in worship? What will you do to improve the profile of the church in the community? What will you do about the falling numbers at Wiles Green?"

Her answer to all those questions had been, "Nothing. I will watch, and wait, and listen. Nothing for a year, at the very least. Then, when I have seen enough to understand, where change seems helpful, it can begin. But at first, nothing. Until they trust me. Let them get familiar with the sound of my voice."

One of the strangest and most surprising things to Esme in her first probationer appointment had been the unsettling accuracy of the simile describing a congregation and their pastor as sheep and shepherd. The relationship centers in the voice of the shepherd. "My sheep know my voice," Jesus had said once, long ago, and Esme had grown up thinking that to be a reference to spiritual call, but she had found it in practice to be simpler and more basic than that. When a faith community comes to know and trust a leader, that leader's voice can bring them to peace. As the pastor's voice opens the worship of the community, the trust implicit in the relationship gathers the people of God into one, so that their prayer and praise arises in one peaceful drift of incense smoke finding its way to heaven.

In her first year and a half with her new congregations, already there had been the usual trickle of domestic tragedies and small emergencies. A troubled mother had poured out to Esme her concerns about a child truanting from school and making friends on the fringes of the drug world. There had been two bereavements in Portland Street families—one SIDS—and one of her Brockhyrst Priory pastoral visitors had died after a very swift illness. At Wiles Green a much-loved member of the congregation in her nineties had been diagnosed with cancer—Gladys Taylor, a sweet and gentle white-haired lady who hosted the Bible study in her small room in the almshouses by St. Raphaels Church. Gladys, unfailingly kind and understanding, restored Esme's faith in old ladies; it was with a pang of real sadness that she heard of the diagnosis. As Esme spent time with these and others passing through trouble and anxiety, word went around that when they needed her she came. She chaired her business meetings with competence, insisting that they close no later than half-past nine—well, twenty minutes to ten if "Any Other Business" turned out heated. Her stewards in all three chapels worked well with her, and all her pastoral visitors did their work with diligence. The usual cold wars and simmering feuds seemed temporarily dormant: After eighteen months Esme relaxed enough to consider her own life beyond the occasional visit to her mother or day off window-shopping and enjoying a cappuccino in Brockhyrst Priory.

Her minister's diary was printed to span well beyond a year, and though she had begun her new one in September at the beginning of the Methodist year, the old one still lay on her desk, handy when required for transferring details of this year's engagements made far in advance. She intended to trawl through noting down all engagements still forthcoming and all the valuable margin notes of addresses and telephone numbers and personal details; but so far she had not found the time, and last year's diary had not yet outlived its usefulness.

In February, as Lent began, Esme looked in her old diary—the one that had been new when first she sat at her desk on those August days at the beginning of this appointment—to check the memoranda pages for details of services and study courses held jointly with churches of other denominations at this season of the year.

As she flicked through the pages, she came across her long-forgotten entry:

BIKES *Jabez Ferrall, Wiles Green, behind the Old Police House, 50 yards beyond the pub.*

She paused and reread it and looked at it for a while. The watery sun of early spring streamed through the window onto her desk. The tree that overhung her driveway was developing sticky red buds that one day soon would unfurl in crumpled new green leaves. When she drove out to Wiles Green for Sunday worship or to lead the Wesley Guild, the dog mercury was advancing cautious early shoots on the verges of the lanes. The air smelt fresh and inviting. *A bike,* she thought. *Why not?*

Not today, but one day soon. And time went on, but the idea stayed with her, so that on the Tuesday of Holy Week, before the days erupted into the liturgical marathon of Maundy Thursday, Good Friday, and Holy Saturday, culminating in Easter Sunday's multiple Eucharists, Esme made a space to investigate the possibility of buying a bike.

It must be somewhere near here, then.

Nosing through the narrow street, Esme tried to be mindful of the traffic and look out for the Old Police House at the same time. With almost nothing to boast in the way of commercial premises at Wiles Green, the pub stood out proudly, and "A bit beyond the pub, fifty yards, no more— set back a little from the road," Marcus had said.

Esme pulled up at the roadside, just straddling what pavement there was, and found that the square and solid pink painted house, behind the neatly trimmed privet hedge alongside her car, bore an engraved plate: OLD POLICE HOUSE. So the unmade track half-grown with weeds and rutted with potholes that disappeared around the back of the house must be the path she was looking for.

She climbed out of the car and looked up the little lane. Walking up it she passed on her left the Old Police House and on her right the brick wall that formed the side of a house that fronted the road. A few tender shoots of early weeds and the hopeful beginnings of buddleia sprouted from the base of the wall. Ahead of her, self-seeded hawthorns and elder overhung the path. She could smell wood smoke. Beyond the limits of the back-garden walls that flanked the way, the path finished at a low picket fence lichened and leaning with age, pushed out of place somewhat by an unruly planting of lavender, rosemary, and sage; and a confused burden of honeysuckle vines that sprouted the beginnings of their leaves among the dry, climbing, thorny stems of wild rose. Behind this fence, two gnarled apple trees bowed over the tangle of grass and herbs. A few brown hens wandering there muttered to each other and remarked on the finds, their fierce eyes detected in the undergrowth. In the fence a gate stood ajar, opening onto a damp brick path, home to a multitude of small, early weeds, leading directly to the front door of a cottage. The cottage windows were small and low, the walls red brick, and the door painted green. On the lintel of this door, a hand-painted sign said JABEZ FERRAL—BICYCLE REPAIRS. And a grey-weathered table to the left of the door held a collection of jars with a card propped against them that read LOCAL HONEY, alongside a tray of eggs, a cardboard basket of last year's apples, and a jam jar for callers to leave their money.

Esme pushed the gate fully open, half-surprised to find it swung silently, hung precisely on perfectly oiled hinges. She took a few steps along the brick path and stopped, entranced. Whoever lived here? Something in the sight of it tugged at the heart of her. It looked peaceful and simple. Quiet and left to be. And a green fragrance of herbs and earth hung about it all. Entirely still on the path she stood, and took it all in, and loved it.

"Can I help you?"

The quiet voice with its country burr startled her, coming from behind, and she turned quickly, flustered momentarily by a sense that she had intruded—an unfamiliar sensation to her these days, accustomed by years of pastoral visiting to a warm and grateful reception by people in any state.

I am so glad I came here, Esme thought, as she looked at

the owner of the voice. *I am so glad I didn't miss this in my life.*

"Mr. Ferrall?" she said.

Jabez Ferrall looked at her shyly; a little sideways, from under his eyebrows, which were wiry and silver grey. He would have made five feet, seven inches, in his work boots if he had not stood, with the habit of years, slightly hunched. Clothed in faded and shabby green corduroy trousers below a battered brown waxed cotton jacket that was far too big for him, his hair in a waterfall of silver and white almost to his waist, and his beard straggling to a stop somewhere in the middle of his chest, Esme could almost have believed one of the characters from her childhood fairy stories had come to life before her. She gazed at him in delight.

He stood his ground, but something in his habitual stance gave the odd impression that he was backing away from her.

Very bright and clear was his glance when his eyes briefly met hers. A half-formed impression of something very transparent and truthful, and yet wary—no, guarded—no, only shy, Esme thought.

"Yes," he said, and again, "can I help you?"

"My name's Esme Browne. I'm the Methodist minister for the chapel here—" Esme registered in herself a sense of surprise as Jabez Ferrall inclined his head slightly—the smallest movement, but clearly indicating that this was not news "—and I'd like to buy a bicycle. I was recommended to come here."

A flicker of amusement came into his eyes.

"From me?" he said. "Who told you to come to me to buy a bike?"

Esme felt mildly irritated. He didn't seem to be taking her seriously.

"Well, it's what you do, isn't it?" she rejoined crisply, "— bicycle repairs?"

"Yes, but—" he looked at the ground a moment, and when he raised his face to glance at her again, the flicker of amusement had become a lopsided grin, "—come and have a look."

The path was narrow for two people to pass, and Jabez Ferrall hesitated; once again the bright look he darted at her gave her the odd feeling of coming from behind something, from a place of hiding. As though he saw her more accurately than she might have wished but kept himself hidden.

"Shall I come by you?" he asked, and stepped on to the grass to pass in a careful circle around her. "This way." He looked over his shoulder at her, and she followed him along the path, which progressed from brick to gravel and mud between a vigorous growth of assorted weeds, around the back of the cottage to a yard paved with stone flags. They crossed the yard, passing the back door of the cottage, where a cast-iron frame supporting an old-fashioned grindstone stood against the wall, to the entrance of a long, low shed built out from the side of the cottage and in the same red brick. As they went across the yard, Esme looked at the small and antiquated green open truck that stood parked rather haphazardly against the hedge that bordered the yard. *Does he paint everything green?* she wondered. Perhaps he'd had a job lot to use up. A memory stirred somewhere. Hadn't she seen that truck before? Following Jabez into the shed, which was his workshop, Esme stopped for a moment to allow her eyes to adjust to the gloom. A window, not very big, was set into the same wall as the door, but Esme thought he could have done with at least one large roof light.

Inside the workshop, the walls were lined entirely with a combination of shelves storing an assortment of containers—rusty biscuit tins, mostly, and margarine tubs relabeled with paper and adhesive tape—and things hanging from nails hammered into the brickwork—bicycle parts, machine parts, garden implements, and tools. In the center of the workspace stood a zinc bath of water, the surface of the water made a rainbow with a film of oil. Esme looked at it all; at the cluttered workbench under the window which (she thought) would have admitted more light with fewer cobwebs; the bike stands supporting various frames, a sturdy table spread with newspaper on which stood cleaning cloths, a can of three-in-one oil, and some dismantled machinery that meant nothing to her. There was so much to take in, she did not at first register, against the furthest right-hand wall of the shed, a spreading bed of ashes, in the midst of which lay a small heap of smoldering logs, their lazy smoke drifting up into a brick canopy leading into the flue above. No grate. Not even a fireplace in any very structured sense. A large cat lay dozing on the edge of the mound of ashes.

Jabez meanwhile was picking his way through the clutter of machinery that occupied the periphery of the shop.

"I do have a ladies' bike, as it happens," he said, "but it may not be what you had in mind. It's here."

He moved aside a bike stand supporting a frame with no rear wheel, pushed a coiled length of hosepipe out of the way with his foot, and brought into the space in the middle of the workshop a very elderly bicycle, in admirable condition, but definitely a creation of yesterday.

"It's a nice bike." Jabez looked at it thoughtfully. "Got some components added in the '40s and '50s, but a lot of it still original—celluloid-covered bars and mudguards. BSA three-speed hub gear with a panhandle changer. Monitor rear brake. Challis bell—I put that on. I've still got the original saddle, but I thought this one would be more comfortable. New tires, of course. I mean, I've overhauled it properly, stripped it down, and cleaned it, done all that was needed and waxed the frame and everything. Just depends, as I say, if that's what you had in mind."

Again the bright, swift, amused glance that took in more than it gave away.

Esme decided the best course would be to abandon her defensiveness and let him help her.

"I don't know anything at all about bikes," she said. "I mean, I can ride one, but I haven't done for years. I just felt

I had to get some exercise and lose some weight. Why shouldn't I have a bike like this in mind?"

And the honesty seemed to pay off. He looked at her more openly; and this time she saw a kindness that she felt obscurely grateful for. Almost unnoticed, a thought passed the edge of her mind, *This man will never cheat me.*

"Modern bikes, like you might get in Barton's Bikes in Southarbour—which I think is also nearer your home for repairs and such—have more sophisticated gears, much lighter aluminum frames; they make for easier cycling, especially on the hills. Cost you more, of course."

"What are the prices?" Esme asked him.

"Well—maybe you'll pick up a good modern second-hand bike for two hundred pounds, if you're lucky and you don't mind waiting. I'd ask you fifty for this. Because of the tires, and the work I've done on it. I didn't pay for it; Miss McPherson had no more use for it, and she sent it along to me in case I could make anything of it. Nice bike, as I say, but you'd use less puff and muscle on a modern job, there's no doubt about it."

"If I buy this bike from you—" Esme hesitated; she had a feeling this was a man who could see through pretense to ulterior motive; "—would you maintain it for me? Help me look after it, I mean. Because they need oiling and stuff, don't they? You have to know things." *And*, which she didn't say, *I just love this place and you so intrigue me, I must find a reason to come back.*

Esme had rightly detected Jabez Ferrall's capacity for insight, but he had a certain humility that prevented him ever imagining Esme to be interested in him. And he was very familiar with other people's inability to care for their own bicycles.

"It's how I earn my living," he said. "I expect you'll find it easier to do all the routine stuff at home—tire pressures and lubrication, brake blocks, and whatnot—but you can always bring it to me for servicing or if you have any problems or the wheels go out of true."

Esme looked at him aghast. "I don't think I can do *any* of that," she said. "I'm only just about going to be able to ride it without killing myself."

His eyes met hers then with a definite twinkle: "You wouldn't be the only one. I spent most of last Wednesday getting mud and nettle stalks and grass and heaven knows what else out of Mrs. Norman's axles. Mud's a bit out of her sphere of experience it would seem. Whatever. I can help."

"Then I'd like it," Esme replied, "but I'm not quite sure how I'll get it home. Is there a bus that comes out here from Southarbour?"

"Was. But not since 1973."

"Oh." Esme felt a bit out of her depth. "Well … I expect I could ask someone from chapel to give me a lift over here, only …"

He waited, and raised his eyebrows at her enquiringly. To her considerable embarrassment she could feel herself blushing. "I'd just rather they didn't know I was getting a bike. In case it turns out that I never really ride it. I'd feel so silly."

Jabez chuckled. *Smoker's teeth*, Esme registered.

"Are you sure you want to buy a bike?" he said. "Why don't you go home and think about it. I'm not likely to sell this in a hurry."

Then came a moment of inspiration.

"Could I come here a few times and watch what you do to maintain a bike? So I'd feel more confident?"

Jabez didn't reply at once.

"Yes … yes, I suppose so," he said reluctantly, after a moment's hesitation. He seemed a little taken aback.

"Not if you'd rather I didn't."

"No. No, it's all right. It's just people don't come here much; it's a bit of a refuge."

Esme took a deep breath. She was unsure how much this man would understand.

"I promise not to be 'people,'" she said softly, "and I would be very grateful to have temporary admission to a refuge."

Jabez shifted his grip on the bicycle frame and looked down at it. "Let me just put this away," he said, and turned from her to reposition the bike against the wall. Having done so, he stayed a moment longer with his back to her, buried his hands in his pockets as he turned again to face her.

"You would be welcome," he said, "anytime." But it was

quietly spoken and, Esme sensed, somewhat costly. A man who deeply valued his privacy.

"I won't get in the way." Her tone beseeched him, and he sighed, moved his head a little impatiently. He returned the hosepipe back to its original position with his foot. He wouldn't look at her. She saw she had imposed too much on his seclusion.

"Is any time better than another?" she persisted, ashamed at intruding, but determined not to lose this enchanted place.

He shook his head, his gaze averted still. "Anytime."

The tabby cat rose to its feet among the ashes, elongated its body in a long, shaky stretch and ambled across the shed to wind itself around his ankles, scattering a light fall of the ash that clung to its fur. It had a purr like a diesel engine. Jabez bent to scratch its head, and the cat raised its chin appreciatively, closing its eyes in slow ecstasy.

"Thank you, Mr. Ferrall, for your understanding and your help," said Esme.

Straightening, he looked from under his eyebrows at her; appraised her carefully for a matter of seconds.

"I expect it had better be 'Jabez,'" he said.

Esme stowed this treasure in her heart with joy.

When she said good-bye and left him in his workshop, Esme became aware of a happiness that had been absent so long its quality had become unfamiliar. She had become used to the satisfaction of a job well done, and the pleasant company of decent people who were disposed to be nice to her; used to the appreciation and delight called forth in her by a sunny day or dewdrops on a cobweb or the first sight of new lambs in the spring, and used to the comfortable feeling of five minutes longer in a warm bed on a chilly morning, or the relaxation of a cup of coffee enjoyed curled in an armchair at the parsonage after the end of a long business meeting. Life held many comforts and consolations. But not for a long time had she felt this song of delight that came from meeting someone whose soul she recognized as—what? A kindred spirit, maybe? Someone whose being spoke to her destiny? At any rate, someone to whom her own soul gave its unhesitating "yes."

I think, she reflected as she paused by the front door of his cottage to buy a pot of honey and half a dozen eggs, *Jabez Ferrall is going to become a friend.*

As she motored peacefully back along the narrow lanes in their dappling of sun and shade, through the wooded hillsides and pastureland around Wiles Green toward Southarbour with its banked terraces of Victorian red-brick dwellings clinging to the steep coastal hills, Esme decided to disregard her standard plan of preaching from the lectionary so as to offer an ordered but varied theological diet of careful scriptural exegesis. Once Easter had gone, and they were back to ordinary time, as a change, she thought she might preach on contentment. Something about the wisdom of staying where you are, being at peace with what life has offered you, living quietly and simply, recognizing when you have enough, and finding satisfaction in daily work, in what is ordinary—even, maybe, a little old-fashioned. Philippians 4 would do nicely as a scriptural basis. The whole of it—possibly trimming Evodia and Syzygus off the beginning and the same with Epaphroditus at the end. And for a text, majoring on the assertion, "I have learned how to be content with whatever I have." She might even have a point to make about the countryside with its little cottages, and the virtues of the bicycle as compared with the motorcar—always recognizing of course that some people needed cars and even small trucks to fulfill the requirements of their occupations. Worth pointing out though that bicycles have an important part to play in a green future. Especially the older, recycled, less garishly painted kinds of bikes.

Changing down to negotiate a sharp bend, Esme slightly adjusted her thinking to lower the profile of the bikes in her sermon plan. The spiritual potential of cycling she felt sure might be considerable, but its theological application was perhaps limited. Though there again … Her thoughts were interrupted as she pulled out of the bend and spotted ahead of her a line of cars behind an elderly tractor making valiant progress but nonetheless creating an obstruction. On an ordinary day this might have irritated her. Today she chose to regard the tractor as a form of angel, a protective escort gentling the excesses of accelerated modern living, promoting longevity in the rabbit population and inner peace and patience in the lengthening queue of motorists in her rearview mirror. Esme hummed a little tune and felt disinclined to overtake even when the opportunity came.

As the traffic became more congested in the approach to the town, so also the road signs proliferated and the view changed to one of faded advertisement hoardings, bus stops, edge-of-town supermarkets with huge parking lots and adjacent garages, all huddled in against the railway station with its taxi rank and little fruit stall and the inexplicable piles of rusted metal girders and broken-up concrete. Esme felt its familiarity challenged by a new sense that the small country chapels and the village communities in which they were set had a special value, deserving at least as much pastoral attention as a larger town church. Possibly more. The town church could probably look after itself. Up to a point.

When Esme got in, she found thirteen new messages on her answer-phone (all countering her notion that a larger town church could in any sense manage its pastoral or administrative tasks without the assiduous attentions of its minister) and a late mail delivery comprising of a complicated letter about changes to the ministerial pension scheme, the local preachers' quarterly magazine, and the draft minutes and agenda for next month's meeting from the church council secretary.

Esme applied her usual solution of a large mug of coffee and a chocolate flapjack. And then another chocolate flapjack. She felt even guiltier and disliked the round contours of her face and the disappearance of her ribs, but it staved off the moment she had to go into her study, begin returning telephone calls, prepare her Sunday sermon, and give a little advance attention to the agendas of her three forthcoming church general meetings.

Easter. Light. Morning light dawning into the darkness of the tomb. New life coming with the light. Living. Living lightly, she thought. *The way of the poor carpenter of Nazareth: simplicity, anonymity. Detachment from all the baggage that weighs down human beings: complications of material possessions and relational possessions too—just of being possessive. Jesus let things go maybe; perhaps that's why they let him go too—the way parting to let him walk through death into life alight and unlimited. His presence reversed cling and effected freedom. Death could not hold him. He lived lightly. He arose. Jabez Ferrall,* she thought, *you are a most extraordinary man. Easter. Light. The power to be free. Simplicity. Soaring. Flight. Even the sparrows are numbered. Do not be afraid to live simply. Do not be afraid to soar and to fly. Easter. Living lightly. Simplicity. Do not be afraid. Jabez—in the Bible, isn't it? Where is that?*

She leaned back in her chair and reached across to the shelf her concordance shared with several translations of the Bible, the *Constitutional Practice and Discipline* manual (volumes 1 and 2) of the Methodist church, its Worship Book, and its Minutes of Conference and Directory. Her favorite translation of the Bible was seriously in danger of losing the cover to its spine, and the cello tape patches holding the concordance together had long since yellowed and lost their grip. *Must get a replacement copy—I think I can set that against income tax—darn! I haven't filled in my tax return form,* she thought as she turned the fragile browning pages to the "J" section. She found Jabez in 1 Chronicles, in a complicated genealogy of the lineage of King David. He had only a sentence or two, but it had to do with relief from distress. His mother had so named him because of the pain and distress she experienced in giving birth to him. And Jabez prayed to the Lord asking that the divine hand might be stretched over him—but here the texts differed as to the desired outcome; some making the prayer a plea for protection from distress in his own life, others a plea for his own distress to cease, but one curiously interpreting his words as a prayer for God's blessing to restrain him from evil, so that he would never again be a cause of pain. *How strange,* Esme thought, as she pondered the texts; *I wonder why Jabez Ferrall's parents chose …? Or maybe they just liked the name Jabez.* Anyway, the prayer of his life seemed to be directed toward healing and peace, and in 1 Chronicles God had granted what he asked.

On Good Friday, Esme had an afternoon service out at Wiles Green. It was a circuit tradition to hike the four and three-quarter miles across country along the footpaths from Brockhyrst Priory. The walkers were joined at Wiles Green Chapel by the lazy and the infirm and kept watch for an hour in a vigil meditating on the cross and passion of Jesus before emerging into the Sunday school room for a robust bring-and-share tea.

Along with two or three others, Esme left her car at the chapel and returned as a passenger to the start of the walk. The wind blew chilly but the sun shone, and Esme enjoyed chatting with the various members of her churches, getting to know them a little better as they strolled along the hedgerows or stopped from time to time to admire the pastureland rolling away from the brow of a hill. As they walked together, Esme asked two of her church members, a husband-and-wife couple who ran the newsagency at Brockhyrst Priory, if they knew of Jabez Ferrall. They laughed, saying, "Oh yes, Mr. Ferrall, yes, known him for years." Before he retired, when Maeve, his wife, was still alive, they said, he'd had a newspaper delivered regularly, but like so many of the old people he had to cut back once he became a pensioner. They asked where Esme had come across him, and she said Marcus had mentioned him to her. They agreed that Mr. Ferrall was a bit of an oddity; then to her excitement Esme spotted a bullfinch, and the conversation moved on to recent sightings of birds.

On arrival at the chapel, the walkers had an opportunity to refresh themselves with a cup of tea before the service. Esme reflected that the sheer quantity of teacups washed up in the course of the afternoon overall required a stoicism worthy of Good Friday on the part of her Wiles

Green congregation, nearly all of them well over seventy. As she came in through the door of the chapel, where the trestle tables ready with teacups and milk jugs and huge brown enamel teapots stood in the Sunday school room that formed an anteroom to the worship space, Esme paused to watch her church treasurer, Miss Lucy Trigg, divesting herself of her felt hat and plum-colored tweed coat. Miss Trigg, local preacher and senior steward at Wiles Green, had the entire congregation under her thumb. Though she was raised as a Strict and Particular Baptist, she had found her way to this chapel when still only a teenager and unstintingly lavished her considerable energies upon its spiritual welfare ever since. The Southarbour circuit preachers' meeting had neither the backbone nor the foresight to refuse to accredit her as a preacher and had suffered the effect of her extraordinary gospel of chimera and retribution ever since. Esme had heard Miss Trigg preach, on one of the Sundays in August before she had taken up her appointment. Miss Trigg always came in handy for August. Ministers might be moving, preachers with schoolchildren in the family necessarily taking their holiday then; but you always could rely on Miss Trigg.

Esme remembered the sermon, vividly. Miss Trigg had preached about the Virgin Mary, with reference to the lamentable slippage of traditional interpretation in the credo of the modern church.

"The Lord Jesus Christ was born of a pure virgin," she had asserted, more aggressively than was necessary judging by the nods of agreement here and there in her congregation. "He had to be born of a virgin, because if he hadn't have been, his blood would have been the same kind of blood as yours and mine. And our blood's no good—no good at all for salvation. Jesus Christ wasn't born with blood like yours and mine in his veins. He had God's blood—God's blood that had to be shed on the cross for our salvation, to save sinners like you and me from the eternal punishment that awaited us. Quite rightly awaited: 'Deliver us from evil,' the Lord's Prayer says, and note that word *evil*. Evil is not just knocking folks on the head and bumping them off but a hundred and one little things that you and me get up to every hour of every day. We are born evil, sinners from the day of our birth. Little children are evil, however innocent they may look. You leave a child alone in a room with a bowl of sweets on the table, and you can guarantee that child will eat one, for children are thieves and evil by nature until they are saved from the thrall of Satan by the precious blood of the Lamb; and brought to the mercy seat by the free grace of Jesus Christ who gave himself a sacrifice for sin and laid down his life in our place: For the wages of sin is death and only his blood could atone as an acceptable offering to a holy God. 'Vengeance is mine,' saith the Lord. We are not called to understand, only to accept. Never be ashamed of the virgin birth."

Esme had listened to this in some amazement but had over the months come to a workable relationship with her

Wiles Green senior steward. Miss Trigg disapproved of her appointment because Esme was not only a woman but also a divorced woman. But she was gracious enough to relinquish none of her offices and maintain her usual grip on the life of the chapel at Wiles Green. Sometimes Esme felt that grip amounted to a stranglehold and was occasionally tempted to the view that if the congregation justified its existence in nothing else it did so by the community service of keeping Miss Trigg contained in the chapel. Still, she kept the books well enough, lived nearby, and was always willing to let in the builders and the man from the electricity board. She terrorized the leaders of the Mothers and Toddlers group that met in the Sunday school room every Thursday and the cleaner employed to come in on a Friday (not today, Good Friday, but that lady was expected to attend the act of worship instead).

Once free of her coat, Miss Trigg got busy with the teapot. Her scones were her own recipe and her tea hot and powerfully strong. *Much like the gospel she preaches then,* Esme thought as she approached the trestle table, saying, "Lovely day, Miss Trigg—thank you for all this; I know what hard work it is. Half a cup will be plenty, I'll add some hot water from the urn in the kitchen."

Sometimes Miss Trigg remembered that smiling was her Christian duty; today she was concentrating on pouring the tea. Age made her hands a little unsteady, but she scorned to acknowledge this. She wanted the Lord to find her at her post when he came again. The second coming caused her a certain amount of consternation because of the amount of traffic on today's roads, which would inevitably be thrown into mayhem by the selective nature of the rapture. She walked to church when she could, on the days when her sciatica didn't play her up too badly.

Silently, she held out a half-filled cup to Esme. Their eyes met. "Nice day," said Miss Trigg gruffly, prompted by the requirements of Christian charity. "Enough?"

Esme knew that shameless flattery and many expressions of solicitous concern for her health could melt that seemingly implacable exterior, but today she felt disinclined.

"Yes. Thank you very much," she said, taking her drink with her to the refuge of the small and spotless kitchen where some of the ladies of her congregation stood chatting, with dishtowels at the ready.

"I've got some neat tea here, needs diluting," Esme said as she made her way to the urn. They laughed. Esme thought it an undeserved kindness that her church members would usually laugh at her jokes, however feeble. They had many ways of surrounding their ministers with tacit encouragement. She stayed with them, enjoying their good-humored company, while she drank her cup of tea. It occurred to her to ask them about Jabez Ferrall, whom all of them knew. They told her how his wife had died some five or six years ago, and how they thought the bereavement had aged him. They agreed on his devotion to her,

especially in nursing her through three or four years of gru-
eling illness; terrible, they said; started in her breast and
went to her liver in the end, poor woman. They mused for
a little while on his avoidance of chapel people; they said his
mother used to be a member at Wiles Green Chapel, years
ago, and Mr. Ferrall's name must surely be in the baptism
register somewhere. But they thought there'd been some
kind of upset with members of the prayer group while his
wife was ill—not that that had stopped him coming
because he never came near the place anyway. They agreed
that he was a funny old so-and-so and that the old lady who
lodged with him was even funnier than he was, and they
chuckled as they considered the household. But they all
agreed that Mr. Ferrall would be the man to go to if she had
any household repairs needing attending to—"He's handy
is Mr. Ferrall, and very honest," they concluded. Then they
took Esme's cup to wash up as she went into the church to
prepare for worship.

They sang the passion hymns of mourning and told
again the terrible story of Christ's betrayal and agony, and
this year as every year, despite the resolute habits of ordinary
cheerfulness that conditioned their lives, the dark narrative
took them down with itself into the eerie dank silence of the
tomb.

It was right to remember, Esme thought afterward, but
right also to restore people afterward with the conviviality
of a chapel tea. This annual event was well supported by all

the chapels in the circuit and was an important highlight of the year for Wiles Green.

Eventually, having circulated well and spoken to almost everyone, and having thanked the ladies in the kitchen, Esme slipped away to her car, parked out on the road where others could not box it in.

"Home to finish my Easter sermon," she said to herself, but she knew she wasn't going home quite yet.

She could have driven out along Chapel Lane down the back way to Southarbour, but instead she drove into the village, as far as the Old Police House, where she drew up, parking carefully to keep well out of the way of passing traffic but leaving enough space for any pedestrians to pass on the inside as well. For a moment she sat in the car, undecided, unwilling to intrude where she felt unwelcome, aware that such a short time had gone by since last she had called in.

She put her hand on the keys still in the ignition, almost went to turn them and fire the engine again, but instead took them out and got out of the car.

The cottage had all the enchantment of her first visit. She hesitated on the path, wondering whether to knock at the front door, choosing instead to follow the way around to the backyard and the workshop. As she came around the house, she heard the clank and scrape of metal on stone and coming around the corner into the yard, she found Jabez squatting on the ground brushing clean the underneath of a rotary mower that lay on its side in front of him.

He didn't look up at first, when Esme said hello. For a few seconds, he continued brushing the odd corners and the bottom of the engine without speaking. Esme began to wonder if he had heard her, when he said, "You're back. Welcome. I can well do with a second pair of hands in a moment when I'm sharpening these blades."

He glanced around at her briefly. "Unless you'd rather not. You're not really dressed for stripping down a lawnmower."

Esme smiled. "I'd like to help," she said, perching on the edge of a kitchen chair standing out in the yard. She felt a bit self-conscious in her clerical collar and her neat black skirt but was pleased to be not entirely superfluous.

She watched Jabez lay aside the brush and reach for the metal key to undo the nut holding the blade in place. "You got to have it turned this way so the oil doesn't run into the carburetor," he remarked, as he laid the blade aside with the nut placed carefully beside it and began to loosen the sump plug under the engine.

"Been at church?" He shot a glance of friendly inquiry at her as he got to his feet and lifted the lawnmower upright over a battered enamel pudding basin to bleed away the old oil.

"Yes," she said. "It's Good Friday."

He looked up at her. "I do know," he said. "I thought about you in the service."

He had an old glass meat dish handy for his next task,

which was flushing out the sump, after which he set the machine on the ground again and squatted down to dismantle the air filter attached to the carburetor on the side of the engine. "Excuse me a minute," he said, and carried the outer gauze of the filter in through the open door of his kitchen. She could hear him at the sink, not far within the door, the tap running, and scrubbing, the tap running again, and then he reemerged patting it dry with a dishtowel, and propped it against the house wall at an angle so the air could finish the drying.

He blew the dust off the cardboard section of the filter and set it aside with the gauze. Then, moving light and quick, he crossed the yard to his workshop from where he returned with a big box wrench for the spark plugs.

As he bent over the machine, examining the plugs, he remarked, "I sit in the porch sometimes and listen to the hymns. Even to the service in the summertime if they leave the doors open. I don't come in, but I sit in the porch sometimes."

He cleaned off the carbon deposits carefully, fishing in the back pocket of his trousers for a piece of fine sandpaper to rub everything clean.

Esme watched his face, bent over his work, giving nothing away. She felt the by now automatic response of her soul going on alert. This happens to ministers, she had discovered. There is a professional interest that sends a shaft down into the fabric of a minister's being as tenacious as a dandelion root. "Why don't you come in?" she asked, with what she hoped was a casual air.

Jabez smiled at the transparency of her proselytizing but continued to concentrate on resetting the gap using his thumbnail as a gauge as he replaced the clean plugs. He dusted the terminals, brushed them lightly with his sandpaper, and refitted the high-tension lead.

"Because I don't like the church," he said.

Esme watched him as he checked and blew clean the carburetor jets before he began to reassemble the filter. She liked the composure and focus of his face as he worked.

"But you believe in God?" she ventured.

He glanced up at her momentarily.

"I believe …" he hesitated, searching for the words to say what he wanted. He turned aside and reached for the sump plug, replaced it. "You got to make sure this is tight."

He paused in what he was doing, rested his weight forward on his knees on the stone flags of the yard. "I believe in the stories you hear of people who died and were resuscitated. Those stories about a long tunnel leading up to the light. And the light is full of love and truth. I believe that. Light that sears and light that dances, exquisite to take your breath away, blinding bright. Light that could cut like a laser but also nourish and heal and clean like sunshine. I believe in that. And that one day I will find my way home there. Or maybe not. Is that God—what I believe in?"

Esme stared at him. "Jabez, that's beautiful!"

Irritation twitched somewhere in his look, because he hadn't meant beauty, he'd meant truth.

"You ready to help me with this blade, then?" he said, reaching down for it without looking at her, getting to his feet again, and crossing the yard.

He showed her how he wanted her to turn the handle on the grindstone that revolved in a water bath supported by a cast-iron frame. As she did so, he held the blade against it for sharpening.

"But it doesn't matter what I believe, I still don't like the church," he said, with a sort of stillness of determination that Esme guessed ran very deep.

"Did we hurt you?" she asked, gently. She hoped her tone sounded ingenuous. It wouldn't do to let him know she'd had the gossip of several church members about him, but she wanted to know about his wife and what it was the prayer group had done to upset him.

Jabez looked suddenly very tired. Sharing his soul had become unfamiliar. He felt unsure about this intrusion.

"That's fine, you can stop," he remarked, as he lifted the blade and turned back to the lawnmower again.

Esme wondered if her question would be left unanswered, but as Jabez knelt to reposition the blade on the mower, he glanced at her narrowly from under the wiry silver eyebrows, saying, "I think you may know a bit more about me than you pretend."

That moment was a crossroads for them. Esme had to

decide then whether she wanted Jabez to be an acquaintance or a friend, whether she was to be the minister of the chapel to him, or just herself, Esme.

It is understood that a pastoral relationship is without the quality of truthfulness that a friendship has. The transactions between ministers and their flocks are ritualized; there are expectations and therefore pretenses. This is understood and part of the world of formal relationships undertaken by people in the public eye. But a friend approaches barefoot with needs as unadorned as a beggar's bowl, or the gift of self like a flower held in the hand.

She might have stayed as a minister then, evaded his rebuke with a joke, retreated to safe footing—"Oh! Sorry! Didn't mean to intrude!" Esme knew it was possible to make comments of that sort in just such a tone as to imply the other is prickly, oversensitive; there was no need to admit one's own dishonesty. She might have taken that course, but in her few years as a minister she had learned to know how rare a thing it is to be offered the chance to be truthful. Reality is always so demanding. Not many attempt its rigors.

Jabez refitted the blade as she considered this and tightened the nut with his key, afterward slipping it into his pocket.

"Yes, I do know a bit about you already." Esme felt ashamed as she said it. "I've asked several people about you. I know you were married, and that your wife died; and that something happened there to do with our chapel prayer group. I wanted to find out about it. Just nosy I suppose. It's none of my business. I'm sorry, Jabez."

And as simply as that, they crossed over into friendship—his offer of truthfulness and her shamed acceptance. Esme thought later, what slight moments are the occasions of human transformation.

Jabez sat down beside the lawnmower and felt in the pocket of his jacket for a tin of tobacco, inside which were also cigarette papers. He rolled a cigarette, carefully, very thin, and patted his pockets to locate the matches with which to light it. Esme sat on the edge of the wooden chair again and waited for what he would say. Recovery time needed, it seemed. He drew on the cigarette.

"My wife, Maeve," he said, affecting a hard and matter-of-fact tone, "died of cancer." He paused, and looked suspiciously at his cigarette, and with good reason, because it had gone out. Esme waited while he relit it. He drew on it, looked at it, and flashed her one quick glance.

"It was awful. Horrible. She lost her hair, and she had a lot of pain. Her arm swelled and her medicines made her sick—desperately sick—and her belly filled up with fluid, and she smelled bad, and she knew she did, and she got so thin she looked as though her teeth didn't belong in her face anymore. She wanted to stay here, so I nursed her."

He stopped. Esme waited. He drew on the cigarette, relit it because it was out again. Esme waited.

"And then—we were clutching at straws I think—someone

from the chapel," he did not look at her, but gazed steadfastly ahead at nothing, "asked if a group of them could come to the cottage and pray for Maeve and me. I don't know what possessed me to agree to it, but—well … perhaps you can imagine. We were short on hope."

He stopped speaking for a moment, his face set and still, remembering.

"So they came. Here, in our cottage, they came. Not Miss Trigg, she isn't into all that, but a woman that twittered and a woman with a silent enigmatic smile and a man who stood too close when he talked to me and a little bald bloke who was deaf. To pray for Maeve and me. Maybe you know them. I don't. I haven't been to chapel for years, and I think a lot of those that worship there now aren't the old ones but run out from Southarbour to keep it from closing down.

"Anyway, they said could they lay hands on her for healing, and she wanted it so I said yes. I didn't want to raise Maeve's hopes but, you know, her eyes that had been so dull and enduring suddenly looked alive again. I felt angry and helpless because I knew it would be no good. But I went along with it. I helped her into a chair in the middle of the room, and the four of them jostled around her into a group with their eight hands plastered on her thin, wasted shoulders and her poor bald head. A bit excessive. And they started to pray. D'you know the kind of thing? Do they still do it? 'Lord, send your Spirit, Lord, to heal and bless her, Lord; make her free from pain, Lord, blah, blah, blah.'"

He drew on his cigarette. It was out. He didn't bother to relight it, but let his hand come down to rest on his knee. He glanced at Esme, but only for a moment.

"I remember it sinking in with such appalling clarity that Maeve was going to die. I hadn't really faced it till then, till I heard their church-speak full of unreality and realized what reality held for us. I was standing by the table, an onlooker, trying to get under control the grief that was suddenly going crazy inside me. I was trying to put it on one side to deal with later, when the deaf man must have found his moment to get a prayer in edgeways because he startled me by booming out like a foghorn, I mean really in capital letters, 'OH LORD, WE PRAY FOR MAUVE!' And it was at that moment that I lost it all. To that extent I suppose he prayed with power, because his prayer certainly had an effect on me. 'Mauve!' Inside me it all muddled together; all at once something laughed and something wept and something died. Apart from her funeral and sitting eavesdropping in the porch some Sundays, I never go near chapel nor church. Well, to be fair I hadn't anyway, not for years."

A brief, wry grin twisted his face. "You'd have been proud of me though. I made them a cup of tea before they went. And I gave them a biscuit."

The desolation of this story moved in the center of

Esme's soul. She felt the sharpness of its anguish and was at a loss what to say.

After a moment, "What did Maeve think of the prayer?" she asked. "Did she find it helpful?"

Jabez nodded slowly. "She did. She did, but she died."

He looked thoughtfully at the lifeless remains of his cigarette in his hand and flicked it back over his shoulder in the direction of the orchard grass that grew down to meet the flags of the yard.

"Esme, I don't like the church. I don't like its hypocrisy, and its need to be right and to control everybody. It works by fear and manipulation and doublespeak and to be honest I got no time for it at all. Now if you'll excuse me—" he got up and lifted the lawnmower into the back of his truck and fetched a can to decant the used oil for recycling; "—I must take this mower down the road to Mr. Griffiths before the afternoon's over. It was nice to see you."

There was a definite dismissal in his tone that went beyond the requirements of the afternoon's tasks. Esme stood up and straightened her skirt. She looked at him, but he didn't meet her gaze.

"Am I a part of all that, then?" she asked. "The church?"

His eyes flickered, and he stood looking down at the metal can in his hand, slowly screwing down the cap.

"Well, yes," he said, quietly. "I guess you are."

Esme felt a sharp pain of disappointment: The moment of honesty that brought intimacy between them seemed to have been lost, and the clarity between them had slipped away, leaving them back as they were, little more than strangers.

"But it's still okay to come here?" *Leave it, Esme,* a voice inside her warned. But somehow she couldn't leave it; she had to be sure.

He sighed, impatiently.

"I run a business here," he said, adding with a quick glance around his yard and an involuntary laugh, "if I may be permitted to dignify it by calling it that. Anyone can call in anytime. You asked to see how bikes are maintained. That's all right. Apparently you're interested in lawnmowers, too. As far as it goes, that's all fine. But—look—I'm not a mission field. Can we be clear on that?"

Esme felt her color rise. He was denying the pure truth that had shone between them, and she felt belittled and shut out by the way he spoke.

"Most certainly," she shot back defensively. "You make yourself perfectly clear. I won't hold you up any longer."

She left very swiftly, without looking back.

THREE

J abez moved about his kitchen slowly and stiffly in the half light of the dawn. It was just after half-past five, and he felt weary still. He hadn't slept well. He had added some dry kindling to the dying remains of yesterday's fire in the Rayburn's firebox, seen it crackle and blaze up nicely, pushed some chunkier bits on top, filled the kettle, and set it on the hottest place of the stove's hot plate. He turned his back on it and leaned against the dishtowel rail on the front of the stove, glad of the warmth as he listened to the water begin to stir. He leaned forward and reached for his tobacco tin on the kitchen table, and he rolled a cigarette as he waited for the kettle to heat up. The radio muttered quietly in its corner. He fumbled in his pocket for matches, and lit the cigarette. He looked at the end of it glowing ruby in the cold, uncertain light of the morning; and he thought it beautiful, that small red glow.

After awhile, as he heard the first sounds of the water

heating increase to something more determined, he pushed away from his resting place. By the yard door he struggled his feet into his Wellington boots, and went out of the kitchen across the yard for the faded plastic bucket he mixed the hen food in. The tabby cat appeared at his side, winding itself sinuously around his ankles, and he bent for a moment to scratch its ears affectionately. The weather had changed, the sunshine had gone, and today's northeasterly wind carried a cold, thin rain. In the small wooden shed where, in with various gardening implements and a bale of straw for his nest boxes, Jabez kept the hen food, he scooped some meal into the bucket from the tin mug inside the paper sack and refolded the top with the absentminded methodical precision of habit. He carried the bucket back to the kitchen, the cat running at his heels, and added half the heated water from the kettle to the meal, set the kettle back on the hot plate, and took the bucket to the sink, stirring in the water and some scraps left from last night's supper with a spoon that lay on the draining board. Then he carried the steaming mixture out into the yard, shivering in the slanting drizzle borne on the unrelenting wind, up through the orchard to the chicken house, where his brown hens, shut in securely against the visits of the fox, were still fast asleep, but willing to wake up for their breakfast. He propped the hen house door back and scraped their meal into the aged and dented aluminum bowl that lay on the grass there, watched them tumble out of their house in haste to find their food, checked the laying boxes—

not expecting and not finding any eggs so early in the day—
and turned back down to the yard, where he could hear the
kettle beginning to whistle in the kitchen.

He left the bucket in the shed, kicked off his boots at the
kitchen door, grateful to step out of the wind, and went in to
make his tea, strong and dark, the way he liked it. He sniffed
at the milk he found in the fridge and paused reflectively.
Sniffed again, and after a moment's hesitation, resigned himself to pouring some into the stained and chipped mug he
had rescued from its fellows on the draining board. He
poured some into the cat's saucer on the floor near the sink.
Opening the door of the Rayburn, he added a split log to the
fire, closed it up again, and adjusted down the draught.

Then tea in one hand, cigarette in the other, Jabez moved
in that quiet way of his from the kitchen into his living room,
making for the refuge of his fireside chair. Nothing in the
grate but last night's ashes, still faintly astir. He put down his
tea on the hearth. Sitting on the edge of the chair, leaning
forward, his left hand rested on his knee and held the glowing cigarette while he took up the poker in his right hand,
riddled the ashes through. He straightened up with a sigh,
then sat for a moment with the poker dangling inert in his
hand, his face as grey and hopeless as the ashes on the hearth,
just still and letting his mind wander, until a cough shook
him and he grimaced, recalled to the present moment, laid
the poker down, and went patient on his hands and knees to
lay kindling, roll the pages of the free local newspaper into

firelighters, set a match to begin what was, for him, always a clinging to hope, warmth, life, and home; a fire to sit by, gaze into, brood upon.

There came a moment between kneeling to contemplate the yellow-orange flames beginning to devour the twists of paper, and rising awkwardly back into his chair, when something sharp and painful slid obliquely along Jabez Ferrall's soul; a simple blade of acknowledgment—so abysmally lonely. But he turned from it before it became self-pity, to the last half-inch of his cigarette and to the comfort of tea still hot.

In his sixth year as a widower and the sixty-ninth year of his life, Jabez kept that economy of movement, inner stillness, of those who prefer to disturb the deep barren ache of living only as much as must be.

It was, he reflected, as he drew on the last of the cigarette and flicked the butt of it into the flames, a luxury really to light two fires, especially now that spring had arrived. Still, the stove had to be kept in to keep the house dry and warm and in readiness for cooking meals and heating dishwater. And this fire to sit by was a small and temporary delight; just for a moment, the space it took to sit awhile and drink a cup of tea before the day began. Primitive, really, he thought; not much advance on the Stone Age or whenever in human history they had lit fires to keep away the wild beasts and the evil spirits. For here he sat, keeping his own demons at bay with the comfort of a fire's light; setting something bright and living between himself and the shades mocking his inadequacy and his entrenched, habitual gnawing of grief. Well, loneliness. Nothing to assuage it. No help for it. But firelight is something of consolation, essentially alive.

As he drank his tea, folding his hands around the mug and sitting forward in his chair toward the fire's warmth, Jabez reflected on his conversation with Esme yesterday. The memory embarrassed him. How had he come to give so much of himself away? He regretted his bitterness and his frank contempt of what after all was her way of life, the context for most of what she did. "I shouldn't have said those things," he murmured, ashamed. He felt the stirring inside him of the bad stuff—the self-reproach and uncertainty, the sense of inadequacy and weakness. What are you supposed to do with it, all that stuff? Where is it supposed to go?

After Maeve had died, he had just kept himself to himself, managed it all as best he could, the tearing, eviscerating misery of grief. Now he had grown a flimsy carapace over the first rawness but hadn't gotten further than that really. It sufficed for the day-to-day, but when, as yesterday, he came to talk about any of it, the despair came back as fresh as ever, uncontainable. And what are you supposed to do with it?

Jabez sat a moment longer, his face drawn into haggard lines of weary bewilderment. Then, irritated at himself, he shrugged, inspected the quantity of tea left in the mug, knocked back the dregs of it, and got to his feet to begin the day. There was work to be done.

❖

The day did not improve but continued in fitful showers and keen, persistent wind.

Through the morning Esme finished off her Easter sermon and worked through a pile of correspondence. She had one more Holy Week house communion to do, at Gladys Taylor's almshouse out at Wiles Green. Facing her sickness with dignity, Gladys never complained, and greeted Esme on her visits with warmth and kindness; but Esme saw the pinch of fear underlying the set of Gladys's features and heard the resolve of courage that had entered her voice. She called when she could with cartons of high-calorie, complete-nutrient drinks and magazines, and today for Holy Week, the bread and wine of communion.

She stopped briefly at Brockhyrst Priory on her way there and bought a bag of six currant buns and a loaf of bread, mindful of the closed shops in the coming public holiday. She took in a bun for Gladys—who would not eat it, she suspected, but might like to be thought of, and maybe would manage a taste. She was shocked by the deterioration of Gladys's health; a new frailty, and blue shadows circling her eyes—"Let me call the doctor," she said, but Gladys, surprisingly stubborn, refused to disturb her doctor until normal office hours resumed on Tuesday.

When she came away from the house, Esme sat in her car for several minutes feeling upset and adjusting to the evident reality that Gladys would be with them very little longer.

As she drove back through the village, she went more slowly, and stopped eventually, outside the Old Police House. *I can't go back again*, she thought; *that's three days running. I mustn't—I can't* ... and she slowly took the keys out of the ignition, took the bag of currant buns from the seat beside her, and got out of the car.

As she followed the muddy path around the cottage, early weeds heavy with rain wetting the legs of her jeans, Esme became aware she was treading very cautiously— silently, actually. In one hand she carried the bag from the baker's: a peace offering.

She came into the yard. The shed door stood open. Esme stole closer and stood uncertainly in the doorway. Inside, Jabez was crouched over his zinc bath in the middle of the shed, running an inner tube slowly through his hands under the water, checking for a puncture. He did not look around. Apparently he hadn't heard her. His hair was tied back, but she couldn't see his face; still his movements were as always calm, methodical. He didn't look cross. She stood in the doorway, watching him.

After a few moments, "You're standing in the light," he said, and she answered, softly, contritely, "I'm sorry."

He looked back at her briefly, an unreadable look, and stood up, holding the dripping inner tube over the water.

"For standing in the light? That's quite all right."

"No, Jabez. For trespassing on sore places. For hurting you."

He hooked the tube over the handlebar of a bike propped against his workbench and rubbed his hands dry on his trousers. He lifted his hand to his face and with the back of it wiped away the drip that had gathered on the end of his nose.

Esme took in the wrinkled, shrunk look to his skin, presently various shades of mauve and blue except for his nose, which was rather red.

"Jabez," she said, "you look absolutely freezing."

"I am," he replied, and, looking absently around for some mislaid item, he added, "and ready for a cup of tea." And suddenly he looked up, looked directly at her, looked her in the eye—which in that moment she realized he rarely did—the bright flash of a glance that reminded her of every wild creature in a hedge whose eyes had ever met hers: "Would you like to come in for a cup of tea?"

On an afternoon of pastoral visits, a minister can be awash with tea. No village chapel meeting, not even the church council, can proceed without a cup of tea. Esme had lost count of the cups of tea she had been offered in Wiles Green, Brockhyrst Priory, and Southarbour since she came to live there. But here she had the feeling of being offered something most precious and rare. Jabez, she thought, would not give his hospitality lightly.

"I would love to," she said, "and I brought you some buns. To say sorry."

He was rummaging among the jumble of things pushed

against the wall at the back of his workbench—sandpaper and bits of chalk, oily rags, spanners, and old margarine tubs, holding assortments of different-sized nuts and valves.

"To make peace with me?" he said.

She did not answer, but watching him she began to wonder if truly he had lost something or just found the rummaging a refuge from too direct a meeting. And he stopped suddenly, placing his hands on the edge of the workbench, rough, red, cold, chapped hands, resting there in absolute simplicity, stood with his head bent, adding quietly, "Because there's no need to. Ever."

And again that quick glance that shot like dark fire from his soul to hers. *You and I,* she thought, *have known each other for a thousand years. You're right. Nothing could break the peace between us.* And then she thought, *My goodness! Where did that come from?* But she said only, "Thank you."

And he withdrew his hands and left his ruse of searching, came out to her and into the yard, switching off the light, and pulling the shed door closed behind him.

Around the middle of her solar plexus, Esme felt a childish effervescence of excitement. For she so wanted to see inside this cottage.

As she followed him across the yard, clutching her bag of buns, Esme had the curious sensation of being once more about four years old: eager, inquisitive, excited, happy, and alive.

He pushed the kitchen door, which stood ajar, fully open,

and stood back for her to go in first. She stepped inside, taking in at a glance its smallness and friendly clutter—a paper feed sack printed with the words *Layers Mash* lay down as a doormat; the saucer for the cat with its rim of congealed yellow milk; the shabby wooden table, two stools and a chair roughly drawn up to it; the wall above it fitted with shelves to house miscellaneous crockery and grubby jars of oats and rice and pulses, and dried fruit and herbs and brown sugar. She looked at the Rayburn that stood against the inner wall, giving off a steady comfort of warmth and a faint smell of wood smoke and ashes, and dishtowels set on the rail to dry at the front of it. She saw the clothes rack drawn up to the ceiling, a few garments still hanging there, and the various boots left higgledy-piggledy by the door; the deep white ceramic sink with its sturdy old-fashioned taps and wooden draining board, where various pieces of crockery stood propped to drain, and a cracked and grimy bar of workmanlike soap waited in a saucer near the taps. Everything was functional, comfortable, and plain; and, for no reason she could identify, it made Esme feel very peaceful, very welcome, and very much at home.

"I'll just wash my hands," Jabez said, "and then I'll make you a cup of tea."

He kicked off his boots and went to the sink. Esme sat down on one of the stools at the table, and she watched him; the stoop of his shoulders and the long tail of silver hair that hung down his back; the quiet focus of his absorption in washing his hands—soap, nailbrush, thorough rinsing; and yet she could feel him aware of her, even though his back was turned.

He was done and came across to the stove to rub his hands dry on a dishtowel. He did not look at her, and she sensed him suddenly shy. He took the kettle of water from the back of the stove, lifted the hinged cover back from the hot plate, and set the water to boil.

"It'll be awhile," he started to say, "but—" The door that led from the kitchen into the rest of the house opened, and Esme turned her head to find herself looking into the eyes of the old lady who had accosted her outside St. Raphaels Church on the first day she had visited Wiles Green.

"Good afternoon," said the old lady, who looked as disreputable and as extraordinary as she had at their first meeting. "Where have you parked your car?"

Her face as she asked this regarded Esme impassively, but in the almost black, sharp eyes Esme saw a mocking twinkle that stopped her in time from taking the question too seriously.

"Down on the road," she replied. "Well, half across the pavement actually. I do what I can to make life difficult."

The old lady nodded. "I thought as much," she answered. "Are you making tea, Jabez? I'll have a cup if so."

He looked at her, his head cocked to one side, not smiling, but a certain wry amusement in his face.

"Not 'please Jabez'; not 'thank you'; not any such thing.

Esme, this is Seer Ember. She lives here. But I get the impression you've met."

Esme smiled, and Jabez looked at her, sharply, then at the old lady. "Ember, you weren't rude to her, were you?"

Esme was puzzled. "Forgive me," she said, "but *what* is your name?"

The old lady's face wrinkled in a grin—"Foreign, you think?" She laughed. "*Seer.* 'Tis a word, you know, you a holy woman. One who sees, a seer is. Inside sight. And I expect you come across an ember before today. The embers is all that's left when a fire dies, but the real heat of the fire is there, under the ashes. Embers look like nothing, finished—but woe betide you if you don't treat 'em with respect. 'Seer Ember.' See?"

"Yes," said Esme. "Yes, I certainly do see. I'm sorry to be so obtuse—do you mind if I just get this straight? Which bit of it's your surname and which is your Christian name?"

Ember's eyes had depths like jewels, and her bright regard held Esme in mocking consideration.

"I had a father once and I was born under his name. I was given to a man in marriage, and I came under his name. He left, and good riddance: He found another and I hope she brought him the luck he well deserved. I was baptized in a church and given a Christian name; but my ways parted from the ways the pious tread in long ago. I bow my head to Jesus Christ, for he walked, and he stopped, and he was nailed; he understood the speed of love. Love burns slow. Enduring.

But I want my own name. I'm nobody's property. I am what I am, and my name's my own self. *Seer Ember.* I sit in the ashes now, but I still got a spark, and I know reality when I see it. Will that do you?"

Jabez, listening to this conversation with his arms folded, leaning against the rail along the front of the stove as he waited for the kettle to boil, offered the comment, "I tried to tell her that Tsunami was a pretty name that would have suited her just as well, but she wouldn't have it."

Ember took no notice of this remark at all, her eyes challenging Esme with an insolent sparkle that Esme found endearing but imagined might be hard to live with.

"So—" Esme persevered, "I'm sorry not to be quicker on the uptake—'Seer' is a form of address, like 'Mrs.'? And I call you 'Ember'?"

"You got it. Jabez, you been to the shop? I don't know what there is to eat in the house to go with a cup of tea if we got a visitor."

"Oh!" Esme held out the bag of buns. "I bought these from the baker at Brockhyrst Priory. It seemed like an afternoon for holing up with a hot cup of tea. They might be nice with some butter if you have any."

Ember peered into the bag with interest. "Smells good. Yes, I don't doubt we got butter. I've laid a fire in the house for the evening. Shall we light it now and toast them?"

Jabez, moving about the kitchen washing up mugs and finding milk and emptying the cold dregs from the teapot into the compost bucket, nodded in assent. "Yes, I'm ready to sit down. Take Esme through and light the fire, Ember; I'll be there with the tea in just a tick."

Ember turned on her heel and retreated the way she had entered, Esme following her into the living room, which looked friendly and shabby, the furnishings reasonably clean, but old and worn. On one side of the fireplace a long sofa with squashy, untidy cushions stood under the low, square window where potted plants grew on the deep sill. An armchair stood to the other side of the fireplace, and another smaller chair atop a confusion of knitting, newspapers, and spilling piles of books also faced the fire. The tabby cat Esme had seen before in the workshop lay curled in this chair.

"Sit you down while I light the fire—try the sofa," said Ember.

Esme sank into the feather cushions and watched Ember as she kindled the crunched paper and split sticks to begin, her small, plump figure dressed in its approximation to robes bent over as she waited the moment to add larger pieces of wood. She wore her hat still, even indoors. *You look extraordinary*, Esme thought, and Ember turned her head to look at her.

"'Tisn't usual for Jabez to ask somebody in. He doesn't trust easy. Must have taken to you."

Having got the fire going to her satisfaction, Ember turned to the smaller armchair, unceremoniously routed the cat, and sat there herself. Jabez came into the room carrying a tray with mugs of tea and the currant buns cut in two and piled beside a dish of butter.

He set the tray down on the floor, gave Esme her tea, for which she thanked him, and Ember hers, which she received without comment.

Sitting down opposite Esme in the armchair next to the fire, Jabez took up the toasting fork that lay on the hearth, and spiking a half currant bun on it, held it to the flames for a while, turning it when the first side was done.

"Help yourself to butter," he said, giving her the first one completed and beginning to toast the next.

Esme found herself feeling wonderfully content. The homeliness and simplicity of this place permeated her being. The world of committees and computers, of safeguarding practice and health and safety regulations, of tactful ingratiation and carefully worded preaching seemed to have receded to a very distant place, and she felt more relieved than she would ever have guessed.

"This is lovely," she said. "It feels like being on holiday."

Jabez smiled, handing Ember a toasted bun. Fitting the third one onto the toasting fork, he glanced at Esme, drew breath as if to speak, and then changed his mind.

"Well?" said Ember, not looking up from spreading butter on her currant bun.

"I think—" Jabez kept his eyes on what he was doing, "—I think I owe you an apology, Esme."

"You do?" She was startled.

"I must have sounded bitter and contemptuous yesterday—"

"That's nothing unusual for you," Ember interjected, which he ignored.

"—and I'm sorry if what I said was hurtful. I didn't mean it so. There have been some bad times. Thank you for giving me another chance."

"That's smoking," said Ember nodding toward the teacake he held to the fire, adding with some curiosity, "what did you say to her, then?"

Jabez laid aside the fork and reached across to butter his toasted bun. He sat back in his chair, a mug of tea in one hand and a currant bun in the other, looking into the flames of the fire.

"I was rude about the church," he said quietly, "and just generally prickly and unfriendly."

"The religious establishment is fair game, generally speaking," said Esme, with a grin. "I mean, even Jesus called religious leaders 'whitewashed tombs and a viper's brood.' Why would anything change in two thousand years?"

"Well, you may have something there." Jabez shot her an amused glance. "But then again perhaps it's not for me to say so."

"Okay," said Esme, "so you've told me what you don't believe and what you don't like about the church, and I have to admit I sympathize. Tell me about what you do believe as well."

THE CLEAR LIGHT OF DAY

His brief, expressive grimace communicated the daunting nature of this prospect, and he took a bite out of his bun, chewing it thoughtfully.

"I tell you one thing Jabez believes," remarked Ember, before he was ready to speak. "He read a book on macrobiotics while he was nursing Maeve, which gave him all kind of ideas about the yin and the yang of his table, and put into his head the idea that every mouthful should be chewed thirty times before 'tis swallowed—and you may take it from me, there's no sillier sight than a macrobiotic convert doing his best to chew porridge. So between trying to chew that bun and trying to chew his cup of tea and trying to describe the Cosmos According to Jabez Ferrall, you'd better take over toasting them buns or it'll be a mighty long time before you get your other half."

Jabez's eyes closed briefly in silent dismissal of this speech, but with a smile Esme took up the toasting fork. She could see Ember had a point.

"I believe," he said eventually, "in the mysteries of Christianity, don't mistake me. Where I stand in life I can well see the cross, and I comprehend its power to transform. I see the resurrection, too, how it lies at the heart of things. If a thing is true, then its truth runs through all of the universe; you take soundings anywhere and you'll find the same truth. Every winter and spring, every sunset and sunrise is the melody of resurrection, and the Christ sits at the heart of it like the pip at the heart of the cherry. There's a deep reverence in me for who Christ is; I know him. I know. But when I told you I got no time for the church, I'm speaking about the house of cards that's built on the top of the mysteries. I'm not interested in all of that. It interferes with the nature of things like Victorian corsets interfere with a woman's body. What I live by is the interweaving and interdependence of all life. The vitality of Spirit is in all creation like sap or blood or breath—even in the stones and the dust and the light, everything. So I believe in treading gently; in healing it where it's hurt and holding it where it's in danger; not using up too much, not taking what isn't given. I think I'm not separate from anything that shares life with me; if I hurt you or disrespect you, I diminish myself, whoever you are—a mouse, a sapling, a river; or another human being. We are all one thing, the being of God expressed in creation, most lovable, most profoundly to be adored. To me 'integrity' means the out-living of that oneness in accountability; looking after things, being trustworthy, keeping faith."

"He hardly knows what hot food is," observed Ember, which prompted Jabez to take a mouthful of tea and another bite of his bun. "Have you done with the butter?" she added as Esme passed her a newly toasted half of teacake, and "Toss a stick or two on that fire, Jabez."

Jabez obediently added some split wood to the fire, and Esme leaned down and pushed the butter dish along the rug in Ember's direction.

Esme felt a sudden, unfamiliar quickening of joy in listening to Jabez. The biggest and most unexpected disappointment for her, in pursuing the path of ordained ministry, had been the reluctance to engage in conversation of spiritual things among the people with whom she lived and worked. She found the aspirations and yearnings and adventures of the human spirit caused universal embarrassment, except among those whose lives would very soon be at an end. To find here, in this simple cottage, an apparently uneducated man discoursing with ease on all the matters she had longed to explore further, the things that were closest to her heart, delighted her.

She leaned forward eagerly. "I suppose what you mean," she said, "is the relationship between holiness and wholeness. In the Lord's Prayer, 'hallowed be thy name,' the word *hallow* means holy but comes from the same root as in the Old English greeting *wes hal!* which means 'be thou whole!' and is the basis for our modern *hallow*. Healing, completeness, come from Spirit."

Jabez nodded, wiping a trace of butter from his fingers onto his trousers as he completed the chewing of his teacake. He swallowed, his eyes kindling with pleasure at her ready interest, and said, "The Native Americans' tepees are circular dwellings arranged into circular villages because they believe the movement of power is circular, like the roundness of the sun and moon and sacred earth, the cycle of the seasons and the curving arc of life that comes back on itself from the helplessness of infancy to the helplessness of great age. Life has a circular dynamic. What goes around comes around. There is no escape from what we put into life; one day it will return to us again."

"Do you think, then," asked Esme, "that there is a separate God—a God over and above us, like the Father of the Christian faith, essentially other, standing apart from creation and watching over it? Or do you believe that there is divine Spirit diffused through everything like perfume or smoke?"

Ember had spread butter on the second half of his currant bun toasted for him by Esme, and put it in his hand. Having just taken a bite of it, Jabez shook his head.

"No," he said, when he had finished it, "neither. I believe we are held in God. It is all sacred because it is held in the mind of God and maintains its being because it is held in the heart of God. We are in God as the wave is in the ocean; and God is in us as the ocean is in the wave."

Ember grinned. "You want to watch out for my wave, it's got a stingray in it," she interrupted. Jabez looked at her, but wouldn't be drawn.

"When I was a child," he continued, "Mother had a text framed on the chimney breast there, IF GOD FEELS FAR AWAY FROM YOU—WHO MOVED? After Dad and Mother died, I took it down because I never liked it. Because I think if you feel far away from God that's just part of the loneliness of being we all suffer. Maybe it means you need a hug or a cup of tea with a friend or an early night, but it can't possibly mean you moved away from God; I mean, where would you go? 'Whither can I go from thy Spirit?' God wouldn't be God if God had finite being—love you could stray outside of. Ember, is there any more tea in that pot—would you like another cup, Esme?

"I read a story once," he continued, as Ember gathered their mugs and bent over the tray to pour more tea, "about a Zen monk on pilgrimage, who sat down at the site of a holy shrine and put his feet up on a statue of the Buddha. I expect I'm telling you what you already know if I say that in the East it's a grave discourtesy even to sit with your feet pointing toward something sacred—you got to keep them tucked back underneath you. So this monk was in trouble, and a fellow pilgrim passing by reproved him for his shocking disrespect, which was fair enough except, as the monk said, 'But where shall I put my feet that is not holy?' Is that tea too strong—I like it that way, but you might find it a bit overpowering?"

"So everything is good?" Esme said. Jabez glanced at her briefly, but said nothing in reply. Ember grinned and drained the remains of her tea from her mug.

"And if everything is good," Esme persisted, "where does the force behind greed and corruption and oppression come from? If we all live in God and all are holy, where do torture chambers fit in? If you take away the balance of heaven and hell, God and the Devil, you have an awful lot of explaining away to do."

Jabez smiled, and looked into the fire. "Yes, I know," he said. "There's lots of ways of resolving this, isn't there? 'The problem of evil.' The Parsees—Zoroastrians—who were very big when the Bible was being made, so that lots of their thinking was woven into it, believed in a universe at war. They posed two supernatural giants, Ahura Mazda, the creator of light and order and peace, and Angra Mainyu, the creator of darkness and disharmony and disease. These two were eternally at war, and the whole cosmos was caught up into their battle. Every single thing every single one of us does would serve to advance the battle in one direction or the other. Every word or action or thought contributes toward the eventual supremacy of light and wholeness or of darkness and disintegration. It's interesting that, as far as I can tell reading the Old Testament, the ancient Jews didn't really have a formal belief in life after death. The immortality of the human soul is the concept of a different culture— Hellenistic, I suppose. The ancient Jews made little distinction between the individual and the community; you lived on in your descendants. Your living being came from God's breathing—he breathed out, you were created; he drew breath in, you died. But the Zoroastrians seem to have intro- duced a belief in spiritual orders of beings—demons and angels—which became culturally incorporated into our Testaments. Then of course, also, they divined wisdom astro- logically—like the magi in Matthew's gospel, who would have been Zoroastrians. Matthew wrote from Syria, fairly

THE CLEAR LIGHT OF DAY

near their territory, and like the book of Isaiah, which speaks so highly of Cyrus of Persia, there's a lot in his writing that resonates with Zoroaster."

"Such as?"

Esme, fascinated and astonished by Jabez's easy erudition, wondered how he had come to such a familiarity with things most people she met knew nothing about, even ministers. She waited, intrigued, to hear what his reply would be.

"Oh," he said, "in Isaiah, the rough places being made smooth—the Parsees believed the world should be perfectly round. The lumps and dents are Angra Mainyu's work. And in Matthew the broad way and the strait and narrow way—it's a reversal of a Zoroastrian teaching. But anyway, what I'm trying to get round to is that if you go back to ancient Judaism, you have a concept that all that comes our way comes from the hand of God to train and shape and discipline us—everything, 'weal and woe.' I suspect this demons and devil stuff came from a different culture—very strong in Matthew, as I say, who seems to be much acculturated to Zoroastrian thought. For myself I'm quite interested in what William Blake said about the polarization of reason and energy, as an alternative concept to good and evil. I believe that everything has a circular flow, coming from good and returning to good; the circulation of God, maybe. When we try to go against the flow, we run into trouble; life hurts us then—it's a learning opportunity, a chance to find the direction of God's love. But then you'll ask me, how should we try to go against the flow if we're part of it? We make mistakes, don't we, awful mistakes, and we wound each other terribly. But I still believe in the goodness at the core of every human soul and the center of all living being. I believe it's all a chance to channel energy wisely. I believe every agony, every cruelty, every adversity is a chance to learn wisdom and compassion, a better way. Patience. Like the paintings that show Christ's hands open, with the nails in their palms. Not clenched. Agonized, but open. It isn't how it must have been, physically; it's an icon of the spiritual wisdom of the cross. And even while I'm struggling to explain, I know it doesn't all tie up neat. There's just some things I don't understand. But in my heart I feel it."

Jabez stopped speaking suddenly and glanced at her, anxious. "Oh dear, I'm sorry—I'm going on too much. Esme, I'm so sorry—you must be bored out of your mind. I get carried away. I'm sorry."

Esme sat looking at Jabez in some amazement. She had never met anyone quite like this. He flushed slightly under the intrusion of her gaze and looked down at his hands, gripped together in sudden embarrassment between his knees.

"What did you say you do for a living?" she said. "*Mend bicycles?*"

And Jabez's head shot up—stung, he flashed a glance at her, affronted.

"That's right," he said, on the defensive. "That's me. But

I can read and inform myself as well as any man. And I can think. Is that okay?"

"No, no! I didn't mean—of course it's okay—I didn't mean to imply there was anything wrong with that, I'm just surprised you haven't chosen to—er—"

"Make something of myself?" There was a dangerous glint in Jabez's eye.

Ember, who had taken up her knitting while Jabez was talking, said, "Sixty-nine years ago in January, the immortals in their grand stupidity made the blunder of entering Jabez Ferrall for the Human Race. All he done ever since is dawdle along admiring the buttercups and the vetch that grow alongside the track. He won't be coming in second place, he won't be coming in third place, nobody even suggested he might try for first place. If the gods are kind, they'll watch over him wandering along to the finishing line and give him a rosette saying 'I had a go.' He's got all his grey matter intact, in a funny order be that as it may; but you could hardly accuse Jabez of being an achiever."

Esme smiled. "I suppose it depends what you mean by achievement. I've no idea what academic qualifications he may have, but he clearly has the intellectual capacity for anything! And I don't think I could make a living with the work of my hands like he does. I simply haven't got the skills. Speaking of which, Jabez, it occurs to me—should I have the lawnmower at the parsonage looked at before the summer? Or will it just be all right?"

Jabez, relaxing, relieved to be let off the hook, placed a small log on the fire and asked, "What did you have done to it last year?"

"Last year? Nothing. I mowed the lawn once or twice when the grass got long and emptied the clippings onto the compost heap, and then I just put it back in the shed."

"Did you clean it?"

"Well—no, I didn't actually."

"Last time I serviced that mower was two summers before you came. Is it running all right?"

"I think so. I mean, I didn't find it very easy to start, and it coughs and splutters a bit—but it cut the grass. Would you—should I have it serviced? How often do you do Marcus's?"

"I look it over before he starts cutting in the spring and before he puts it away in the autumn. Are you asking me to come and see to yours?"

"Well, if that's okay. If you don't mind. How much do you charge?"

"Oh, well … pass me your mug." Jabez began to gather the things together on the tea tray. Esme had an odd sense of seeing his spirit furling, of withdrawal, and a quiet shuttering of his soul.

"Thursday be all right for you?" he said. "I got to go into Southarbour then to have a look at the window frame in the bathroom at your superintendent's parsonage. I could come on after. Be about three o'clock I expect."

"That would be really helpful," said Esme. This sounded like something of a dismissal, and she stood up, concerned not to outstay her welcome.

"It's been ever so kind of you to invite me in for tea. It feels like, well, sort of like home here. You've done me no end of good."

Jabez straightened up with the tray. He looked pleased.

"Next time you come," said Ember, without looking up from her knitting, "you can bring some more of they buns if you pass through Brockhyrst Priory. I liked 'em. It's nice to have a treat. Maybe they do coconut macaroons?"

"Ember! For pity's sake! You can't—you mustn't—" Jabez blinked anxiously, and Esme couldn't help laughing at him.

"They do, as it happens," she said. "I'll bring both."

Ember nodded, continuing serenely with her knitting.

Jabez took the tea tray out to the kitchen and Esme followed him. She stood in the doorway to the yard. The rain had stopped, but the wind still blew cold.

"Thank you, Jabez," she said, turning back to face him before she went on her way. "It's felt so nice being here today. I mean—" she hesitated, feeling shy; "—like being with friends."

Jabez stood with the dishcloth in his hands, looking down at it. He nodded.

"I'll see you Thursday, then," he said.

"Esme!" he called after her as she went out into the yard.

She stopped. "Esme, when you come again, bring your car up into the yard. There's room. Don't leave it parked on the road."

"Oh, I think it's okay there," she said. "I know it blocks the pavement a bit, and I know Ember doesn't like that, but I park it carefully so pedestrians can get by."

"Yes, but ..." He shrugged his shoulders and buried his hands deep in his pockets, offering her a brief sideways glance. "Traffic comes by close sometimes and besides that ... Bring your car into the yard, Esme; don't leave it parked on the road."

"Well, okay, if you think so. Thanks anyway. Bye-bye!"

As she went on her way, Esme felt a warmth of acceptance and belonging somewhere at the center of her being. *Next time you come ... When you come again.* She stowed their words away as a secret treasure of belonging. *I love those two. They're amazing. I love that cottage,* she thought. She walked cheerfully down the path to her car, smiling at the thought of Ember looking forward to macaroons.

Jabez went back into his kitchen, checked the firebox in the Rayburn, and threw in a couple of small logs from the basket. He picked up the tin of tobacco from the table and rolled himself a cigarette. He stood leaning against the stove rail, smoking reflectively, very still.

After a short while Ember came into the kitchen. She washed up the mugs they had used and emptied the teapot.

"'Tisn't like you to invite somebody in," she remarked,

drying the crockery and hanging the mugs on their hooks beneath the shelf beside the table.

"I like her, Jabez," she said.

Their eyes met, and he held her gaze, but he said nothing, had no need to.

"You want to roll 'em thicker," said Ember. "That thing's gone out."

Though she and Marcus worshipped at Brockhyrst Priory, on the afternoon of Holy Saturday, Hilda Griffiths took a large armful of daffodils and a generous mound of greenery from the garden to help decorate Wiles Green Chapel for Easter Day.

She returned from this mission to find Marcus relaxing in the sitting room with a cup of tea and the *Saturday Telegraph*.

"Do you know, my dear," she said conspiratorially, "I've just seen Pam Coleman in the village as I was coming away from the chapel."

"Really?" Marcus tried unsuccessfully to sound impressed.

"And, do you know, she says she's seen Esme going into Jabez Ferrall's place three times this week! Parks her car right outside on the road!"

"Well, I should think she's wise to do that," Marcus murmured vaguely. "I expect Jabez's yard has been cluttered up with bits of lawnmower belonging to people like me with the first sign of fair weather."

Hilda perched herself on the chair opposite him, and leaned toward the screening *Telegraph*, not to be put off.

"I said to Pam, 'I expect she's looking for a bike, dear—I know she was interested to find one; Marcus recommended her to try Mr. Ferrall.' But, really! Three times in one week! I think it's a bit indiscreet! In a person of her standing—don't you think she should know better? After all, an odd-job man! And right under our noses in the village! What's more, Mr. Ferrall must be twice Esme's age!"

"Twice her age?" Marcus lowered his paper, disregarding the crumpling of its pages, his eyes vaguely aglow. "Twice her age? Then, my dear, the time must be auspicious for them, if your surmise is correct, and they have embarked on a now deepening friendship. Because only in one year of your respective lifetimes can you be twice someone else's age."

"Marcus, whatever are you *talking* about?" Hilda's tone grew petulant, and she flung up one hand in a gesture of frustration. "He's twice her age and he always will be!"

Marcus's gaze rested its lambent gleam upon her.

"Not at all, my dear, you are surely not considering. Supposing Esme to be thirty-five and Jabez to be seventy— though I am not as convinced as you are that the gap is so very great; I should have put Esme more nearly at forty myself. But, taking these ages as correct—for surely Jabez Ferrall is not eighty years old, then he would indeed be twice Esme's age. Yet, in the year Esme was born, when no doubt Jabez would then have been already thirty-five, he was clearly at that time far more than twice her age; as he would have been when she was eight—or sixteen. But, as she grew older, she would have gained on him, until she has this year, if you are right, achieved the triumph of becoming half his age. Therefore, by the time *she* is seventy (given that is his present age, though as far as I am aware he has not in reality celebrated his seventieth birthday yet), she will be two-thirds his age, for he will by then be only a hundred and five. And, should he live to be 140 (though by the sound of his cough now I think he may not), why by then she, at 105, will be three-quarters his age; time thus perhaps moving more slowly for Jabez Ferrall than it does for Esme—as indeed the thoughtful observer might in any case deduce from the relative tempo of their lifestyles— though no doubt it seems to crack on fast enough to him. Who knows but, if he could only live long enough, she continuing thus to gain on him, one day she might so far advance as to be twice as old as he is!"

Hilda eyed him with uncertainty and suspicion.

"But …" she paused to compute in her mind, "that couldn't happen, my dear," she said firmly, adding, after a pause, a note of uncertainty creeping in, "could it?"

But Marcus had returned to his paper, declining to take further part in the conversation. "No …" he murmured absently, his voice barely audible, not the faintest hint of encouragement in his tone.

FOUR

As the days lengthened and warmed, and full summer burgeoned in the great green canopy of leaves, Esme delighted in the sparkle of sunlight on the ocean when she was in Southarbour and the country lanes adorned with wild flowers as she drove out to Brockhyrst Priory and Wiles Green.

With some reluctance, because she would rather have bought something from him, Esme accepted Jabez's reiterated advice to choose a modern, lightweight bicycle. He found her one in the "For Sale" columns in the free newspaper and came with her to have a look at it before she purchased it.

At first, as spring blossomed into summer, she restricted herself to modest cycling forays at quiet times of the day— round the corner to the grocer's or along to Portland Street for worship and evening meetings. Then, more adventurous, in the warmth of the long summer days, she cycled out to

Brockhyrst Priory for her pastoral visiting; and by the middle of August, the seven miles to Wiles Green seemed entirely manageable given a day with a not-too-crowded schedule. She felt stronger and fitter, moved easier. Every now and then she had hopes of losing weight, but cycling increased her appetite. Somehow it seemed less important; she liked herself better than she had.

Her hair went blonde in the sun, and her skin brown, and life seemed good.

She knew that much of her contentment came from her friendship with Jabez and Ember, whom she visited several times in the week. She would call in whenever she passed through Wiles Green; and on her day off, or if she felt lonely or at a loose end. Without ceremony, they made her welcome. Sitting on the floor of Jabez's workshop, watching his capable hands patient on a task, mending and making, coaxing the best out of worn machinery most people would have thrown away, Esme felt utterly at home. On colder days she would light the fire at the back of the workshop, and the cat would climb onto her lap as she sat on the edge of the ashes. Most days, through the summer, Jabez worked out in the yard, and then she would sit in the sunshine, resting her back against the wall of the cottage. They talked about so many things, and sometimes silence lay companionable between them.

Early on in this friendship, Esme had been puzzled by the relationship between Jabez and Ember.

"Are you and Ember—is Ember your partner?" she asked him on the day in late spring that Jabez checked over the bicycle she had bought as she sat on the edge of his workbench, a mug of tea in her hands.

He looked up, startled. "Ember's eighty-six!" he said. "Not that age needs to be a bar," he added, returning to his task; "'tis who you are not how old you are that counts. But … God save us …" He straightened up, gazing sightlessly out through the yard door, a look of absolute horror on his face as the thought sunk in: "Imagine being married to Ember!"

"Somebody was, once," said Esme.

He glanced at her and laughed. "Yes," he replied, "but not for long."

He looked at the bike from all angles, having examined, cleaned, and oiled parts of it to his satisfaction, then pronounced it fit for use.

"You got a good buy," he approved and picked up the almost-cold mug of tea waiting for him beside Esme on the bench.

"Ember's lived in the village forever," he said, "but she gate-crashed my life after Maeve died. I was in a state, then. In pieces, to be honest. Ember turned up at the cottage one evening, asking if I would fill her Thermos flask with some tea. She had a very small clapboard cottage, dilapidated; falling down it was, but she didn't care. She cooked outside on a fire in the back garden when it was fine and on her fire indoors when it rained. I think she did most of what she had to do outside, but she had water laid on there—one tap if my memory serves me right. She came to my cottage because a variety of things had happened all at once. She wasn't very well, which is unusual for her; she'd had an intruder, an unpleasant young man who threatened her with all manner of things when she saw him off, which she did in no uncertain terms. And the washer had gone on her tap. A Thermos of tea sounded a bit insufficient, and I offered her a bed for the night, because it was dusk and she seemed rather vulnerable—" he grinned, "—I didn't know her very well, then! She came in and had a meal, and I thought it was me doing her a good turn, but I was so grateful for someone to talk to. Everything still hurt in a very raw way then, and it all came pouring out, and she listened. She had no advice and no platitudes, which was a relief. I sorted her tap washer for her in the morning, and she went back to her cottage for a while. My place was in a bit of a mess; I'd let it slip, lost interest in life and myself, really; and after that night Ember came and cooked for me and did some basic housework—very basic, is Ember's housework. She wouldn't have any payment, but she ate with me, and after awhile it seemed sense for her to move in. After all, she's getting on a bit. So she sold up her cottage—or in real terms I suppose you'd say she sold the land her cottage stood on, because no one could have lived in that ruin but Ember. That was about four years ago. We get on all right, but no—" he smiled, "—she certainly isn't my partner. There you are, then; that looks good to ride. What hidden faults it has will no doubt show up later." He drained the mug and put it back on the bench. "Happy cycling. You'll get good use out of that."

As Esme gained in confidence and experience in her ministry, establishing her own style as a pastor, her own role in the community, she found that when it drained her, when she was confused or bewildered or discouraged or tired, an evening curled up on the sofa by the fire in Jabez's cottage would restore her and bring her back to peace.

There were times when she needed Jabez and Ember very much. As Gladys Taylor's illness progressed through that summer, Esme spent as much time as she could with her; visiting her in hospital, sitting by her nursing-home bed. She knew it was routine work for a minister, so it took her by surprise to discover how far her soul slipped out of its customary housing to walk with Gladys on the unearthly paths of spirit as Gladys began the long journey out of this world.

Afterward, on the day of the funeral, when the service was over and Gladys's body committed to cremation, Esme shared in the tea and sandwiches that followed at Wiles Green, and then took refuge with Ember in the cottage—Jabez was out fixing someone's hen coop that had been disastrously compromised by a fox. Ember made tea and said little, didn't resort to her usual sardonic banter, listened while Esme told her the story of Gladys's commonplace dying, tears slipping down her face.

"You done well, my love," was the only comment she made.

Esme realized that something had eased in her being; that the ordinary troubles of her congregation no longer chafed on her; her housebound elderly members' anxious preoccupations and fixations with present illness and past relationships no longer irritated her; she had time for them and affection. She wondered if this was because of Jabez and Ember, who asked nothing, but always had time for her.

Apart from the sickness and sorrow to which she was often witness, and the ongoing difficulties presented by the responsibility for aging and decaying buildings carried less and less effectively by aging and dwindling congregations, one of the greatest challenges Esme met in an average week was that of trying to keep the peace between some of the stronger personalities of her chapel communities. Sometimes the personal effort of tact and diplomacy required by this almost exhausted her. At Portland Street, she had made a huge mistake. Her property steward had stepped down from office after nine years of smoothly fielding the emergencies and routine dilemmas of managing the premises. To replace him, she had been delighted to secure the willing services of a quiet and reticent man who had been a manager for a large electrical supplier before his retirement seven years ago. With horror, having appointed her new steward, she watched as, in the intoxication of new power, he blossomed into something akin to a military dictator, so that in turn the leaders of the playgroup, the Mothers and Toddlers group, the Brownies, the Boys Brigade, the karate club, and the women's meeting called on the phone or in person in states of indignation and distress. The long saga of what Esme afterward thought of as The Blutack War took most of her energies for several weeks.

It was easier when she herself bore the brunt of the oddities of her church members. A sense of humor was usually sufficient, even with Miss Trigg.

The chapel at Wiles Green had no central aisle but two aisles on either side of the main block of pews and flanked by the smaller side blocks. At the conclusion of worship, Esme, having blessed her congregation, would make her way from the pulpit down one aisle, through the door at the back into the Sunday school room, where she would be met, greeted, and thanked by the steward on duty emerging from the door at the foot of the corresponding aisle on the other side of the chapel.

This was often a moment of friendly and kindly fellowship—a brief time to comment on the weather and catch up on the steward's home news before the rest of the congregation finished their personal concluding prayers, greeted each other, and made their way out of the church.

This brief moment of fellowship metamorphosed into an ordeal on the occasions when Miss Trigg's turn came on the stewards' duty roster. Zealous, grim-faced, and overlooking nothing, she would greet Esme with a list of the theological shortcomings of her preaching, as often as not demanding an explanation.

The first time Esme ventured all the way out to Wiles

Green on her bicycle for evening worship (Miss Trigg approved this mode of transport, being both arduous and frugal and thus reminding her of her youth) on a dry Sunday after a wet week in early August, her duty steward for the service was Miss Trigg. In the vestry before worship, Esme was as charming as she knew how to be, enquiring solicitously after the condition of Miss Trigg's hiatal hernia, the well-being of her nieces, and the progress of her vegetable garden. Miss Trigg, whose arthritis eased in the summer, in easygoing mood, felt disposed to be pleasant.

After worship, with a kindly smile, she had prepared her compliment.

"When you came to us," she said, advancing to shake Esme's hand as they emerged through their respective doors, "they said you preached good sermons; they said you preached *wonderful* sermons!" She contemplated Esme from under the brim of her felt hat. "Well, I haven't heard any yet. But I thought tonight's was a little better."

"Thank you," said Esme, weakly. Straight after leading an act of worship, a preacher has very little in the way of defenses.

When she had shaken the hands of her congregation, enquired after their various ongoing life situations, and seen them on their way, she found herself alone again with Miss Trigg, who, with an armful of hymnbooks received from the departing worshippers, stood admiring her bicycle. They chatted for a while about the old days before the war, when

Miss Trigg as a young woman had been able to reach terrifying speeds freewheeling down Stoddards Hill, and Miss Trigg enquired genially where Esme had acquired her bike. As they wandered across to the bookshelves and Esme picked up her papers to stow in the basket Jabez had fixed on her handlebars, she explained about the advertisement in the newspaper and added that Mr. Ferrall in the village had been kind enough to look the bike over before she bought it.

"Mr. Ferrall? Oh, so you've met *him*, have you?" Miss Trigg replaced the hymnbooks in the shelves with a certain veiled violence. Esme waited for whatever might follow. She had a feeling Miss Trigg had not finished.

"Backslider, Mr. Ferrall is," continued Miss Trigg with the particular air of vicious relish she kept for matters of disapproval. Esme waited, intrigued. Her imagination was trying unsuccessfully to fit Jabez into the context of this chapel congregation.

"Known him all my life." Miss Trigg slapped the last hymnbook into line with its fellows. "He was in my Sunday school class when he was a lad."

Esme's eyebrows rose. Jabez in Miss Trigg's Sunday school? However old must she be?

"A quiet lad," remembered Miss Trigg, "and quick at his lessons. Quick to learn and to remember. Always had his verse ready, from the week before. 'Course, he had a good start—his mother was chapel. She used to bring him, not just send him, every week: Faithful, was Alice Ferrall. And a true believer. Washed in the blood of the Lamb. From sixteen. But Silas Ferrall, he was a freethinker!" Miss Trigg flashed a glance of absolute knowledge at Esme—"The sins of the fathers!" she explained.

"Alice Ferrall died when Jabez was fourteen." Miss Trigg narrowed her eyes and leaned in a little toward Esme. "And since that day he's set foot in a church but twice. Once to marry a woman and once to bury her. And that was church, not chapel. Backslider. There's no redemption for such as 'e. One who's known the ways of the Lord. Which he did. One who's put his hand to the plough and looked back. He's not fit now for the kingdom of God. That's the Word of the Lord. Have you your key or am I locking up?"

As she cycled home from this encounter, Esme turned it over in her mind, conscious of a divergence of possible responses open to her. She could choose to confront Miss Trigg head-on, taking issue with her strange theology and flagrant bigotry. She had a suspicion that sooner or later this might be necessary, because Miss Trigg's disapproval of her resulted in a steady low-key campaign of undermining that would bring them in time face-to-face—unless her pastoral input in sickness or personal tragedy in some presently unforeseen event should win her that allegiance of gratitude that can bridge any depth of doctrinal mismatch.

Or she could choose to continue with her present course of careful courtesy, agreeing with everything she could find to agree with, persisting with friendly overtures, and working at damage limitation among the members of her flock wounded by Miss Trigg's ruthless promotion of her views, undertaken with unflagging scrupulosity as a biblical witness. Esme disliked confrontation and knew that the way she handled things, sympathizing behind Miss Trigg's back with the enemies she made, was less than honest.

Yet she also knew that, because of the responsibility of authority she held, if she ever took Miss Trigg on in direct and outright battle, it was essential she win the fight, or Miss Trigg's grip on that long-suffering congregation would be unbreakable and would be a problem for any pastor following Esme as well as Esme herself.

There was something more besides. If Esme won that fight, Miss Trigg, who was eighty-one, would be broken and would have to retire from battle in humiliation. Her aggressive religion and self-righteous posturing arose partly from narrow experience of life and loyalty to those she had loved and the traditions they had instilled in her, but also covered, Esme felt sure, a deep insecurity and lack of self-esteem. Miss Trigg was a bully, and bullies are brittle and frail. She must just carry on with her present approach for now—keep things sweet. Time would tell, and the balance of relationships in the faith community was always an evolving dynamic.

When she offered herself to serve as an ordained minister, Esme had not imagined that her energies would be so occupied with the shadowboxing exercise of negotiating the minefield of intricate relationships among the personalities of the chapel communities. She had imagined spiritual battles in intercession alongside dedicated prayer warriors; she had imagined herself empowering the faithful by her collaborative style of ministry; she had imagined a personal discipline of prayer and theological study, refreshed by a rhythm of retreats—not keeping her head down with the low stealth and cunning of a fox in the wily accomplishment of the smallest achievements, along with a permanent low-grade exhaustion that made the tasks of prayer and theological study so unattractive.

Space to breathe and dream and be is the essential foundation underlying any program of reading and prayer. Esme knew this but watched helplessly as every day and all her energy were relentlessly swallowed by the unending round of expectations and jobs to be done. It seemed impossible to claw back the amount of time necessary for an adequate routine of spiritual refreshment. Time and again, in the vestry, before worship began, beneath the prayer the steward offered aloud to God, Esme slipped in her own silent entreaty, *I'm sorry, God, I'm sorry—I haven't given this enough prayer or thought or time. Feed them because they are your flock. They should be fed because of me—but feed them in spite of me, for your love's sake.*

In her preaching, she knew she had added very little of fresh insight in the last few years. She still relied on the resources of her ordination training lectures and was grateful that oversight of three different chapels meant most sermons had a minimum of three runs before they had to be discarded.

Cycling through the fading light of the evening, Esme turned all this over in her mind as she had so many times. On the steep incline sweeping down toward Brockhyrst Priory, preoccupied with the perplexity of how to pick her way through everything with some kind of spiritual integrity, she almost collided with a squirrel that scampered across her path, stopped sharply to avoid hurting it, and felt her brakes suddenly go.

The squirrel dashed to safety, and Esme swerved sideways into the hedge to avoid picking up any more speed on the way down the hill.

Feeling silly, and grateful for the deserted road, she freed herself from entanglement with the twigs and thorns, dismounted, and walked down to the foot of the hill, then cycled the rest of the way home to Southarbour with caution, stowing the bike in the shed with the intention of dealing with it later.

Though August was often a slow month, Esme had a busy week, occupied with hospital visiting, officiating at two funerals on behalf of colleagues on holiday, then a wedding to do on the Saturday. As she prepared her sermon for Sunday morning, Esme reflected that she had been two years in her present appointment, with little so far to feel proud of.

At Brockhyrst Priory morning worship, she thought

about the difference it made to have a cheerful and pleasant steward on duty, as Marcus met her at the door with a smile, unobtrusively available as she organized her papers in the pulpit and spoke to the organist, and ready to accompany her into the vestry when she was ready to go there.

In the vestry, during the ten minutes remaining before the time for Marcus to say a prayer with her and precede her into the body of the chapel, they chatted amiably, Esme enquiring after Hilda's health and telling Marcus about her bike and how much she was enjoying it.

"Yes, I've spotted you from time to time, whizzing by out in our neck of the woods. Did you find Jabez Ferrall any help?"

He nodded as Esme spoke enthusiastically about Jabez's kindness to her, both in his help with the bicycle and with a variety of minor repairs at home.

"Indeed, he's a good man. Very able. Very intelligent. I'm glad you've found him useful. I do myself."

"Yes, I've come across him getting your lawnmower ready for cutting the grass in the spring."

"Oh well—" Marcus chuckled, "—he does sterling work. I always say to Hilda, it's important to take our custom to people in the village if we want a living village community to continue. Otherwise it'll just peter out into a holidaymakers' dormitory. I can't really put much business Jabez Ferrall's way—but maybe enough custom to help keep him in diesel for that old green truck of his—which he seems to have had from time immemorial and keeps on the road by patient determination and consummate skill. I'm glad you went to him. He's retired now really, of course, but I doubt if he has any sort of pension from what he used to earn. And he may look like a leprechaun, but I imagine he is actually flesh and blood and occasionally has to eat some bread with his free-range eggs and his local honey. What time do you make it, Esme? Ten twenty-eight by my watch. Are you ready to pray?"

Esme heard not a word of his prayer, though she did her best to concentrate. Jabez had never asked for payment for any of the numerous small jobs he had done for her, and she felt suddenly sick with anxiety at the thought of him managing on a state pension, undertaking work for nothing for a woman with no dependents living in occupational housing on a stipend that probably amounted to more than twice his annual income.

She followed Marcus into chapel feeling wretched, fluffed her call to worship, and hardly recovered her concentration until two-thirds of the way through the first hymn.

She consoled herself then with the recollection that the failure of her bicycle brakes would require a repair for which, this time, she would offer payment on a proper footing.

When the first prayers were done, as she listened to Marcus giving out the notices, welcoming her to the pulpit and announcing the offering, it occurred to Esme to wonder why he and Hilda worshipped at Brockhyrst Priory and not in the chapel at Wiles Green. She thought perhaps they had lived nearer Brockhyrst Priory before his retirement, and she asked him about this at the end of the service, as she stood with him by the door waiting to greet the people; he having shaken her hand and thanked her, commenting thoughtfully on some of the points she had raised in her sermon.

The second door steward stood a few feet away, replacing unused hymnbooks into the empty shelves.

"The chapel at Wiles Green—well—um—Wiles Green ..." Marcus seemed embarrassed by her question. "I mean, I hope you'll be understanding, Esme, if I say that the chapel style at Wiles Green is just a bit too *holy* for me. I'm an ordinary chap, really. Please don't misunderstand me. My faith is of huge importance to me. But ..."

Esme looked at him. "It's Miss Trigg, isn't it?"

Marcus shifted uncomfortably and looked down at his feet. "Miss Trigg is a force at Wiles Green, certainly," he said, and then, valiantly, "What would Wiles Green Chapel be without her though, eh?"

"A lot nicer," interjected his fellow steward, without turning from stowing the hymnbooks. Marcus looked discomfited.

"I absolutely didn't hear that," he said, his face clouding. "Esme, they're a long time coming out this morning. You stay here to shake people's hands, and I'll go and fetch you a cup of coffee."

As she greeted her flock straggling out of the church and through into the afternoon of that day, Esme continued to brood on the problem of Miss Trigg. She wished something would alter or give in the situation without direct intervention. The church had to have a place for everyone, an unconditional acceptance of even the most awkward personality. The difficulties came when one individual was so hard to relate to that the community as a whole became discouraged, newcomers felt alienated, and the faithful unobtrusively drifted away. Given that Miss Trigg had already lived eighty-one years, a natural solution lay in the not too distant future, but Esme hoped a less negative possibility could be found. Besides which, Miss Trigg looked as tough as baked leather, with plenty of life in her yet.

She was still on Esme's mind after the close of worship in the evening. Esme had been preaching in her superintendent's chapel at West Parade, in the next town along the coast from Southarbour. She drove across country toward Wiles Green, tired at the end of the day. Sunday preaching always drained her of energy, and the habit she had acquired over the summer of spending an hour with Jabez and Ember had transformed the feeling of Sunday evening from a fretful, spent, overweariness to a satisfied sense of completion.

She turned off the road and up the unmade track that curved behind Jabez's cottage into his yard with a sense of homecoming. She felt that she belonged here as she knocked on the kitchen door and let herself in.

In the cottage, although the evening was warm, as dusk approached Jabez had lit a fire in the sitting room, and

Ember sat in her usual chair with her knitting while Jabez had a book on his lap in his armchair by the fire. He had left the Rayburn to go out, and their kettle stood on a trivet, fastened to the grate, that could be swung round over the flames.

Esme curled up in the corner of the sofa and told them about her day. She asked Jabez about being in Miss Trigg's Sunday school class, and he smiled, and reminisced about the other children and their experience of chapel fifty years ago. He spoke about going to evening worship with his mother, about how much it had meant to her, and how pleased she had been by his own devout leanings in those days.

"Yes. I gave my life to Jesus. I suppose he's still got it. I don't seem to have one myself. And I invited him into my heart. And—" he looked at Esme with a sudden defiance, "—he's still there, whatever Miss Trigg may have told you. Somewhere. Bit dusty perhaps. The poor carpenter of Nazareth."

He bent down and picked up the poker, prodded the logs together on the fire, and poked the trivet, on which the kettle had begun to whine, aside from the flames. Then he relaxed his hand and let the end of the poker rest on the hearth.

"Dear Lord, what must it be like?" he said quietly. "All these years. A prisoner in the heart of such as me. 'Tisn't true then, what they say about hell. He's there, too. We were quite a stretch there together."

With a sudden smile of mischief, Esme remembered and recounted to them Miss Trigg's glowering remarks on the state of Jabez's soul, his ignominious condition as a backslider, unfit for the kingdom of God. She laughed at the memory, but Jabez said nothing.

Ember startled them both by spitting with sudden force into the fire, which hissed back at her. She looked into the flames for a few seconds, and then turned her fierce gaze upon them.

"I like to know," she said belligerently, "what kind of kingdom this kingdom of heaven be; all peopled with Miss Triggs and slamming its doors on Jabez Ferrall. Sounds a hell of a place to me. I choose my word with care. No wonder their God's always so miserable. I'd be the same myself if I had the governing of it. Such a kingdom as knows nothing of the meaning of gentleness. Trouble with chapel is all their eternity offers them is a choice of one hell or the other. No wonder they all look as though they got indigestion. 'Tis all that doctrine; it repeats on 'em. Heaven defend us from their salvation if it has no part in the life of such as 'e."

She shut her mouth like a trap on the close of this vehement speech, her small eyes snapping and sparkling with her fury. Then, holding Esme's gaze, less angry but no less compelling, she added, "Jabez is a good man, and you know it well. And if you let that eyesore tell you different and you never contradicted her, then I hope you're ashamed of yourself."

Esme could not think of any adequate reply to this.

Without bringing it into consciousness, she vaguely registered the sense of dragging weariness that underlay everything in the years since she had been ordained. It came in no small part from the inescapable exposure to the relentless expectation and excoriating blame of strong-minded old women. Somehow she had become trapped in a life that forever held her in a direct glare demanding, "Well?"

She could feel herself blushing.

Jabez did not look at her, but he was swift in his rescue.

"I never could stand up to Miss Trigg myself," he said, "and she's right, I am unfit for the kingdom of God. I thought we all were. I haven't even aspired to be fit for it. I'd been hoping for mercy, I think. And Miss Trigg has the edge on me, because I haven't even done myself credit in the kingdom of earth, which is less fussy and more forgiving than the kingdom of heaven. At least she's held down a steady job and earned herself a pension: All I've achieved is a terror of the human race and a lifetime scraping by repairing bicycles. I admire her. She was a doctor's receptionist for forty years and very competent. She nursed her mother fifteen years an invalid in her own home. And she runs that chapel like clockwork."

Silence followed these words, but not for long. Jabez had his head bent, turned away to look toward the fire, but he couldn't ignore Ember's gaze boring like a power drill into the side of his head. He shifted uncomfortably.

"What?" he said defensively.

"Do you lie in bed at night *practicing* these 'umble things to say, or does it come natural?" Ember demanded. "Because they trip off your tongue with an ease that astonishes me. Lucy Trigg is a horrible old woman and you know it."

"Practicing? Ember, that's just not fair!" His head jerked up to look at her, his face flushed with indignation. "Horrible old woman, is she? Well, it takes one to know one, anyway."

Ember grinned at him, taunting, her eyes sparkling. "That's more like it," she said, her gaze holding his with the jaunty confidence of a very experienced combatant.

But Jabez looked tired. Esme could see that whatever he thought of it rationally, Miss Trigg's indictment had found its mark and hurt. She wished she had never mentioned the conversation and felt unsure of how to salve the wound she had made.

"Bike running all right?" Jabez found a way out of the impasse, setting Miss Trigg aside. "You came in your car tonight, didn't you? I thought I heard you turn into the yard."

"That's right—it's partly why I came, actually, but I forgot about it after I got here. I think the brake's broken in some way. I was coming down Stoddards Hill quite fast into Brockhyrst Priory, and I slammed the brakes on for a squirrel out thrill seeking, and they went. I managed okay just going gently enough to use my foot as a brake, but I wanted to ask you if you would fix them for me. Will you be coming out to Southarbour sometime soon? I'm not sure I'd be quite safe coming all the way out here without brakes."

"You certainly would not! Cable snapped, by the sound of things. I thought I'd checked the brakes out carefully; they should have lasted you longer than this. I can come over tomorrow morning—will you be there? Give me the key to the shed if not. I'll just pick the bike up and bring it back here, that'll be the easiest."

"D'you know," said Esme, still mindful of the hurt she had caused before, "it makes so much difference to me to have you here. There have been all manner of things you've fixed and mended for me: You give me tea and toast and you check the oil in my car—you make me feel so safe and well looked after."

Jabez's eyes shone in a sudden smile and then, shyly, he bent to push the kettle back over the fire. "You're welcome," he said quietly as he did this, "you're welcome. You're just part of the family." He glanced across at her, happy but slightly embarrassed. "Would you like a cup of tea, Esme? Ember?"

Esme laughed. "I never knew anybody drink as much tea as you two do—but yes, please."

"Tea's good for you." Jabez took the pot to empty the dregs from their last drink and put new tea leaves in. "It's cleansing for the system," he said, as he came back to the fireside and intercepted the now shrieking kettle.

"Is it?" asked Esme in surprise. "I thought too much tea was bad news."

"You take a peep at the inside of Jabez's teapot, my love,

if you want to see for yourself how cleansing it is," said Ember, who had picked up her knitting needles and was casting on a new row. "His gut's as full of tannin as his lungs is full of tar. I 'spect he got furred-up arteries, too, from living off those eggs from his chickens. Not a tube in his body but will be blocked with some kind of gunk. One way or another his innards is probably coated with stuff a more frugal man could harvest and sell in tins for shoe polish."

"Thanks, Ember!" Jabez stirred the tea in the pot, pouring Esme's first because she liked it weaker.

"I don't like you smoking," said Esme softly, as he handed her the mug of tea. "It's so bad for your health."

Jabez began to look slightly harassed. "I don't smoke much indoors, not when you're here."

"It's not that I mind it for me—I think your tobacco smells quite nice. It's the damage to your body that worries me."

"Don't you fret about Jabez, my love. Smoke? He don't really smoke. You ever seen Jabez with a cigarette properly alight? Besides, he's not got the money to smoke. He rolls they things so thin I could pass one through the eye of a darning needle."

"Oh," Esme laughed. "He doesn't smoke Camels then!"

Ember looked at her blankly.

"Camels," Esme prompted. "The eye of a needle? Never mind, Ember, it's nothing—it doesn't matter. Camels—they're a kind of cigarette."

Jabez sat down in his armchair behind his cup of tea.

"Does this have an end?" he asked, amused but looking somewhat cornered, uncomfortable at being the focus of their conversation. "I haven't got many vices. Compared with shooting crack and hunting foxes, tea and cigarettes is fairly innocuous, isn't it? Esme, are you hungry? Did you have a bite to eat or did you come straight from church?"

She admitted that she was hungry and accepted gratefully the offer he made of cheese sandwiches. While he was out in the kitchen making them, she said to Ember, "Jabez has been so kind to me—and you have. Things get a bit wearing when you're on your own. Really, I'm ever so grateful."

Ember turned her knitting and sipped her tea. "You made a difference to him, too, my love. Do anything for you, would Jabez. You given him a great deal."

"I have?" Esme looked at her in surprise. "I sometimes feel a bit guilty because I come here so much and let myself be fed and looked after and don't give anything in return."

"That's the thing you given him," said Ember, the dark brightness of her gaze amid a thousand wrinkles contemplating Esme over the top of her knitting. "Jabez isn't happy without he got someone to love. Been like giving a puppy to a child, having you turn up here as you did. Done him the world of good. Suits us all."

It was with a sense of well-being that Esme parted from them later in the evening. They had chatted about this and that and nothing, discussed the parasite infection troubling the legs of one of Jabez's hens, and the promising crop of apples ripening in his orchard. Ember described to Esme the various garments she had knitted and the mixed reactions when she presented them as gifts, and her vivid account made Esme laugh. When she went on her way, the concerns of her work had receded, and she felt at peace.

Jabez came out into the yard with her. "Go carefully," he said, as he often did when she got into her car. "I'll be over in the morning, to see to your bike. Just leave the shed unlocked if you go out."

The stars were shining as Esme left, with the first scent of autumn in the night air.

"Your cable's snapped."

Esme had a staff meeting in the morning and returned to find that Jabez had called and taken her bike. She had several visits in nursing homes to make in the afternoon, but drove out afterward to Wiles Green and found Jabez in his workshop, squatting down to examine her bike, his cat stretched contentedly in the ashes by the comfortable glow that smoked under the flue.

"I wonder if it would take one a bit thicker. Anyway, I've been thinking from what you said I might have tightened the pivot bolts too much when I put the brake arms back. It's been so wet and muddy for the time of year, more wear and tear I expect—I better look at them. Don't want you having an accident. Put another stick or two of wood on the fire, and sit you down by there—it won't take me long."

He lifted her bike onto a stand, and knelt down beside it, looking critically at the brake system. "Can you pass me the Allen key?" He looked up at her swiftly, smiled at her blank incomprehension, and got to his feet to fetch it himself.

Esme pushed together the glowing remains of firewood in the bed of soft grey ash and added some small twigs to rekindle a flame.

"You were very nice about Miss Trigg last night," she said.

The dry sticks caught fire, and she placed some larger pieces in a pyramid on top.

"I believe in being nice about people," he replied, and she watched his fingers deftly removing the anchor nuts and the wire from the straddle yoke, setting the bits carefully beside him, dismantling its mysteries with competence. "Besides," he added, flashing her a glance of mischief she thought almost reminiscent of Ember, "Miss Trigg's done a lot for me—more than she knows."

"Has she?" Esme looked at him in surprise, pleased and relieved to hear something good about Miss Trigg.

He had the bits on the floor and looked at them all, wiping them with an oily rag, turning them over to look for faults. He reached across to a tin on the ground near him and selected a piece of emery paper, sanded a metal stud, examined it again, sanded it some more, then reached the paper back into the tin and wiped down the part he had smoothed.

"Go on," said Esme. "Miss Trigg."

Jabez hesitated.

"Well?" she said curiously.

He took a breath, uncertain, then proceeded. "I got married in the 1960s. I was twenty-six and Maeve was nineteen. We hadn't been anywhere much, we weren't sophisticated people. Brought up church and chapel, we were—a bit innocent. I don't suppose you remember the 1960s."

"Not much, not really. I mean, I was born in 1959, so I was little while it was all happening. But what's that got to do with Miss Trigg?"

Jabez was satisfied with the state of the bits he had before him, and fetching a length of cable he began to reassemble the cable housing, threading the wire through the hole in the yoke anchor bolt. "At that time, Miss Trigg ran a young people's fellowship at the chapel. I never went and Maeve was church not chapel, but Maeve's friend Susan always used to go." He pulled the tin toward him with his free hand and rooted in it for a spanner. "Although you were only a babe in the '60s, I'm sure you know it was a time of revelation to us young folk then. There were books and magazines and things—pamphlets even. 'Things you always wanted to know and never dared ask.' Are you with me?"

"Yes," said Esme. She sensed a certain reticence in him, and felt so curious as to what he was going to tell her that she hardly dared breathe in case he thought better of it and withdrew.

"Yes. Well, Susan—I don't know who she got it from, a

girl from work I think; she worked in a dress shop at Southarbour—she had this booklet that had come free with a magazine that told you all kind of things." He rummaged for his cutters and trimmed the wire, then got up to find a cable end-cap from a tobacco tin on his workbench. "About making love," he explained, unnecessarily.

He fitted the cap onto the cable wire and crimped it on tight with a pair of pliers.

"There was everything you could imagine in this little book," he said, "and a few things you'd never imagine and wouldn't like to try."

He tossed the pliers back into the tin. Esme waited, fascinated.

"Susan gave the booklet to me and Maeve for a laugh, you know—'cause we were getting married." He stood up and tested the brakes, shaking his head at them. "That still isn't quite right." He squatted down by the bike. "It had pictures," he added.

"I think I need a smaller Allen key."

He found it and adjusted the little center screw, tested the brakes again, "That's better," and turned his attention to looking over the rest of the bike.

"But Susan, she was a bit of a stirrer, and she enjoyed baiting poor Miss Trigg, who must have been about your age at the time, though she looked ancient to us. That spoke's not right. Darn, where's the spoke key now?"

He searched on his workbench. "Here it is," he said and

returned to the bike, removing the tire and the tube from the wheel.

"So she asked her about this booklet. I don't expect she told her all that was in it—I hope not anyway—but a lot of it, and she asked her what a young Christian person should think of it."

Having laid aside the tube he removed the rim tape he had put in, unscrewed the nipple, and drew the spoke out from the hub flange.

"Miss Trigg, as you might guess, told her it was all the Devil's work, wickedness and sin and a certain road to damnation. Like so many other things Miss Trigg never had the chance at. Dancing and the London theaters and an evening at the pub."

He drew the bent spoke through his fingers, examining it: "How'd you do that then? You been riding off road?"

He took the spoke to the back of the shed and measured it against some that he kept there, until he was satisfied he had an exact match. He brought them both back, laid the old one on the ground. "Bent bicycle spokes and tinfoil make good bird-scarers for the peas," he remarked, and spun the wheel to the place that he wanted.

"I suppose Maeve and me had a bit of rebellion in us, else we wouldn't have left off going to Sunday worship. Anyway, when Susan told us what Miss Trigg had said—" he pushed the spoke head through the eye in the flange and with gentle pressure flexed it to weave in to relation with its fellows, "—we thought we'd have a try at the things in this book."

He threaded the spoke through the eye at the rim and pushed the nipple onto the end.

"Will you pass me that can—not the three-in-one, the synthetic one—yes—thanks. And the little screwdriver. That one. With the red handle. Thanks."

He tightened the nipple, looked critically at the tension, tightened it a little more, then looked round for his file, and worked at the small protrusion of the spoke end on the wheel rim.

"Me and Maeve," he said softly, "we had no idea how much pleasure was in our bodies. The things you could do with hands and tongue—maybe I shouldn't be discussing this with you, but you've been a married woman; I think you know."

He began to turn the wheel, plucking each of the spokes gently at their midpoint, his head cocked like a bird, listening to the pitch of their tension.

"Not all that was in the little book appealed to us. We just liked what was gentle."

He stopped at the spoke opposite the one he had just fitted, tightening it half a turn, listening again to the tension.

"So I think maybe I owe Miss Trigg something for forty years of the sweetest pleasure in my marriage bed. It heightened my respect for God, which I have to say is more than anything else much did in my dealings with her."

He turned the wheel slowly, feeling with his thumb for any protrusions.

"Did you ever make love outside, in the fields, under the sky?" asked Esme, wistfully. He smiled.

"We did not. There's a lot of flint in the ground in this part of the world; and plenty of thistles."

He lifted the bike from its stand and upturned it on the floor to rest on the handlebars and saddle, setting the handlebars straight.

"Making love," he said, squatting down behind the front wheel, checking the alignment with the back one, "should—in my opinion—be done in bed. 'Tis a thing of tenderness, and it should be warm and comfortable."

He stood up and bent over the tin to look for chalk.

"And private." Spinning the wheel, he brought the chalk slowly against it to mark the high points on the rim. "You make your bed in a field and ten to one the likes of Seer Ember will have chosen that hillside for an evening ramble, and have things to say that leave you hardly knowing where to put yourself."

He made some more adjustments to the spokes, loosening, tightening, going over the whole wheel. "That should do it," he remarked, and replaced the tape, the tube, and the tire, and set the bike upright.

Taking the air pump from the frame, he said, "However did we get onto this subject anyway?"

He inflated the tire till he was happy with it and continued,

"You got to keep these tires properly inflated, Esme, or you're more likely to get a puncture. You should go for the pressure level they give you on the tire wall, but don't be too gingerly with it, you could take it to twice that before you blew it off the rim. I think that'll do now, the rest of it looks fine."

She got to her feet and went to admire his handiwork.

He glanced at her shyly. "I hope I haven't been too free in my conversation. I somehow feel I know you perhaps better than I do."

As he stood before her, his roughened, oil-blackened hands resting light on the handlebars of her bicycle, his head a little bent and his eyelids veiling his eyes in awkward modesty, she hardly liked to say that her overwhelming impulse was to put her arms round him and hug him.

"You do know me better than you do," she said, "and you're a darling for fixing my bike."

It is my ambition, Esme thought, as his head dropped still further to hide his face, shy but pleased at what she had said, *to have this man able to look at me for more than two seconds at a time.*

"Shall I put it outside while you tidy the things away?" she asked, just allowing her fingers to touch his as she put her hands on the saddle and the handlebars. He released them from his hands instantly, and took a step back, his heel crashing against the tin on the concrete floor, startling him.

"Thank you," he said, "but just set it against the wall. I think it's coming on to rain again, and—oh, but I'm sorry, maybe you must be going? I was just assuming you'd like a cup of tea. I know I would."

Knowing she would be at his cottage later in the day, Esme had avoided tea all day, drinking coffee at her staff meeting, and declining the offers of drinks from kindly staff in the nursing homes.

In his kitchen, she sat on one of the stools by the table watching Jabez set the kettle to boil and then scrub the oil from his hands at the sink.

"Jabez," she said, with sudden misgivings about the simple question she had to ask, "how much do I owe you for this work?"

Jabez looked at her briefly as he crossed the small space to the Rayburn and took a dishtowel from its rail to dry his hands. "You owe me nothing. My pleasure," he said as he leaned past her to reach the tea caddy down from the shelf.

"No, really, Jabez, this is your living," she insisted. "If you supply free parts, free labor, and free delivery to all your friends, you'll be bankrupt."

He spooned tea leaves into the pot in silence, fetched milk from the fridge, turned to shoo away a hen appearing in cautious inquiry at the doorway, took the kettle as it began to sing from the hot plate, and poured the boiling water into the pot.

"Jabez?" she said.

"You owe me nothing," he repeated, quietly.

He poured milk into their mugs and replaced the bottle

in the fridge. He sat on the kitchen chair alongside the table, pulling the other stool to him, and putting his feet up on its crossbar.

Into the silence, as he waited for the tea to draw, he said gently, "Let me have something to give you."

Esme laughed. "Something to give? Jabez! You feed me, you give me tea by the gallon, you share your fireside, and your friendship. How about me having something to give? Let me pay you for this; it's costing you money."

Jabez poured the tea out into the mugs and pushed hers toward her, without looking at her.

"I think you don't know—" he began, glancing at her fleetingly, but thought better of it and shook his head. "You owe me nothing," he said again. "Here's to drier weather in the autumn," and he raised his mug to her in a toast.

"Oh, Jabez," she murmured in reproach.

"I got ideas of my own about money," he said, setting his mug down. It served all right for a refuge, but the tea was too hot to drink. "I believe that affluence and ambition are diseases. Like Saint Paul saying the love of money is the root of all evil and saying for himself he'd learned to be content with what he had in every circumstance of life. And Jesus saying the cares and pleasures of the world are like brambles that choke the light and life out of the tender shoot of integrity and compassion in a person. Human greed is at the bottom of half the troubles of the world. If you aspire toward a spiritual life, whatever religious system you practice in—be you

Hindu or Buddhist, Christian or Humanist, Taoist or Muslim, or Jew; whatever—the gateway to spiritual path is simplicity, and unless you undertake a discipline of simplicity, your spirituality will be like joists with dry rot."

He looked at her momentarily, his glance shy, but eager. That this mattered to him was very clear.

"When Saint Francis of Assisi taught his friends and followers about the way of Christ, he was adamant about simplicity—for that matter, so was Gandhi, so was Jesus, so was Lao Tzu. Francis talked about being in love with Lady Poverty—his bride, he said. He saw a vision of beauty in extreme simplicity; the beggar's bowl, the borrowed donkey shed, walking barefoot. Humility, you know, and offering his time to serve other people as a gift of himself in love. He's a bit of a hero of mine. I'm not man enough to scale the heights he did, but I can make little forays into the foothills. I can manage tiny bits of hospitality and the occasional act of kindness. Not often. And I know that Spirit, life, is a wildflower that doesn't take to cultivation. You try to pick it to make it an image thing, a stylish ornament in a vase, the finishing touch to an affluent setting, and it'll droop and die. To find it, you got to walk the sheep tracks, not ride the motorway. Frugality. Humility. Quietness. Working with your hands and finishing a job carefully and well. Doing what you do mindfully and with peace. Paying attention. Simplicity. Kindness. Looking after things. That's my faith, and I can't call it a religion, it isn't systematic—but it holds together, it makes sense. Dogma and doctrine are too grand and over-stuffed for the house where my soul lives. I'm not poor, Esme. I don't need very much."

Esme drank her tea, watching him. He spoke quietly and unpretentiously, almost with reluctance. What he had said came from very deep within him, she thought.

"So what may I give you in return for everything?" she asked him.

Jabez cupped his hands around the mug of tea.

"If I can choose, then I would treasure your friendship."

"Jabez, that's already given."

"Okay. So we're quits, and you owe me nothing," he said.

FIVE

September was manic.

In a weak moment, which she now regretted, Esme had agreed to take on the management of the annual circuit service at the beginning of the Methodist year. She had invited the guest preacher a year beforehand, but now came the plethora of details to be settled as the event drew near. Esme had to weave into this annual event a moment of stardom for everyone concerned. All the areas of work in her circuit—a sprawling territory with fifteen chapels and a Methodist geriatric residential home, four pastors, and a lay worker—had to be represented. West Parade Chapel boasted a professional musician who had attracted a first-class organist and organized a stunningly good choir considering the raw material the choir mistress began with. In her chapel at Portland Street the congregation had a worship band with guitars and a contentious drum kit (this drum kit never found a happy niche in worship, being always just loud enough to antagonize the traditionalists and just quiet enough to frustrate the drummer). The teenagers from the various chapels had organized into a loose-knit youth fellowship that deserved a voice at any circuit event. The minister in pastoral charge and the lay worker were each expected to have their special area of responsibility in the service. The superintendent had to be allowed to make a speech of welcome at the beginning, but under all manner of threats be required to stick to his time limit, as the mainly elderly congregation didn't like to be kept out late in the evening, the pews were uncomfortable, and if the guest preacher missed the 8:55, he wouldn't get his train back to London till 10:20 on a Sunday night.

Esme sat with a pad of paper charting out the balance of traditional hymns with choruses, choir items with congregational singing, and apportioning the readings (chosen by the preacher to support his theme) and the prayers to the staff and circuit stewards. She hesitated over the offering. There had been a row last year because the youth fellowship had been invited to take up the offering, much to the chagrin of the West Parade stewards who had a "system" and said it hadn't been carried out properly. She hesitated also over the readings. The guest preacher had requested a modern translation of the Bible, which meant not using the special lectern King James Bible recently dedicated at West Parade Chapel in memory of the senior steward's wife, who had died after a miserable and protracted illness the previous year.

Then she remembered that she had ages ago invited a youth leader from Brockhyrst Priory to sing a solo. This secured the loyally supportive attendance of a number of leaders from the guides and scouts, but also put a greater weight to the desirability of a relevant, accessible act of worship, which didn't matter so much if no one was coming except the Methodist diehards who simply wanted to sing some rousing Charles Wesley numbers and enjoy the visit of a dignitary from London.

Esme sat at her desk with her head in her hand, trying vainly to think of ways to fit it all into an hour-long act of worship. Eventually, in a fit of temper, she screwed up her sheet of paper into a tight ball, threw it across the room, and went out to the kitchen to make a cup of coffee. While the kettle boiled she ate a flapjack. She knew how many calories they contain, so once the coffee was made she restricted herself to a plain biscuit to go with it. And a second one to save her coming back for another, knowing perfectly well she'd have finished the first one before the coffee had cooled enough to drink.

She returned to her study. The most difficult part about organizing the circuit service was that the draft had to be submitted to the superintendent, who would ask for a multitude of minor details to be adjusted, and then ask to check the redraft and make further alterations before she could type it up and print copies.

Esme made a list of the people to be phoned. The youth

fellowship wanted to do a drama but could only manage one they'd practiced already, which wouldn't necessarily relate to the overall theme. Nonetheless, their title should be on the printed order, whether or not they changed their plans at the last minute. The choir mistress, she knew, would be ready with a list of beautiful but obscure and highbrow music—anything from Byrd to Birtwistle if the last two years were anything to go by—for Esme to dispose around the various liturgical moments of introit, offertory, anthem, recessional, and anything else she could think of. And she had to check the availability of her proposed readers, intercessors, and stewards.

And, Esme reflected, she'd better get on with it because it was happening in three weeks time, and as it was late this year, she had three church council agendas to put her attention to at the same time, as well as the pastoral committees, the finance and property committees, the mission and neighborhood committees, and the stewards' meetings for all three chapels. Then, she suddenly remembered Portland Street had decided to hold their covenant service in September instead of January this year, and she had undertaken to make the necessary phone calls and publicity fliers to elevate it into an ecumenical occasion.

Her phone rang. Marcus asking if she was ready with Sunday's hymns yet—no, she wasn't, she said she'd phone him back. As soon as she'd replaced the receiver it rang again. One of her pastoral visitors from Portland Street—had she heard that Mrs Whitworth's sister-in-law had gone into hospital for an operation on her varicose veins? No doubt Esme would be grateful to know. *No, I'm not,* Esme felt like saying. *The woman doesn't even come to church and doesn't know me from Adam, and now you've phoned me, I'll have to go and visit her, as if I hadn't got enough to do already.*

"Oh, right, thanks so much for letting me know," she heard her voice saying cheerfully. "With a bit of luck I can get up to the hospital this afternoon. Which day did you say her op is scheduled for?"

As she made a hasty trip to the hospital toward the end of the afternoon, logging her mileage for her expense sheet, Esme noted with amazement the distance she had traveled since last her car had been serviced. In a circuit straggling along the south coast, journey distances mounted up astonishingly, and she made the fourteen miles round trip from her parsonage in Southarbour out to Wiles Green often enough to make an appreciable difference.

Sunday came before she drove out to call on Jabez and Ember that week. By Sunday evening she felt frayed and bad tempered. The week had been too full, and she was exhausted. She preached at Brockhyrst Priory in the evening, and then drove on to Wiles Green. As she turned into the track and stopped in Jabez's yard, Esme felt a sense of profound relief. Spent and weary, she longed for the homeliness of the cottage and accepted hungrily the welcome that met her as she tapped at the door and let herself in.

Curled up in the corner of the sofa, as Jabez ascertained that she hadn't eaten and went to make her an omelet and Ember lit the fire in the gathering dusk of the evening, Esme began to relax.

"I've been so busy, just so busy, running around like a headless chicken!" she said to Ember. "There hardly seems a moment to stop. I get up at half-past six, I crash out at half-past ten at night, and there's hardly a minute unfilled. My garden's full of weeds and my house is filthy. There's a list as long as my arm of old people I haven't visited, and don't want to, and should have. When I'd been to do my hospital visits on Thursday, I called at the supermarket on the way home, and they'd done a huge swap-round of all their stock—nothing was still where I expected it to be. I was wearing my dog collar still—you know, minister, a professional nice guy—standing in the middle of the shop barking at the assistant, 'Where are the ready-meals? Where are they?' I was too tired and too short of time to go and look for them. I had to have my hymn list ready before choir practice and then fit in supper before a wedding rehearsal and the playgroup steering committee. There was no time for a treasure hunt in the aisles of the supermarket! Oh—thank you, Jabez; thank you so much."

He held out to her a plate of steamed vegetables and an omelet cooked to perfection.

"I'm not volunteering for housecleaning, but I can have a little go at your garden if you like," he said gently.

Esme looked at him and burst into tears.

"There's never any time!" she wailed. "No time for anything important—life, love, walking in the beautiful woodlands! The world is torn by war and greed, and our country has a big part in that. But there's no time to make changes, because changes take thought and time; and all the thought and time are taken up with churning out papers and satisfying expectations and meeting targets and millions of detailed thingummies that use up every single second—anyway, why can't Mrs Whitworth's sister-in-law's own blasted people go and visit her? What's the matter with her, hasn't she got any friends?"

Jabez sat down on the sofa beside her and took the plate off her lap as she dropped her face into her hands and wept.

"Here. It is clean." She felt a handkerchief being held against her hands, and she took it obediently and wiped her eyes and her nose.

"Come on, sweetheart. Eat your supper. I'll make you a cup of tea. You'll feel better in a minute."

"I tell you what." Esme looked up at Ember's face, an odd mixture of sympathy and mischief. "Give me your visiting list, my love, and I'll go and see 'em. I reckon we can soon cut it down."

Esme had to laugh, as the vision of Ember as pastoral visitor sank into her imagination.

"Jabez makes a good omelet," Ember added. "I'd eat that, my love, while it's still hot."

A great sigh shook Esme's frame, and she began to eat her supper, feeling comforted and understood. It was delicious. Afterward, holding her mug of tea in her hands, she said, "When I very first came here, Jabez, you said this was a bit of a refuge, and so it is. It is for me."

He nodded. "Well, it's here for you."

Esme pondered this thought for a moment, and then she said, "How do you do it, Jabez? How do you make it like this, a place of sanctuary? Everything feels calm and on purpose here. My life should be like this, peaceful and orderly and quiet; that's what spiritual people are supposed to be like. My life should be like a candle burning, beautiful and recollected. Instead of that I'm just rushed off my feet and guilty and resentful, tired and cross with so much to—"

"Ssh, ssh. Calm down." Jabez smiled at her. "One thing at a time. Can I pontificate for a minute while you eat your supper? Stop me if I annoy you. First thing: Right now, I mean right now this very minute, apart from being tired and a bit burnt out, what problems have you got? I mean, have you got a pain, or an appointment? Are you expected somewhere else? Are there any more deadlines to meet tonight?"

Esme stopped and thought about this, her fork in her hand. "No," she conceded.

"Then be here. Don't give away this time to tomorrow or let it be soured by yesterday. Time may come when you're incontinent and diabetic and alone, frightened and hungry, riddled with osteoporosis or arthritis or cancer. Tonight you're warm—I hope—and fed, and comfortable on my sofa, and with people who love you. That's to treasure, I think. I'm certainly treasuring you being here. Tomorrow will come with all its tasks and demands, but it's a way off yet. D'you know—Esme, am I wearying you? Tell me to shut up if you don't want to hear all this."

"I'm listening." She smiled at him.

"My hat, that was an opportunity missed," murmured Ember, resting her chin on the rim of her mug as she gazed into the fire.

"Well, what I was going to say—when they found the Cullinan diamond, the biggest one ever, they didn't realize what they'd got at first. The chap who discovered it brought it into the office, and the story I heard was that the bloke in there laughed at him, said, 'That's not a diamond!' and chucked it out the window. The thing is, a diamond is just a rock among rocks if you don't look with a seeing eye. And moments are the same. Among all the dusty bits of rubble that make up the ordinary life, there's a scattering of diamonds. The important thing is not to throw them out of the window when the miner puts them on your desk. Today was hard work and by the sound of things so is tomorrow. Don't lose this little bit that comes in between. Keep your balance; stay poised on this moment. You're here, with us; we love you, it's peaceful. Chill out."

"Okay." Esme nodded. "You said that was the first thing. What's the second thing?"

"Hang fire, how long is this list?" asked Ember. "Where's me knitting?"

"The second thing is about simplicity. Simplicity is the key to everything."

"Short and sweet, simplicity is," Ember interjected. Jabez frowned at her.

"The whole thing about practicing simplicity is you got to mind your boundaries. Don't let other people give you the runaround. They got expectations—so what? Let 'em keep them. You don't want their expectations seeding into your patch. Expectations breed, grow like wildfire. Thanks but no thanks to anyone's expectations. Don't fulfill 'em and they'll fade away. Expectations is like stray cats—don't feed 'em if you don't want 'em. In each day, attempt one thing in the morning and one thing in the afternoon, and leave the evening for peace when you can. Okay, you got meetings at night. Have a sleep in the afternoon then. Visit not so many people but spend more time with them when you go. Plan times to enjoy."

Esme sighed. "It sounds wonderful, Jabez, but I wouldn't get half as much done."

"No, you wouldn't. You'd get twice as much done, and it would be better quality."

"Slow my life down? You know, I've noticed, when I go out and about on my bike, I see more people. I can stop easily, so I pause to chat and I go into the little shops and see the people that live near the parsonage. Perhaps I should get rid of the car—I seem to spend half my life in the car."

He shook his head. "You got to be practical, Esme. You have responsibilities and a living to earn. Go on the bike when you can and use the car when you must. Don't be all or nothing; give yourself a break."

"Okay," she said, with sudden resolve, rooting in her bag for her diary. "Give me some principles. When I'm rushed off my feet and I've no time to stop and think through it all, I need some principles. What are the principles you live by? Go on. Number one?"

Jabez laughed. "Esme, really, I don't think—"

"Yes you do, you never stop thinking. Go on; I'm waiting."

"Well, all right then. Number One: Simplify. Your home, your wardrobe, your possessions, your ambitions, your schedule, your whole life. Simplify. Everything. Number Two: Schumacher's dictum—'small is beautiful.' Own few things, eat plain food in moderate amounts, avoid clutter. Keep meetings short. Avoid Southarbour High Street like the plague. Refuse to be a consumer. Buy what you must have from small, family businesses. Eat food grown locally. Brings me to Number Three: Cherish the living earth. Avoid buying things that have traveled a long way in manufacture and production. Remember the earth is our home—our life and breath. It's to be held in deepest reverence, and loved and respected. Eat food grown by farmers who nourish it and live alongside the wild creatures in peace.

Don't use many chemicals in your household. Almost every manufacturing process wounds the earth, so recycle, reuse, and don't buy much stuff in the first place."

"Okay. Number four?"

"Bless the community where you live. Whenever you spend money, meditate on the journey of the coin you spend. If you spend it at a small local family firm, it will be reinvested in that local community. Big business carts money away in barrow loads and impoverishes the community like a cuckoo in the nest."

"Got it. Five?"

Jabez thought for a minute. "Gandhi's maxim—thinking globally and acting locally. A knock-on effect of doing business with small local family firms is that not only does our custom give us influence in local trade practice, but also it leaves other parts of the world free to do the same. We think the bad old days of slavery and the empire are all gone, but they're not. We still keep slaves. Slaves make our clothes, our fireworks, provide our sugar and tea—but they're slaves to a huge worldwide system of which we're all a part. Cash crops and monopolies and big business are bad news the world over. Things like tea and coffee and chocolate and sugar that have to come from overseas, if we insist on having them, we should at least make sure they were fairly traded, so the people who produced them had a decent living and basic health care and education. Anyway, what goes around comes around. There is only one world. We're all in it together.

Sooner or later whatever we put out into this life will return to us. We reap what we sow."

"Gandhi … think globally, act locally. And?"

"Watch your boundaries—what I said before; your soul boundaries, life boundaries. We live in a speeded-up, cluttered, exhausted, stressed society. People love fly-tipping their problems. If you got an empty hour, an empty garage, a space to think, someone with a cluttered life will be agitating to fill it up for you. You do them no favors if you allow them to extend their own disastrous agenda into your life. You're a spiritual teacher, and you should be teaching peace by example, and peace comes by minding your boundaries and saying 'no.'"

"Okay. Any more?"

"Well—choose what is handmade with love. Minimize the influence and involvement of machines in your life. Avoid mass-produced stuff, especially stuff produced by ruthless big business in places out of sight and out of mind. Things made in small numbers, by hand, with pride in the work have a soul quality beyond price. And if you make things yourself, at home—bread, your clothes, your supper, anything—it builds up the light intensity in your soul. Digging the garden, kneading dough, scrubbing the floor are activities all contemplatives prioritize. Zen monks sweeping the steps or Poor Clare nuns turning their compost, or hermits collecting firewood in the forest. Okay, they got computers and sewing machines these days, but they know the connection between spirituality and manual work, physical effort—and these people aren't silly."

"That's it?"

"That's the philosophy I live by. That's it."

"So: Simplify; small is beautiful; cherish the living earth; bless the community where you live; think globally, act locally; watch your boundaries; and choose what is handmade with love. Hmm. There's a lot about where to do my shopping and nothing about quiet times and meditation. And I would have thought if I forgo my one-stop supermarket shop and start running around market stalls and farm shops, I'll need two lives running concurrently. But you reckon, if I do these things, my life will run smoother?"

"Well … Yes, actually, I really do. Anyway, it's wholeness. Attending to integrity in the ordinary daily things is what spirituality is. It *is* a meditation by itself. But the most important thing of all, to have in focus every day, is simplicity. It helps you create slow time, and sidestep all this rush and tear that's wrecking friendships and families. Time was an ordinary bloke could do an ordinary job and feel a pride in his ordinary achievement. Give it five more years at the present acceleration of targets and clock-watching, and all the ordinary blokes will be chronically sick with shame and failure and depression, their multitasking wives will be full of hatred born of too many adrenaline toxins from running on empty, and there won't be enough supermen to juggle the management and supervise the machines. Simplicity lets your soul catch up with your body. Prayer, making love, good conversation, gardening, home cooking, manual skills, quality of life; they grow only in slow time, which is created through simplicity. That's me done, I've talked too much, I'm saying not another word."

"Ember," said Esme, "do you have things like that, that you live by? Was there anything you wanted to add?"

"Yes." Ember laid her knitting down in her lap, and her small dark eyes winked like jewels in the lamplight. "Don't eat food you don't like. Don't be deprived of firelight. Don't take anything seriously. Don't let the blackguards grind you down."

Jabez smiled as Esme jotted this down in the back of her diary. "I don't know why I bother," he said. "That's it in a nutshell. I heard a thing on the radio last week, it was a program about China, and they were saying, 'Among our people, the old are respected for their wisdom'; and I thought, *I like that, that's how it should be.*"

"Rubbish," said Ember, in brisk contempt.

"Pardon, Ember? You don't agree?"

She stared at him irritably. "How many old people do you know? If you know someone who's old and stupid—and I could list you a few in this village alone, starting at the chapel—and you revere them for their wisdom, then you know one more stupid old man which would be you, Jabez Ferrall. Get a grip. In any intelligent society, the *wise* are respected for their wisdom. Goats, for example."

Esme started to laugh.

"I feel completely different now," she said. "I feel all keen and full of hope. I'm still tired, and I think I ought to go home to bed, but I feel sleepy-tired and relaxed. I don't feel cross anymore."

She looked at the list in the back of her diary.

"Simplify; small is beautiful; cherish the living earth; bless the community where you live; think globally, act locally; watch your boundaries; choose what is handmade with love; don't eat food you don't like; don't be deprived of firelight; don't take anything seriously; and don't let people get you down."

Ember looked at her curiously but said nothing. Esme snapped her diary shut and slipped it back into her bag, and then searched in its depths for her car keys.

"Right. I'm away. Tomorrow I'm doing assembly at the infants' school and a funeral in the afternoon. In the evening we've got a circuit leadership team meeting. There seems to be one thing after another for the best part of three weeks, but I've no doubt I'll be round before long—if only to complain about time-tabling all this extra integrity activity into my life."

She stopped and looked up at Jabez and felt rather disconcerted to meet his brown eyes contemplating her. But as soon as she looked at him, his eyelids flickered, and his gaze shifted to the glow in the grate.

"Aren't ready-meals a form of simplicity?" she said. "They certainly simplify my life."

"What are the containers made of that they come in?" he asked.

"Well—plastic or metal, usually, with a cardboard or plastic film top and a cardboard sleeve."

"And what happens to the containers when you've eaten the food?"

"That's the simplicity of it. I just throw them away."

Jabez nodded.

"Is it still simplicity if there's no such place as away?" he asked quietly.

"I suppose one kind of simplicity precludes another," Esme said. "I mean, going to one big shop instead of three little ones is simplifying in a way, isn't it? And it's simpler to get all the ingredients in one ready-made meal than to have to buy them all separately in their separate bags and packets."

"Where do they come from, these meals?" he asked. "Who makes them? Do they make them there in that shop?"

"Goodness, no! I've no idea where they come from, or who makes them! Does it matter?"

"Well—it might. Look, Esme, I don't want to criticize. You got a lot to get through and you can only do your best. Still, for tonight you had food cooked by me, with love: my hens' eggs seasoned with herbs from Ember's patch, cooked in Squirrel Farm butter, with Bill Patterson's potatoes, and Mrs. Willard's carrots and greens from the farmers' market."

"How about the tea?" She grinned at him.

"The milk in it came from Squirrel Farm same as the

butter. The tea comes from Kenya, but it's fair-traded, so is my sugar."

He glanced at her, serious.

"I think it matters. To me, my religion, it's not going to church, it's the little things. Keeping faith with all else that lives. Their lives—your life—is entrusted to me, same as my life has to trust them, and you."

"Okay, you win; I see you've more than thought this through. I'll give it a try." She got to her feet. "Good night, Ember."

Jabez came outside with her into the yard, which lay bathed in moonlight.

"I love the earth and the moon and stars. I love the rain and the wind and the night air full of the fragrance of the plants," he said. "Take time to love it. Good night, Esme. Go carefully."

Driving slowly home, thinking about all he had said, Esme felt unsure if it would be of the slightest use to her. It seemed all very well, but it went against the grain of modern life entirely. She could see the point he made about simplicity; and the modern shortcuts of e-mail, text messaging, edge-of-town supermarkets, takeaways, and Internet news summaries seemed to be the way to bypass time-consuming traditions of going to market, cooking, writing (and buying stamps for and posting) letters, spending time with people, and reading newspapers. She wondered if it was just that Jabez was getting old, had time on his hands, and had been too poor and too out-of-date for the electronic revolution. Still, she thought she would bear it in mind. Some of his ideas seemed impossible—after all, where would she buy fairly traded coffee if she didn't shop in a supermarket? *Unless … I wonder …* she thought, as she drove through sleeping Brockhyrst Priory and the country roads widened into the faster approach to the town … *if someone at Portland Street— and maybe Brockhyrst Priory, too—not Wiles Green, Miss Trigg would never let us trade on a Sunday … but maybe, in the other two, somebody—Susan Marsh perhaps at Portland Street, maybe Margaret Somers or Annie O'Rourke at Brockhyrst Priory—would be willing to set up a stall as a Fair Trade rep, and we could make some money for chapel funds at the same time. I wonder …*

Esme thought it could be very uniting, very positive, and help the congregation to find a clearer awareness of the world about which they prayed earnestly but were only hazily informed. *Okay—well done, Jabez!* she thought as she turned into the drive at the parsonage: *I'll check out the Web site after the leadership team meeting tomorrow.*

As she went to bed that night, Esme found herself beginning to feel again for her work the hopeful enthusiasm and alert interest that so often fell casualty to the endless detail of administration, diplomacy, pastoral visiting, and liturgical responsibility that created a treadmill if she allowed it to. And it was hard not to, because all those things were so pressing, requiring so much attention that it was easy to lose the broader, more fundamental vision of Christian mission, the grounded, realistic outliving of Christ's command to be known as his disciples by a life of practical love.

Inspired, she got up early and found the Web site of a supplier of electricity from sustainable, renewable resources, and the Web site of a bank who handled investments in strictly ethical projects—microcredit in poorer parts of the world, organic farms, self-employed craftsmen, social housing, and community ventures. She printed off the information from both sites, enough copies for everyone at the circuit leadership team meeting. *We could do this,* she thought: *Our circuit chapels and parsonages could run on electricity from sources that respect the environment. Our deposit accounts could be shifted to investment in ethical enterprises. Jesus would like that.*

Excited, she stapled the printed sheets into packs, slipped them into a wallet file that she stowed in her rucksack, and set off to cycle across town to her superintendent's parsonage for the meeting.

The agenda, apart from essential routine business, was short. Esme asked for time under Any Other Business to present a suggestion. The main business item was circuit restructuring—beginning seriously to consider the future life of some small and shrinking country chapels, their viability now, and the implications of that for future circuit staffing.

The discussion was long, careful, and detailed. Her two

colleagues with pastoral responsibility in outlying rural areas spoke of tentative plans for amalgamation or even simply closure in four of their chapel communities. Members continued faithful, hardworking, and supportive, but old age brought shrinkage by death, and three of the chapels had fewer than ten members, all over seventy and not all resident in the communities the chapels served. Closures seemed inevitable, such that next time one of the ministers was due to move on, instead of reinvitation being suggested, a cut in numbers of pastoral staff would be necessitated. It seemed desirable that the three remaining full-time ministers should care for the larger chapels, with possibly an active supernumerary or (had they had one) a homegrown minister in local appointment rather than a full-timer appointed in from elsewhere, to mop up the little rural causes while they still soldiered on.

The delicate question to be tackled—which of the staff would be the one to forgo reinvitation and move on—came next under consideration. Esme had two years to run on her present appointment. The superintendent's reinvitation had already been agreed at the spring circuit meeting. One of her colleagues was nearing retirement and hoping to see out his active ministry without another move. The fourth minister of the staff had an elderly mother in a nursing home nearby, a husband who had only recently established and built up his own business, and children coming up to public exam years: So she was also anxious to stay as long as possible before moving. Everyone at the meeting sat and pondered in silence. The superintendent got up and put his head round the door to call his wife to make more coffee. Esme realized they were all waiting for her to volunteer to be the one to move on. She had no dependents nor was she tied by a husband's work commitments. Although all three of the chapels in her section were still viable and in good heart, Brockhyrst Priory and Portland Street being positively robust, with impressive attendance figures, nonetheless she saw that she would have to be the one to go.

"Well," she said brightly, "I expect a change would do me good."

And smiles of relief all round the room rewarded her.

They spoke to her encouragingly about the positive benefits of frequent moves for gaining experience in ministry; about the wide range of possibilities—chaplaincy in schools or hospices or hospitals; overseas posts in Sri Lanka, the Bahamas, the Shetlands, or Malta—or opportunities in the central London offices or in some of the challenging inner-city missions.

Esme listened with mixed feelings. She had grown to care about her church members in the Southarbour circuit, but not so much that it would break her heart to leave them behind. She found the prospect of new forms of ministry exciting. When she honestly consulted her heart, she knew that she had just one serious reservation: She could no longer imagine life without Jabez and Ember. She could no longer imagine life without the refuge of Jabez's cottage or the encouragement of their friendship always there for her. Yet, surely, this was what all ministers experienced when the time came for them to move on? And if she had been one of the ones to stay on, when after three years extension to her appointment the time eventually came for her to go, it would very likely be even harder to leave them.

Esme made a deliberate effort to put aside the misgivings that began to fill her mind and pay attention to the discussion about the redistribution of the sections in the circuit once the number of ministers with pastoral charge had been reduced. A new animation had entered the planning now that everyone knew which minister would no longer be continuing.

Eventually, when it was growing late, the superintendent began to draw the business to a close, pleased that the outcomes had been so harmoniously agreed so far, and relieved to have no ill feeling among the staff over the question of who should move on.

Glancing at the scribbled notes on his agenda, he suddenly remembered that Esme had given notice of something to raise under Any Other Business.

Esme took out her file with the notes on ethical investment and suppliers of electricity from renewable sources, but somehow the whole issue felt less relevant now than when she had printed them out this morning. She had observed in the past that issues of environmental or social concern were viewed as nonessentials, dilettante intellectual luxuries to be made the subject of a seminar and forgotten as quickly as possible. She had been at synod and witnessed resolutions passed determining that all Methodist church members would do their best to affirm and promote fair trade and social justice—which made everybody feel good and committed them to nothing. Even as she spoke about the importance of caring for the living earth and in our practice and choices working positively for a more equitable world, whether or not that was less financially rewarding than following the crowd, she knew she was wasting her breath. The chance of the circuit stewards getting their electricity from any supplier but the cheapest or lodging the advance fund with any bank other than the one offering the highest interest, was slender at any time. Today, when their minds buzzed with administrative and pastoral restructuring, only politeness made them pay any attention at all. They did not even turn over the pages of the notes she distributed. Esme saw it was not going to happen and closed the matter in her mind without pushing for any real consideration of the issues, too disappointed to allow herself to dwell upon it.

Later in the week, as she prepared to meet with her chapel stewards to draft the business of her church councils and break the news of the changes ahead, she wondered whether it would be worthwhile now to put the suggestion of beginning a stall for fairly traded goods. Would it be better simply to let that go? After all, there was very little more than eighteen months left before she would be leaving.

Esme thought about it, gazing out through the window into the front garden of the parsonage as she sat at the desk in her study. Undecided, she took a break from thinking to make herself a cup of coffee. *I suppose*, she thought, reaching absentmindedly for the biscuits as the kettle boiled, *that it would be a start to buy fair-traded coffee for myself. I wonder if they do biscuits, too.*

As she returned to her desk, she opened her diary to the memoranda pages at the back. *BIKES Jabez Ferrall,* she read with a smile, and, turning a few pages further in, past hastily jotted details for funerals and contact numbers for wedding couples, she found and read again Jabez's list of principles. *Think globally, act locally.* She remembered him saying, "I think it matters. To me, my religion, it's not going to church, it's the little things. Keeping faith with all else that lives." And she thought, *Oh well, why not? Let's go for it. There's still time.* She added to her stewards' meeting agendas for Portland Street and Brockhyrst Priory a note to propose the commencement of fair-trading. As she sat reading through the notes she had made, it occurred to her that at Wiles Green, apart from Miss Trigg who would certainly oppose it, the congregation would most enthusiastically introduce and support a Fair Trade stall. She frowned thoughtfully at her agendas. To avoid conflict and confrontation in general seemed only wise, but she felt her life being directed and reshaped by Miss Trigg's convictions and prejudices. "Mind your boundaries," Jabez had said; "don't let other people give you the runaround." She added a note to her Wiles Green stewards' meeting agenda—"Fair Trade stall and rep." She reflected that she might as well have written down "Cause trouble" and accepted the necessity of some kind of a show-down with Miss Trigg.

She liked the principles of life Jabez had outlined, but at the same time she felt conscious that contemplating them created dissatisfaction with her choices; she was a minister of an institutional religion. Is it ever possible for an institution to express simplicity? The restlessness that disturbed her soul intensified as she thought about the gulf between the way Jabez had sketched for her and the inescapable requirements of professional ministry.

Several times that week, Esme came into the parsonage at the end of a long evening meeting, switched on the fluorescent light in her tidy, impersonal kitchen, made herself coffee, and took it into the sitting room to drink in her arm-chair beside the gas fire, turning it on low to dispel the chill of the evening. She looked at the deep-pile, grey-and-purple nylon carpet—a generous choice by the circuit stewards who had furnished the parsonage and had selected similar tones in the easy-care polyester curtains and inoffensive wipeable, embossed wallpaper. It had been kindly done by practical and thoughtful people; but her mind wandered to Jabez's cottage among its apple trees, the smell of wood smoke, the simple pine table his father had made, and paper sack door-mat in the kitchen, the floorboards more or less covered by an ancient rug of faded pattern in the living room with its low ceilings and shabby furnishings illuminated by lamplight and firelight. *That's where I'd like to be,* she thought. *Somewhere like that.*

Her drink finished, she checked all the windows were fastened and the doors locked, and made her way up the stairs, past the closed doors of the three empty bedrooms. Behind the parsonage, through the gap next to the house whose garden backed onto hers, and just beyond the low garden wall in front, streetlights shone all night, so that it was never really dark inside, and outside it was possible to see the moon but very few of the stars. In the corner where the ceiling met the wall, the sleepless red eye of the security alarm system flashed and winked as she moved about the bedroom.

Very tired and somehow dispirited, Esme climbed into her cold bed. She felt too tired to read and too tired to relax. The Methodist church, chronically addicted to incessant bureaucratic change as one of the less helpful outcomes of its democratic structure, had altered its stationing procedure twice since Esme had last gone through the process of appointment and come to Southarbour. She had asked her colleagues what the new system was, without very coherent result. She thought she'd better get in touch with her district chairman for advice.

Every night that week, she lay for a little while waiting for the bed to warm up, wondering what the future might hold and what she was supposed to do next. She thought about her colleagues and her congregations. She thought about parsonages and about how long it takes to get to know a new neighborhood. She thought about what makes a house feel like a home. She wondered about the possibilities of her churches espousing the principles of fair trade. And she thought about Jabez. But before long, each night, sleep came.

On Sunday night Esme presided at a Eucharist at Wiles Green, Miss Trigg on duty as her steward. She preached a straightforward expository sermon from the lectionary readings set for the day, avoiding controversial interpretations or any remarks Miss Trigg might construe as flippant or inappropriate. The congregation was tiny but the atmosphere peaceful. Esme wondered if they would miss her when the time came, sooner than she had planned, to move on. She wondered if she would miss them.

Afterward, turning out of the car park, she glimpsed the new poster in the Wayside Pulpit, saying REMEMBER YE THE SABBATH DAY TO KEEP IT HOLY, and thought of her forthcoming stewards' meeting with misgiving. She drove up Chapel Lane and turned into the village street, then with a lightening of her heart into Jabez's yard.

He had anticipated her coming, and a bowl of homemade vegetable soup with bread and cheese awaited her. Happily she curled up in her corner of the sofa, beside the fire that Ember had recently lit.

"This feels more like coming home than when I go back

to the parsonage!" she said. "It's so nice of you to take care of me like this."

"Ah," said Ember, "'tis rare to find a kindness without an ulterior motive. Even here. Jabez don't cook for everybody. Not even for himself, some days."

She shook out her knitting, a vast stripy thing using a motley assortment of ends of yarn.

"Ember, that's colossal! What are you making, anyway?"

"'Tis a jumper for the winter," Ember explained. "I likes my clothes baggy," she added unnecessarily.

For a while, silence lay between them as Esme devoured her soup and bread, surprised to find how hungry she was once she stopped to think about it.

"Delicious!" she pronounced as she finished it. "Thank you so much."

She reached down and piled her crockery on the floor beside the sofa. She wondered if now would be the time to tell them about the move she had agreed to but somehow felt unable to bring it closer by discussing it. Instead she chose to stay in the temporary reality of the present.

"Jabez," she said, "I've been thinking about all you said to me last week, and it's given me an idea—I thought I might see if we can begin to sell fair-traded things in the chapels I pastor. But I can't do that at Wiles Green without taking on Miss Trigg. Have you got any ideas about how I might sort her out?"

Jabez laughed as he considered this. "I can far more

readily imagine her sorting out me than the other way round," he said. "But surely Miss Trigg will be in favor of fair trade?"

"I expect so," Esme replied, "but not in favor of buying and selling on a Sunday. Once when my car was in for service and I went to chapel in a taxi, she remarked that it was okay because I was digging my donkey out of the ditch."

Ember gazed at her, perplexed.

"You know—necessity. From the thing Jesus says about 'Which of you if your ass or ox falls into a pit on the Sabbath day will not pull him out?' But I strongly suspect that trading on the Sabbath, fair or otherwise, will be strictly off limits. Although, mind you, if I could only remember where it comes in the Gospels, Jesus speaks about doing good being lawful on the Sabbath, doesn't he—and if fair trade isn't good, I don't know what is."

"It's in Matthew 12," said Jabez to her surprise. "'It is lawful to do well on Sabbath days.' Don't look so amazed. I only remember it because my mother used to quote it to excuse my father going fishing while we were in chapel. She said he fished well but his hymn singing was atrocious. While you're at it there's Saint Paul as well, 1 Corinthians: 'All things are lawful unto me, but all things are not expedient: all things are lawful for me, but I will not be brought under the power of any.' So provided it's expedient to hold your Fair Trade stall on Sunday after church, you got a backer in Saint Paul. It's lawful, and you're not to be brought under the power of Miss Trigg, on good authority. And you got an authority in Isaiah 1, 'Bring no more vain oblations; incense is an abomination unto me; the new moon and Sabbaths, the calling of assemblies, I cannot away with; it is iniquity, even the solemn meeting. Your new moons and your appointed feasts my soul hateth: they are a trouble to me, I am weary to bear them … Learn to do well; seek judgement, relieve the oppressed.' And Saint Paul picks this up too, doesn't he? Um— Romans 14. 'One man esteemeth one day above another: another esteemeth every day alike. Let every man be fully persuaded in his own mind. He that regardeth the day, regardeth it unto the Lord; and he that regardeth not the day, to the Lord he doth not regard it.' And Jesus says in Mark, 'The Sabbath was made for man, not man for the Sabbath.' You got every authority. Tell her she's being carnally minded."

Esme blinked at Jabez in amazement. "*Tour de force* or what!" she exclaimed. "How on earth have you remembered all that?"

"Oh, well …" Jabez looked embarrassed. "I'm sorry; I wasn't showing off. It's just—maybe you can imagine it—there was rather a lot said about the Sabbath in this house when I was a child. Quite a few heated arguments. My father wouldn't go to worship, but he was brought up chapel, and he knew why he wouldn't go and what he wasn't going to. Quotations from the Scriptures fired between him and Mother like arrows between crack archers. That was one of the first things that began to put me off the church I think, really. Everyone I knew used the verses of the Bible like a pile of rocks to hurl at each other in an endless battle of one-upmanship and self-righteousness. You get sick of it after awhile. It's a rough game, and a spiteful one, with a lot of losers."

"But you think it's the way to handle Miss Trigg? I mean, if you were in my place—if you were her minister—is it what you'd do?"

"Stone me, Esme! That's a bit unfair! Tell you what, I'll do you a swap. Marilyn Prior's son was out on his bike in the lanes after school during this week. He hit the edge of a pot-hole while he was going downhill quite fast. His chain sprang the cogs, the bike leapt forward, and he was thrown. Something else must have happened—I'm not quite clear what—involving him and a tree. He hasn't bent the forks, but he's crumpled both the top tube and the down tube. He's got a bump on his head. I've got his bike. Okay. You tell me how to fix Danny Prior's bike, and I'll tell you how to fix Miss Trigg."

"Tell his mother to buy him a new one," said Esme. "Your turn."

Ember chuckled. "That's my girl."

"Well, all right, I reckon if it's only ideas as bright as that you're looking for, I may well be able to help you with Miss Trigg. Cup of tea first?"

Having made a pot of tea and poured a mug for each of them, Jabez resettled himself in his chair. "Don't forget to chew it," muttered Ember as he sipped his tea. Jabez ignored this.

"Miss Trigg, then," he said. "As far as I can see you got three problems. One, she's lived in Wiles Green all her life, knows nothing but the folks and the attitudes she grew up with, so she's got small-life syndrome. Two, she's hooked on fundamentalist religion, and her security is its rigid framework that acts as a splint and an exoskeleton and a steel corset of the soul—like those African ladies with all the rings round their necks—they'd have been better off without them but if you took them off now they'd go all floppy. Three, she was brought up by a tyrannical mother and a father who beat her; she worshipped the ground they walked on but she takes it all out on the rest of the human race. She's weak, she's a bully, she's always right, and she's having fun nipping your ankles—is that it?"

Esme laughed. "You know her very well. I think you have it exactly. Heaven knows, she's not all bad, she works like a slave for the chapel, and organizes all sorts of good events, but …"

"All right. Well, in gratitude for your excellent advice about Danny Prior's bike, I'm going to give you my equally valuable opinion about Miss Trigg. First thing is, have you heard her preach?"

"Oh yes," said Esme.

Jabez grinned. "Me, too, many times. Would you be prepared to preach the kind of ideas Miss Trigg preaches and upholds?"

"Well, of course not!" Esme exclaimed. "She preaches a

lot of nonsense, she does really! And it's harmful, dangerous nonsense too. And it's so off-putting! You know, if I could persuade some of the mums from Mothers and Toddlers to come to worship one Sunday when Miss Trigg was preaching—not that I can persuade them to come at all because they've all met Miss Trigg—I'll bet you any money you like they'd never come again."

"Seems reasonable," said Jabez. "But surely then, asking for the freedom to be yourself implies offering the same freedom to other people—even to Miss Trigg."

"Oh, that's all very well!" Esme was sitting upright, annoyed. "But Miss Trigg isn't letting the other members of the chapel be themselves or the toddler group mums—or me!"

Jabez shook his head. "Miss Trigg's a lot of things," he said, "but she's not a witch out of a fairy tale."

"You sure?" interrupted Ember.

He laughed. "No, but I think so. She can't put a spell on you to make you be a frog or a donkey or a statue; neither can she put a spell on you to make you angry or afraid. That's your choice. D'you remember last week I told you—oh Esme, I *hate* this—" he broke off in dismay, suddenly horrified at the thought of himself regularly offering advice. "This is so didactic, I can't hold forth like this; it's like a course of instruction!"

"Correct," said Esme. "Go on."

He shook his head. "I can't. It's embarrassing, I feel such a fool, I—"

"Oh, get on with it," said Ember as she turned her knitting round to begin a new row. "Just say what you think without drawing attention to yourself so much."

Jabez looked absolutely furious. He closed his eyes and didn't speak.

"You were saying?" said Esme. "Being angry is one's own choice?"

Jabez began to laugh. "Thank you! Yes it is—yes, it is. Okay. Last week, one of the things I suggested that you wrote in your diary was about minding your boundaries. A really important part of any spiritual tool kit is the ability to keep soul boundaries—a poise that falls to neither domination by others nor subjugation of them by you. Being with Miss Trigg is probably the best chance you'll ever get to hold your radiance steady in the turbulence of other people's energy. Anytime you find yourself in a tug-of-war with her, just let go of your end of the rope. I know you're the pastor of the chapel—but that gives you a real authority she hasn't got. You're in a position to offer them the chance of a Fair Trade stall, but if Miss Trigg terrorizes them into turning it down, don't panic. If you aren't choosing to fight, you don't have to win. Ministry is responsibility, but all the people share the responsibility of ministry, not just you; it's all of you together; so they got to learn to mind their boundaries too, not let Miss Trigg annex their lives and decisions to her own.

"Words are power, Esme. Breath energy is spirit; it's not to be squandered or used in violence. It's important not to speak unless you really have something to say and others are ready to listen. You can speak softly, and the universe will still hear you, your words will make a difference. And there's no need for hurry or impatience, you can take your time—the earth waits. Time is flexible, elastic. The ark of God doesn't sail without the unicorn."

Ember sat with her knitting in her lap, staring impatiently at Jabez. "Whatever are you talking about?" she said.

Jabez said nothing in reply.

"I think he's saying that even if it doesn't seem likely, gentleness is enough, and there isn't another way. I just have to keep my nerve." Esme ventured. Jabez nodded.

"That's right. D'you want another cup of tea?"

"One more; that would be lovely, then I ought to be on my way. Thank you, Jabez. And d'you think you can fix Danny's bike, too?"

He smiled at her. "I'm sure I can. If I take my time, and think about it; look at it carefully and only try to do one thing at a time."

As Esme drove home that evening, she wondered if she should have told them about the proposed changes in the circuit structure, and her volunteering to move. She told herself that the business of the circuit leadership team had to remain confidential, but she had a feeling that was not the reason she hadn't told them.

It was a long, long time since she had known anyone who would talk with her so freely about walking the paths of the spirit. She felt that she had found something—a kinship, an understanding—too precious to discard and leave behind. Still, she had volunteered to go, and it had been the right thing to do, and she could think of nothing that could be done to change it. She had her living to earn and no home but a parsonage to go to. There were no other choices that she could see. She resolved to be practical and make the best of it; there seemed no other way to stop the spreading stain of sadness, the quiet, persistent grief that wept in her when she contemplated losing this friendship.

She avoided introspection by immersing herself in her work. To her pleasure and surprise, all three church councils embraced her proposal of a Fair Trade stall with enthusiasm, almost unanimously. Even Miss Trigg was remarkably restrained and contented herself with abstaining from the vote.

Six

Esme, watching October come and go, with its church council meetings and Harvest Festival services and suppers, felt uncomfortably detached from her congregations.

I shall be leaving, she thought, *I shall be leaving, and you don't know.* Not until the following spring did the leadership team plan to inform the circuit meeting and the chapels of their decision to reorganize the circuit. In the smaller chapels, keeping going felt no worse than the struggle it had been for so long. In Esme's congregations, even Wiles Green having enough members to remain viable until death took its toll of the elderly congregation, it had crossed nobody's mind that in the event of a cut in staff their minister would be the one to go.

She had spent time reading up in her bulky (hitherto pristine and unopened) current edition of the *Constitutional Practice and Discipline of the Methodist Church*, so as to appear appropriately informed when she asked her chairman

of district about stationing her for her new appointment. He
had reassured her that nothing would happen until next May
at the very earliest; nothing would be known until the following September—a year before she would make her move.
"So don't panic yet!" he boomed, in his jovial way.

Esme could see nothing to panic about. She could see
that her churches would be well served by her colleagues
when the time came for her section to be parceled out into
their neighboring sections. She could see that time was
being given for careful decisions to be properly made. She
could even see that, in the long run, she might come to look
back with gratitude; as the other members of the leadership
team reassured her when they met a second time to discuss
the redistribution of the circuit, the forthcoming move
could broaden her experience and enrich her life. It was just
that, listening to the others discuss possibilities, and to her
church councils talk about futures that only she knew she
would not be sharing, something of the old ache of weariness began to return. In the last year, confidence and
enthusiasm had grown along with a sense of belonging, in
part because the people in membership of her chapels were
now familiar to her and she to them. She knew their histo-
ries, and their family connections now, the places where they
worked, and what their homes were like. Preaching on a
Sunday had a deeper pastoral significance. She knew her
sheep, and they had come to know her voice, and trust was
growing. And then, Jabez ... Ember, too, but, especially,

Jabez … As she contemplated moving, she began to be more and more unsettled, until the parsonage that had never felt really like home began to seem positively distasteful. Esme stood in its sitting room, looking at the wallpaper and curtains chosen by other people with the criteria of sticking to a tight budget and giving offense to nobody. She looked out through the replacement windows with their hideous aluminum frames onto the square lawn and modest herbaceous beds designed for easy maintenance at the back of the parsonage. There was nothing to complain of and nothing to delight in. *I don't belong here,* she whispered, and that was true now whichever way you looked at it.

When Esme had first offered for the ministry, she had been a married woman, and it had been late but not too late to think of having children someday. At that time, her sense of belonging had derived from her marriage. That had gone. The demands of her work ensured minimal contact with her parents, her sisters, and brother, all tied themselves by work and family obligations. She had grown away from them anyway now, in her own soul journey; lonely, her heart longed for someone to be her kindred. *Who will I be?* she asked herself now. *Whose sister am I, and whose child? Who will love me, and where will I belong? What will my home be—just myself, maybe?*

She wondered about looking for some sort of pet. She thought that a dog would require more attention and companionship than her work would permit her to give: But she toyed with the idea of buying a cat—Siamese cats, she had heard, were like dogs in some respects, affectionate, but with the advantage of in-built feline independence. She wondered if having a cat might help to create a sense of home.

Then numbly, standing still, gazing without seeing through the window, Esme thought, *I should pray about this. That's the thing I really ought to do. When you pray for things, they come out right. Well, maybe better than they might have done otherwise. At least, if it's awful, I'd have the comfort of knowing it was God's will.* She frowned, puzzled. *Then ... does that mean then ... if prayer—well, is God looking after me or am I looking after God? Is there a pattern? At all? And if so, does it really rest on my initiative so much, if there is a God? Does prayer really make a difference if all of it is God's will anyway? And if it's not, does that mean God isn't infinite—or all-powerful—after all?* With a sudden, peevish, restless sense of irritation, and an inexplicable but deep-rooted mutiny against the duty of prayer, instead Esme went into the kitchen to make herself a cup of coffee. She looked in the tin. No flapjacks left. She thought back to last week when she had stowed a bar of fruit and nut chocolate in the top drawer of her desk, and thought she'd settle for that.

As she poured boiling water onto the instant coffee granules, she reflected wryly that however big her next congregation might be, any move away from Jabez would involve a reduction in her intake of tea. And she surprised herself by starting to cry.

Hastily wiping her eyes and blowing her nose, refusing to look too closely at what leaving him meant to her, Esme took her coffee into the study, and more from force of habit than for any specific intent, sat at her desk and turned her computer on. The past weeks had been so busy, an evening opening up suddenly free left her at a loose end. She had no need to prepare a sermon for Sunday; they were back in Ordinary Time, she was preaching in a different chapel from the previous Sunday—last week's sermon would do. The church councils were done, as were the circuit meetings and the Synod, and the Harvest Festival produce was all satisfactorily distributed to various worthy causes.

She supposed that now would be the time to pray or to read or to sit quietly and invite God's holy presence into the restlessness inside her. But somehow she found it impossible to settle to anything requiring focus and a clear spirit.

Esme played seven games of solitaire and finished her coffee.

Without really thinking about it, she found herself telephoning Marcus. By virtue of being himself more than through office held in the circuit, Marcus served on the circuit leadership team. Esme thought maybe he would be a helpful person with whom to discuss her proposed move. Perhaps he would have some suggestions, help her to frame a more positive outlook on the prospect.

Her call was answered by a lady from a house-sitting firm, hired for a month to look after their home and their dog. As soon as the lady began to explain her residence in the Griffiths' house, Esme remembered that the date of the most recent leadership team meeting had been conditioned by Marcus and Hilda's forthcoming late holiday in Italy. They were traveling, she recalled, through Switzerland, and staying for a few days in a hotel by the Italian lakes, before stopping off for a week in Venice, continuing to Tuscany and on to a favorite spot in Florence, flying home from there. They would be away a month.

Esme thanked the house sitter and ended the conversation.

She wondered about going out to see Jabez, but decided it would be too late for that household by the time she arrived. The following day she had promised the afternoon for pastoral visiting, but the morning was still free. She thought if the weather remained fine she would cycle over to Wiles Green in the morning, just to say hello.

Esme played five more games of solitaire, looked at various Internet sites she had listed for a free moment, and then decided on an early night.

After breakfast in the morning, she cycled over to Wiles Green and found Ember returning down from the orchard with the hen-food bucket as she came round the corner of the house into the yard.

"Mornin'." Ember watched her dismount and prop the bike against the wall. "You welcome as always to a cup of tea if you fancy my company, but Jabez gone to Shropshire to see his son. Went Monday. He'll be back for the weekend."

Esme looked at her in surprise. "I had no idea Jabez had any children!"

"Two sons he got. Hardly ever sees 'em. He got no money to travel. They got no money to travel. He writes sometimes."

"Oh. Are they married? Has he got grandchildren?"

"One was married but his wife left him, took the kids with her—you know how 'tis nowadays. The other one sits the other side of the church; he won't be marrying." She swung the bucket, making the handle rattle. "You having a cup of tea? I got the kettle just on the boil."

"Thank you."

"I'll just stow this pail back in the shed. Don't you let on to Jabez you caught me feeding his hens this late—he'll be ticking me off. Don't see why. Hens likes a lie-in same as I do."

Esme doubted this, but didn't say so. She followed Ember across the yard into the kitchen and sat at the table, watching her make the tea.

"Jabez's sons," volunteered Ember conversationally, as she peered into the brown depths of the pot and stirred the tea, "is, as you might expect, not unlike Jabez. Achievements and qualifications all about as spectacular as his. Samuel, the oldest one, he got a BA—failed—from York University. Enjoyed prowling around the North York Moors, investigating ancient archaeological sites, and studying up on *The Dream of the Rood* and Old English as I gather, but not so enthusiastic when it came to George Eliot or Milton. Young Samuel says Milton is good for sterilizing nappies and that's about all. According to Jabez, unless you got a good nodding acquaintance with the Gospels, the Psalms, and the Catholic Mass, you got no understanding of any English literature up until the 1970s anyway. That's what he says. If 'tis so then it's hardly surprising Samuel missed his mark—never been near a church in his life, not even baptized. Adam now, his younger son, he never failed anything on account of he never went to any college in the first place. Adam says he's like his father—got a hereditary DNA in Getting By. Seems to be the case, he can turn his hand to most things. If life has a manual or a rule book, nobody ever told those three.

"'Tis Samuel was married. Well, if this ain't brewed now, it never will be."

Jabez usually poured the tea through a strainer into the mugs. Ember didn't bother. She said an occasional tea leaf to chew made it more interesting.

"I suppose I should find a few days to visit my family sometime soon too," said Esme, with less enthusiasm than she had intended. Ember watched her, attentive and shrewd.

"I'm sorry—that sounded as though I didn't look forward to seeing them. I do—I mean, they're my family. It's just, I don't know what exactly, somehow they make me feel a bit of a failure. They're not Methodist. I was brought up Church of England. They think chapel is quaint and unsophisticated and a bit vulgar. My parents came to hear me preach once. I remember it. I gave my best shot at quite a complicated expository sermon on the teaching structure of Saint Mark's gospel. Afterward, my mother said—I can only imagine the remark was one she'd dreamed up earlier to have ready, and she'd slept through the actual service— 'Ah, you Methodists; a simple belief: *Just have faith.* How comforting. I wish I could be like that, but the Anglican Church is a thinking church, intellectual.' They never came to hear me again. One of my sisters is the headmistress of a girls' private school. She went on a conference last March, where they were told how important it is to give themselves little treats to reward all the hard work they do—she says she works a hundred-hour week. So she did treat herself. She bought herself a state-of-the-art wall-mounted CD player. Goodness only knows how much it cost. My other sister is a doctor. My brother is a research chemist. I'm not quite sure what he's doing at the moment. It's all covered by the Official Secrets Act. They're very sweet to me, fond of me. But with the same affection they might show to a much-loved poodle, one that's been in the family a long time. I've dreamed sometimes of becoming a superintendent and then a district chair and then the president of the conference—just to show them. Even if I managed it, I'm not sure they know what the president of the conference is, or does. Actually, I'm not sure I do myself. I think they vary wildly between the ones that deliver impassioned speeches expounding radical political views and the ones with nice smiles that have trouble finding a place to put their handbag down while they bless the winner of the sandcastle competition."

Ember chuckled. "Something been upsetting you? You sound a bit curdled today."

Esme didn't reply. She felt unsettled and restless and sad. Eventually, "Ember," she said, "do you pray?"

Ember considered this question without surprise.

"I light fires," she offered, after awhile.

"Pardon? Fires? Where?" Esme looked at her, slightly startled, waiting for enlightenment.

"Anywhere. In the orchard. In the little hearth in my bedroom. At my old place I lit 'em in the garden near the hedge. Under the stars is best. Fires is fragrant, and calls to the Being at the heart of it all. Twig by twig I makes 'em. I takes my time—just little fires we're talking about, not roaring great bonfires. On the burning I lay dried pinecones from the woods and the roadside. Slips of rosemary, dried sage. In the smoke is all my yearnings. Dreams that never came to be. My sense of home. In the smoke is the brown bears, kept in cages, their gallbladders tapped for bile for Chinese medicine. And foxes, running for home, not knowing their earth is blocked by the hunter. And the forests, cut down for loggers and cattle ranchers. And the streams, fouled with factory effluents and sewage and corpses. In the smoke is the bluebell woods and the daffodil woods, the brilliance of the moon, and a bird singing after dusk on a warm summer night. The sound of the surf on the shingle, and the wind in the tops of the pines. I sits by the fire, and I says nothing, although sometimes I weep. I'm not sure what deity is, my love; but life is sacred, life is wise. One day, if my smoke finds the way home, and wakes the great Spirit, then the face of life that is death will come speeding silent like a hunting owl, and take the cancer of humanity off this poor, stripped, raped mother Earth, take it silent and quick, no more than a squeak of alarm; and the mountains will have their peace again, and the oceans give back the heavenly blue. The guns and the cars will rust, and the televisions will be quiet at last, and the factories and schools and government buildings will be for the bramble, the rat, and the crow. Is that what you call praying? Or is it just fires?"

"I think it's what I call praying," said Esme. "Ember, I just can't pray anymore."

There are very, very few people to whom a minister, whose house and income are linked inextricably to the willingness to pray, may make that deadly confession. Ember seemed like one of the few. Esme heard her own voice sadly and hopelessly speak the words; and it came as a relief.

"Another cup of tea? I think we'd squeeze one more each out of this pot? Yes?"

Ember poured out the tarry, cooling dregs.

"What do you call praying, then, my love; that you can't do?"

Esme sighed. "Well, just the usual things. I should have a quiet time in the morning; read the Bible. Maybe use the prayer handbook or the district prayer calendar to intercede for the world and the church. I should confess my sins and pray for the sick; I should pray through the pastoral list. I might use the Order for Morning or Evening Prayer in the *Methodist Worship Book*. There's lots of modern resource stuff I could get to help me, if only I could get by this terrible inertia. I could do Ignatian visualizations or meditate on a short text or use the words of a hymn."

"I'm not surprised you got trouble praying!" Ember sounded impressed. "You got the same trouble I get buying food in a supermarket. Better with an apple from the orchard or the egg new-laid from under the hen."

"But what am I going to do?" Esme cried out. "I'm a minister, I can't carry on just not praying; I'm a fraud!"

"My mother was born in Wiles Green," said Ember, with apparent irrelevance, "but my father didn't come from this part of the world. My hat! This tea tastes foul, don't it! Let me throw that out, and we'll start again with a fresh pot."

The slops went in the compost bucket, and Ember drew fresh water, which she set to boil.

"My father came from some mountain part on the border of India, I think. He grew up in one of they villages you see on calendars, houses with the roof made out of grey stone shingles. He had a pilgrim soul, my father, didn't stay with us all that long; but after he moved on he used to write to me now and then. He sometimes used to speak to me about Siddhartha, the Buddha. My father told me this word

Buddha just means someone who is awake. He said that Siddhartha taught people only to wake up. To pay attention, be present—'as I am to you,' my father used to say—to live mindfully. My father spoke about life lived on purpose. When he walked, he walked slow, because his feet kind of loved the ground. Every step he took, he gave attention to. He said whatever I was doing, I was to do it with all my attention, even just sitting quietly, watching, or listening. He said you got to have presence of mind. When I was podding peas, he taught me to gaze on my hands and love them working. He said that in the peas were sunshine and rain from clouds and dew and earth. Our mother spoke about the garden having good soil for growing peas, and he used to say, 'Not soil; soil is a word that means dirt. Say earth, not soil; for the earth puts out living plants from the living body of her sacred being. Reverence the gift. Reverence the earth.' He would take up a handful of earth in his hands, rub it, and sniff it, and he'd nod in satisfaction. 'Earth is clean and good,' he told me. And he said to our mother we children were to have earth and air, fire and water to play with, which fortunately wasn't hard in the part of the country we lived in at that time. He often told us to practice the yoga of reverence, until when I was a teenager I asked him what he meant by it. He laughed at me—almost everything made him laugh; not unkindly, he just didn't mind about things. He said it meant seeing into the heart of whatever you had before you until the fire of its divine life revealed itself to you.

Anything—from a cut finger to a plate of steamed cabbage to a sinkful of washing up. A vase of perfumed lilies or dog mess in the yard. The eyes of your bridegroom when he gives himself to you in marriage and the eyes of the same man when he tells you he's leaving you. He said we were to be present to every being we encounter with absolute respect, and treat ourselves with the same respect. I can remember him now, he spoke softly always, saying, 'Every living being is present to this moment, therefore you are a part of everything because you are also in this moment. Therefore you are holy because this moment pulsates with the divine. Your only responsibility is to bring your attention to this moment; when you do so, you will perceive the radiance of divine light illuminating everything that is.' He said all kinds of stuff along those lines. I never saw him praying as such—but I saw him peeling potatoes sometimes, and I believe it was much the same thing."

Esme sat quietly and thought about what she had just heard. She drank her tea Ember had made and poured out and set before her as she was talking.

"I think my congregation would expect me to have a daily quiet time," she said at last.

"Then take quiet time every day," Ember replied. "Invite your God. Say, 'God, have you noticed the quietness of this time? Have you got your full attention on this moment? Good. So have I.' I tell you what isn't prayer, my love. Worrying isn't."

Esme smiled. "No—you're absolutely right. I can see that."

The conversation remained with her through the week—she realized that it had been the first time she had talked with Ember at any length. She felt that in Ember she had encountered something very solid and uncompromising and strong, very wise, too. Esme had mentioned how helpful she had found it to spend time with Jabez, to have the fresh view of his perspective on life, and to hear what he had to say as they sat and chatted in his workshop or by the fireside in the living room of his cottage. Ember had looked at her, a look that Esme couldn't read.

"Jabez?" she had replied. "He got plenty to say to anyone with the same interests. And sometimes, my love, you do well to listen to what he doesn't say—especially to you."

That puzzled Esme. Had she been insensitive in some way? As she looked back on the many times they had talked, becoming easy with each other as the months went by, Esme felt the sudden upwelling of sadness again; she did not want this move, without really knowing why.

In early November, once Marcus had come back from Italy, the leadership team met again. It was decided that after Christmas, Esme could talk to the stewards in her section churches about the changes to come. Then alternative plans for the future would be presented to the church councils and to the circuit meeting in the spring, the implications of the decisions there being returned for consideration at the annual church meetings. As they disbanded after an evening of animated discussion, Marcus said to Esme, "You rang us while we were in Italy, my dear. Was it something in particular? Is all well?"

Esme shook her head. "No problems, nothing to worry about. I just had a thought that maybe I could come and see you, to talk through where I might go, what I might do next."

"Why don't you join us for supper, Esme? Tonight is good if you have no other engagement and feel you can face any more on the topic today."

Esme accepted, gratefully. That evening, driving through the dark lanes to Wiles Green, she reflected on how quickly the summer seemed to have come and gone; the seasons like a wheeled thing rolling downhill, picking up speed as it goes. *I suppose it's because the summer was so chilly and wet this year,* she thought. *I haven't had enough of the sun, I feel so tired and dispirited; I'm not ready yet for the winter.*

Hilda, on the lookout, saw her approach, and stood framed in the warm light of her open doorway as Esme climbed out of her car.

"Welcome! Come in, my dear, come in! Such a dreary night, come in by the fire, come in!"

As Hilda took her coat, Esme asked how the trip to Italy had gone.

"Oh, marvelous, my dear, but just marvelous! It was so lovely to have Jeremy with us—our youngest son, did you know he came? It's never easy for him to get time away from that business of his, it seems to gobble up his living daylights, but just for once he could snatch a few weeks—he had to fly home from Venice of course, and I would so much have liked him to be able to enjoy Florence, but well—I'm sorry, Marcus? Did you call? No, of course we're coming, just a moment of girlish chatter—wine I should think if you're pouring. Come along in, my dear, I'm just dying to show you our photographs—unless of course you absolutely detest other people's holiday snaps—well, it can be tedious, don't you think? Of course it can. There now, in you go, make yourself comfy, that's right, here's Marcus with your wine. Oh, and nuts—I shouldn't know Marcus at a party without his nuts, a very pressing host sometimes—take a handful, there you are!"

Esme admired the photographs of lakeside hills and wayside shrines, the Venetian squares and bridges and waterways, and the glories of Florence. She learned that Jeremy, who appeared in some of the snaps, a youthful clone of his father, ran a small chain of juice bars catering to health-conscious executives in the West End of London. Hilda again expressed concern about how hard he worked and how time-consuming his business commitments were. Required to corroborate this, Marcus expressed the opinion that possibly Jeremy's attitude to his work was a little less languid than it had been to his studies at school; but Esme could see how proud of the young man his father felt.

"And of course now Sophie has her little gallery in

Piccadilly, it's much more handy—she and Jeremy can both be based in the London flat now, and it does save so much running about. Back and forth to Paris was no joke in the long term."

Esme said she could see that this would be so. Gathering the photographs into neat piles again, she replaced them in the envelopes on her lap. "Those are beautiful. What a wonderful trip," she said.

"Oh, it was! Last year in Russia," Hilda threw up her hands in horror at the memory; "well, Marcus *would* go. Leningrad it had to be. Oh, I admit we saw some splendid things but, dear me, icons *ad infinitum* and the acrylic alphabet that nobody could make head or tail of. I was honestly just glad to come home! Now then you must be famished— I've a nice little casserole, just the thing for a cold night. You and Marcus can talk over your church nonsense while I flap about in the kitchen. It's so nice of you to look at my photographs, my dear—you know how it is, people just fall asleep looking!"

Marcus, ensconced in the comfortable depths of his armchair on the other side of the fire, sipped his wine reflectively.

"Are you happy about your move?" he asked Esme, when Hilda had gone out of the room.

She responded cautiously, "Well, if this hadn't come up, I think I should have hoped for a reinvitation to stay, but it all seems practical; I am looking upon it as an opportunity."

Marcus nodded. "But you—" he bent and placed his

glass on the corner of the modern York stone hearth, which looked remarkably at home in this old house with its antique furnishings, "—you had no particular reason why you might have preferred to stay on with us at Wiles Green?" he asked.

Wiles Green? Esme thought of Miss Trigg. *How strange that he might think I had a special attachment to the chapel at Wiles Green. He can't face worshipping there himself!*

"No? Just a question of finding the right way forward? I had thought—" he hesitated, "—I had thought the suggestion I might offer for restructuring would be to combine Southarbour with the little chapels that remain to the west of it, leaving Brockhyrst Priory and Wiles Green to the north as a tiny section suitable for a half-timer; which could be a supernumerary just retired looking for a few more active years or a minister in local appointment who might welcome half a stipend."

"I suppose it's possible one of our retired ministers would take them on, but those two chapels are no doddle to run," said Esme. "And we haven't got a minister in local appointment."

"No," Marcus admitted. "Not at the moment, but you never know."

"Well, but we've got to plan for what we have now," said Esme, perplexed. "Unless you know something I don't know."

Marcus shook his head. "It was only a thought," he said. "And I'm quite sure you know more about it all than I do.

You feel there are no ties for you here then, beyond the natural preference for spending a while longer with the congregations you have come to know?"

"Yes, but somehow … well, if I'm honest, I'm sad to be going; but it's clear I'm the obvious choice if one of us has to leave. And after all, I'd have had to move on eventually, wouldn't I? I'm getting less and less convinced that it's part of the vocation, but the reality is that it's part of the job."

"Yes." The curious, speculative way Marcus was looking at her suddenly reminded her of the way Seer Ember had sat considering her in Jabez's kitchen.

"What?" she asked, feeling slightly unnerved.

Marcus smiled. "I feel not entirely happy about these decisions for change. It seems to me the discussions might have waited until a moment of natural parting. I'm going to go ahead and make my suggestion to the team, Esme; that we make a small section suitable for, say, a minister in local appointment. We may attract somebody. It isn't only older people who go for local appointment. Sometimes folk feel called to ministry who, for reasons of family commitments or other ties to a local area, are looking for something more stable, more rooted maybe."

Why is he telling me this? Esme wondered, bewildered. *For heaven's sake, I know what local appointment entails. Why is he insisting on pursuing this cul-de-sac when there's no one here it applies to?*

"Ah! Ready, my dear?" Marcus got to his feet and stood

politely waiting for Esme to accompany him to the dining room.

After they had eaten, as Hilda disappeared to brew some coffee, Esme asked Marcus for some advice in choosing her way forward.

"It's funny," she said, "there seems to be no particular area or type of ministry that calls to me—all I know is, I'm quite happy here. I think I'll try for somewhere not too far away."

Marcus had no advice to offer, however, and as she mulled over their conversation on the way home, Esme concluded he was probably sensible; people have to accept responsibility themselves for the choices they make.

November, overcast and cold, damp with recurrent drizzle, persisted dismally in the direction of Advent. Esme gazed out of her study window at the cheerless sight of her front garden clogged with a sodden mat of fallen leaves, the earth of its borders between the skeletal rose bushes interrupted by the broken, awkward shapes of dead plants blackened by night frosts.

She sat planning the format for Portland Street's service of Advent Light scheduled for the first Sunday of December in ten days time. Piled on her desk were files of previous Advent services, carols-by-candlelight liturgies, Christingles, and school end-of-term winter services, intended to offer her inspiration. So far none had.

She pulled a lined pad toward her. "People, Look East,"

she jotted down, and "O come, O come, Emmanuel" and "When the Lord in Glory Comes." Changing tack for a moment, she reached for her card file, flicked through to find the telephone numbers of the choir mistress at Brockhyrst Priory and Southarbour's worship bandleader; these she wrote down in readiness at the bottom of the sheet of paper. Suddenly, her attention was caught by something green pulling up alongside the pavement beyond her garden wall. "Good Lord! It's Jabez!" she said aloud, wondering as she left her desk and went to open the front door, if it was right to feel so pleased at the interruption.

"Hello!" she called out to him, happy at his unexpected arrival. He had been about to take something out of the back of his truck, but hearing her call, left it, and came toward the house. Esme delighted afresh in the curious, shy, "I'm not here" mode of his approach. *How does he do it?* she asked herself, smiling at the sight of him in his huge waxed jacket and rivers of silver hair.

He lifted his eyes in one bright glance as he came to where she stood on the doorstep. "I thought you might be glad of your leaves raked," he said, nodding toward the damp mass obscuring her small front lawn. "And round the back," he added. "I popped in yesterday while you were out, but no rake in the shed, so I came back today. All right?"

"Oh, Jabez! You are a darling! That would be absolutely wonderful! Would you like a cup of tea first?"

He smiled. "Well, you put the kettle on while I make a

start on these. Cup of tea be most welcome, but I haven't come to hold up whatever you're busy with."

Esme shook her head, laughing. "Oh, no! Please do! I shall be glad of an excuse to stop! Have you got a rake then? Is there anything else you need?"

"No, I got all I'll be wanting in the back of the truck. Esme, you got no proper compost bins here, have you? If I find a spare morning and I can pick up some forklift pallets or something somewhere, shall I pop in and knock up a place for leaf mold and for your kitchen compost down the end of the garden? Rots down better if it's properly contained."

"Does it? Well, yes, that would be lovely." Esme didn't dare tell him she recycled nothing and threw all her kitchen waste out with everything else for the dustman to take to the landfill site—or that there wasn't much kitchen waste anyway because most of what she bought was ready-meals in the first place. "I'll put the kettle on then," she said, changing the subject.

When, having made a cup of tea and put some flapjacks out on a plate, she returned awhile later to the front doorstep to invite him in, she found him with the leaves raked into neat piles, which he was collecting onto a tarpaulin he had spread on the tarmac drive. She observed that he had brought a yard broom with him, and presumably, intended to sweep up the fallen leaves thickly edging the driveway, too.

"With you in a minute," he said, glancing up.

In the once or twice she had seen him since his visit to

Samuel in Shropshire, Esme had at some point mentioned in conversation the despair she felt at her inability to tend her garden adequately. "It's such a tangle," she had said. "I quite like gardening, but it's a bit big for me, and there are so many other things to be done. The minister before me never did anything in the garden, but the one before him was a real enthusiast, so there are all these dead things and weeds that have colonized the bare earth of the veggie patch. Really horrid weeds too. Ground elder and bindweed and things with deep roots. And now the leaves are falling, I don't see how I'll ever be able to catch up with it."

"I am just so grateful," she said, as he perched on the high stool at her built-in Formica breakfast bar. "Have a flapjack. Have two. It's so nice of you. It feels like the cavalry coming over the hill. Whoever else in all the world would turn up out of the blue to rake up all these blessed leaves for me? Thank you so, so much."

Jabez blinked, pleased and slightly embarrassed.

"Steady on," he said. "I got a free afternoon, that's all. I'm glad to be of some use, I rarely enough am."

Esme smiled at him. "You've a large crumb of flapjack lodged in your beard," she observed.

"Have I? That's nothing new." He felt for it and fished it out. "There are some things that don't go with beards, like professional advancement and spaghetti bolognaise," he remarked, "but it's handy for catching the crumbs, it saves on shaving stuff, and I get up quicker in the morning."

Esme laughed. For a moment there was silence between them.

"D'you know," she said then, "nobody else comes to help me with the difficult things like you do. I've thought about it often, because it's a curious thing about women in ordained ministry. Sometimes the question is raised as to whether it's more difficult for women to be ministers, whether there are practices of discrimination or prejudice that we should attend to. In my own experience, I have never met any sense of individuals intentionally making life difficult—I mean, there are plenty of people like Miss Trigg, but then as you said, she's entitled to her point of view as much as I am to mine. And yet … oh, it's hard to put my finger on what the difference is, it's just little things all the time; ordinary, mundane things that nobody notices—even I don't notice most of the time. You know, I've sat in the Synod at lunchtime, and all the ministers are undoing their sandwiches, opening their plastic boxes and their cling-film packets—and I've heard the men saying things like 'What's this then? I've never had one of these before'; which makes it clear they didn't pack their own lunch, nor yet did the shopping that enabled the packed lunch to be made. Once I made a remark to a male colleague comparing one grocery store to another; he smiled with a sort of polite interest and then said he didn't really know because he hadn't been in any of them—his wife does all the shopping. That man's wife doesn't sit at home polishing her nails the rest of the time either; she's a community psychiatric nurse. And our super-intendent, at a staff meeting, will look at his watch and say, 'I'll have to be back by one, because Jean will have the dinner ready.' I've sat in a committee at Westminster, a roomful of men and me the only woman except one—and she was the secretary of one of the men, there to take notes, you know? And we sat round the table before the meeting began, polite chat. The talk was all about recently visited London art exhibitions and the latest computer software. A couple of the men were having hard times. One of them said his secretary was off sick, and the other one said his computer had crashed—or was it the other way round? Then the door swung open, and into this elegant chatter—I mean, the committee was to discuss poverty in Britain today, and the Methodist church is supposedly a scrupulously egalitarian institution—in walked two black ladies bearing platters of sandwiches. And I asked myself, is this the church of Jesus Christ? Is this how it's meant to be? But, Jabez, what really gave me the creeps is that *nobody else thought anything of it!*

"And in my own life, if I were a man alone—I know this is true from the experience of male colleagues—they'd bring me chocolate cake and ask me round to dinner and offer to help me clean my house. But because I'm a woman, they expect me to help run the bazaar and take an active interest in making the coffee after worship and bake buns for church teas. It's so unfair! If I were a male married minister, my wife would probably do half my pastoral visiting and help me with all the socializing and remember Christmas cards and relatives' birthdays, as well as get the shopping and vacuum the floors and cook the tea. But if I as a woman were married, my husband would go out to work and that would probably be his contribution to the household. Full stop!

"Sometimes as I've been driving seven miles out to Wiles Green along rutted lanes with a fruit salad or a huge vat of soup on the passenger seat, on my way to an event where I have responsibility for all the proceedings as well, I ask myself, *Why am I doing this?* If I whine about it to any other women minister, she just looks at me over her pack of sandwiches (not the one her husband made, the one she stopped to buy at the garage shop when she was filling up with petrol on the way to Synod) and says, 'Well, why are you?' And I'll tell you why, Jabez, it's because although I can preach and chair a meeting and do all that the job requires, underneath it all I'm not a modern woman; I'm not sure of my role, and something in me mourns the passing of tradition."

He looked at Esme. One eyebrow twitched expressively, and there was a smile in his eyes. He said nothing until he was sure she'd stopped, and then, "Um, men do vary," he ventured.

Esme gazed at him hopelessly. "Jabez, I'm so, so tired," she said.

Jabez nodded. He sipped his tea and sat quietly. Esme looked at him, his body relaxed but aware, his eyes thoughtful; she saw a poise in him that she had seen in wild things, not often in human beings.

In the course of her life, Esme had usually had a special friend. When something interesting or important happened to her that she was bursting to share, she would find that whoever she told, she hadn't really told it, not felt she had really been heard, until she told her special friend. Over the last few months she had begun to find, without consciously realizing it, that so it was now with Jabez. Whatever her news or her trouble might be, if only she could tell Jabez, nothing more needed to be said.

"Four years ago, my husband left me." Esme's fingers picked up a till receipt that lay among other discarded papers on the breakfast bar. Absentmindedly, she began to fold and refold it. "I trusted him, you know. He told me he loved me, spun such dreams for me, till I was caught in the silken threads of romance like a fly in a spider's web. He promised me he'd love me always, take care of me. He called me his princess and he said the moon was a silver ball and he'd climb up to heaven and bring it down." She broke off, feeling foolish. Truly she had fallen for the loveliness of it all, the wedding and the happiness of being chosen, of achieving something her family might admire; of being, for a man who had seemed so clever and accomplished and sophisticated, the Only One. Except she hadn't been. "It was all right for a while," she said. "I mean, we managed fourteen years together, just about. We were happy, more or less, right up until the time I was accepted as a candidate for ordained ministry. I don't know what happened, it was as though he saw me as a competitor. He'd always insisted he supported the idea of me following that path, but …"

Her voice trailed away, and she sat for a while remembering. Then she stirred, and looked at Jabez. It intrigued her, the way under a veil of quietness in his face, lights and shadows of his soul dappled and flickered. He sat without moving, impassive, but so alive. He waited for her to speak, but she felt understood; she had no need to say any more.

"Esme, I better get those leaves done," he said after awhile, finishing his tea. He got down from the high stool, took his mug to the sink, rinsed it, and looked round for the dishtowel to dry it.

"My experience is limited," he said, glancing at her with a shy smile as he dried the mug, "but I guess you have to be wary of eloquence. In general, if a man is in love—I mean really, deeply in love—you won't get much more out of him than the bleat of a strangled sheep when he tries to tell you how much he cares for you. Never trust the staying power of a love that can be expressed as 'I *adore* you, darling!'"

Esme laughed. "I see!" she mocked him. "So you could go weak at the knees at the sight of me, and you'd never be able to tell me so!"

He put the mug back on its hook with the others, and hung the dishtowel back on the rail it had come from.

"That's right," he said quietly. "Now I better get on with those leaves."

SEVEN

E sme woke early, with Advent on her mind. Tuesday
today, first Sunday in Advent coming up. Through her
childhood, and as a young woman, Advent had been a season
of excitement and happy anticipation, a magical time of year.
All that seemed to have been crushed out of it now, by the
weight of too many events. She had organized her
Christingle service for Portland Street, with a modest prize
for the child with the best decorated orange. She had contacted the Scout leaders from Brockhyrst Priory to arrange a
small band of instrumentalists for the Advent service of light.
She had appealed for carol singers from all three churches for
carol singing round the village at Brockhyrst Priory. Her
Christmas service details were in to the local paper, and she
had written three pastoral letters for the church magazines of
each of her three chapels, remembering to include a plug for
the Covenant service in early January, there being no January
magazine. The watch-night service on New Year's Eve was

sorted and the Christmas midnight communion, too. The carols services at each of her three chapels had been scheduled so that she could officiate at all three—it meant Wiles Green taking the 4:30 slot again this year, but they didn't seem to mind. In her diary she had noted a number of social occasions; the circuit staff and stewards' New Year's party (all ladies to bring a dessert, the superintendent's wife to provide the main course; Esme was on fruit salad again) and the Portland Street choir dinner at a two-star hotel in a side road a few hundred yards in from the seafront. The choir went there every year, securing at a knockdown price a cheerful evening with a mediocre meal. The youth leader had invited her to the Brownies' and Rainbows' Christmas party, and she had been approached with a request to take a small service for the playgroup that met at Portland Street. She had been invited to the Christmas celebrations of five house groups; in each case Esme was to give a Christmas message, after which there would be a party with finger foods. She had been asked to give the Christmas address for the Multiple Sclerosis Society carol service, taking place in Brockhyrst Priory chapel for the first time this year, and she was to say a prayer at the conclusion of the annual junior school Christmas concert in Portland Street chapel. There remained outstanding some arrangements to be made about the donkey belonging to the livery stables, in preparation for the Living Crib that the vicar of St. Raphaels at Wiles Green masterminded each year. It had occurred to him that ecumenism would spread the burden of forward planning, and he had invited Esme to be part of the proceedings, which involved her sourcing a recently delivered mother, a lantern on a hook, and a reliable donkey. The stable was a regular venue, so nobody had to fix that. On the first Saturday in December, which was AIDS week, Esme had promised to take part in a special service at the Anglican church in the center of Southarbour. She also noted that she had two planning meetings scheduled in early and late December for a bereavement group preparing special intercessions for the hospice anniversary service, which wasn't till February but had to be planned ahead to enable fliers for distribution in the New Year.

Suddenly remembering the preparatory planning necessary for the week of prayer for Christian unity in mid-January and the ecumenical service on Bible Sunday, Esme found herself very wide awake at six o'clock in the morning, which was early for her. Lying in bed mentally reviewing her various commitments and responsibilities for a while hardly seemed to improve them. Fervently hoping that no one would die and require a funeral before the end of the first week of January, Esme got up to make a cup of tea.

Seizing the opportunity offered by an early start to the day, in a moment of resolve she took her copy of the Methodist Worship Book off the shelf and used the set form of Morning Prayer as devotions to start the day. Feeling virtuous, as light came, she decided to go for a ride on her bike as well. She ate a bowl of cereal and left the washing up in the sink for later, locked up the house, and got her bike out of the shed. As she cycled out in the direction of Brockhyrst Priory, encouraged by the emergence of a promise of sunshine after two weeks of drizzling rain, it occurred to her to push on in the direction of Wiles Green and drop in for a cup of tea with Jabez and Ember, who she thought would most likely be up by now. The morning sunlight strengthened as she rode through the lanes. She encountered a number of people out walking their dogs and some schoolchildren walking along to the main road to wait for the bus. She went cautiously, because the postal delivery vans were busy in the lanes at this time, and other vehicles were hurrying to workplaces. Fallen leaves packed on the road surface made the way slippery, and in the places of shadow it was still icy. Esme felt glad to arrive in one piece at the Old Police House. She dismounted from her bike and wheeled it up the path to the cottage, leaving it propped against the wall of the kitchen.

Knocking on the door, and then immediately opening it to let herself in, she found her friends in the warmth of the kitchen, chatting, the early sunlight streaming through the window above the sink that looked up the garden into the orchard. On the table, the remains of breakfast things still stood around the big brown teapot in its multicolored knitted tea cozy (Ember's work). Ember sat in her corner by the stove, and Jabez sat by the table on one stool, his back resting against the wall, his feet up on the other stool. They each held a mug of tea, steaming. It was a companionable sight, and as Jabez put down his tea without question and reached up a hand to the shelf for a third mug, Esme felt a sudden impulse of happiness in the warmth of the welcome always there for her, confidence in friendship given.

"You're abroad early," said Ember. "You had your breakfast, or will I make some more fried bread?"

"Oh, dear, don't give me fried bread!" It may have sounded ungracious but the words were spoken before she thought twice. "I mean, it's ever so kind of you, but I just have to lose some weight. I cycled everywhere during the summer but I don't seem to have lost a pound—it just made me hungry and I ate more."

"I expect it's just muscle then," said Ember consolingly. "Muscles be heavier than fat."

Jabez held out the mug of tea he had poured her and took his feet off the stool, pushing it toward her for a seat.

"It's okay," she said, leaning her back against the edge of the sink, "I'm fine over here. I don't think it is muscle, Ember, I think it's middle-aged spread." She sighed. "It makes me feel so frumpy."

"You don't look frumpy," Jabez said quietly. "Just—" and then he mumbled something in the direction of his tea that Esme didn't catch. She looked at him, intrigued, but he wouldn't look back at her.

Ember, alert, her eyes snapping with mischief, caught Esme's eye. "I believe," she said with a grin, "those words, if that's what you can call 'em, were 'nice to hold.'"

Esme took a moment to register her own delight in the compliment—that it was more precious to her than she might have expected. Jabez took refuge in his mug of tea. Ember regarded them both with intense interest.

"Well," she said, "you bring him something nice to hold, he got the bike shed, what are you waiting for?"

Jabez froze in rigid embarrassment, his hand halfway returning his mug to the table. For a moment he said nothing, just stared fixedly at the space in front him. Then he placed the mug very quietly, deliberately, on the table.

"Ember, for heaven's sake, she's a minister," he said. "That's disrespectful to say such a thing."

Not in the least put out by this rebuke, Ember regarded him with skepticism, leaning forward to say, "Jabez Ferrall, you tell me you look at Esme and see a *minister,* and I'll call you a liar to your face."

Desperate, turning his head away as an animal turns its head from the bars of a cage, not looking at either of them, Jabez said firmly to Esme, "I wouldn't lean against that sink if I were you; you'll get a line of water on your back. Excuse me now, I haven't fed the hens."

Avoiding their gaze, he got to his feet and crossed the kitchen, escaping into the yard and closing the door firmly behind him.

"He has," said Ember, with a grin.

They heard the postman call to him, and Jabez reply; but he didn't bring the letters into the cottage.

"Oh, dear." Esme felt worried. "I think he was really offended, Ember. Don't you think you should maybe go and apologize?"

Ember's face wrinkled into laughter, which shook her small frame.

"Leave him be, he'll come round," she chuckled. "Bring that tea and sit you down here at the table. Jabez takes hisself too serious most of the time. 'Tis a male disease."

Esme smiled, and came to sit with Ember.

After awhile Esme asked, "Will either of his sons come home for Christmas?"

Ember shook her head.

"If you ain't religious that way, then all Christmas brings is expense," she replied. "He sends them a card and what money he can for a present. If he's lucky, they remember to send him a card, at least before January's too far started. We have Christmas very quiet here. Jabez likes to listen to carols on the radio, and when the shops reduce the prices of everything after Boxing Day, we have some stuffing and a bird, a Christmas puddin' and a jar of brandy butter. Last year he gave me some chocolates—that was nice; and I'd knitted him a scarf which he was glad of. I got a book put away for him this year; saw it at a jumble sale in the summer."

"What's the book?" Esme asked.

"Annie Dillard—*Pilgrim at Tinker Creek*. She done a good thing in there about stalking muskrats, and I reckon Jabez'll like reading that."

"I don't think I know it," said Esme. She sat for a while, contemplating the month ahead and shook her head. "I think I'll be lucky to get through Christmas alive! It's just so hectic. The last thing in the marathon will be just a morning service on Boxing Day (being Sunday, but we've cancelled the evening worship); and then I drive up to stay with my family for a few days. Back in good time for the New Year's services. It feels a bit like a treadmill sometimes."

Ember looked at her curiously. "Do you enjoy your work?" she asked.

Esme blinked, surprised. "Do you know," she replied after a moment's thought, "that is not a question I've ever asked myself. I believe in it—I think. It's worthwhile, I suppose. The church at its worst is soul-destroying, but it's the only institution founded on a command to offer unconditional love and that's a wonderful raison d'être."

"A what?"

"Reason for being there. When my husband left me, I lost quite a lot of myself. Hope, you know, and confidence. I have found comfort in the work; if nothing else it keeps me busy."

"You ain't very happy then?"

Esme considered this. "Well—yes and no. I feel a bit restless sometimes, for reasons I can't fully analyze. Something to do with my own fulfillment—I don't know. I seem to achieve remarkably little. But the people are kind, and the work is something I feel able to offer. When I preach, I feel alive."

Under Ember's perspicacious gaze, Esme felt it all sounded very empty and inadequate. "More tea?" Ember asked her, but she shook her head.

"Surely, though," Esme protested then, "that's how it is for all of us, isn't it? Life in the real world is a very humdrum thing; we have only moments of exhilaration. Isn't it the same for you? Like the prayer book calls it—'ordinary time'?"

"I've had good times and bad," Ember said. "I was not much more than a girl when I married; my husband left and good riddance and I never looked for another. Bad news is men, most of 'em. I never had any money nor wanted none. I done bits to get by, that's all. But I had a day when I asked myself, *What is it all? What's it for?* I remember it, I was standing in the lane that leads off the top of Stoddards Hill, high summer, and I just stood there and listened to the heartbeat of it, and I saw that life held out its hands to me, and that in the very core of it all there is joy. Make no difference that you got to grieve sometimes and these things happen that tear the very gut out of you. Makes no difference. Its heartbeat is joy, and it holds out its hands to you, and the only doorway into it is this living moment. Worry and fear and longing and desire is about living in tomorrow, and grief and bitterness and regret and pain is living in yesterday. Life is joy, and joy is never tomorrow. There is only now. If you ain't living now, why, then, you're dead. And trying to please other people slams the door to joy shut in your face. Walk your own track.

Listen to life's voice with your own ears. Don't trust truth in packets, especially the ones got warnings and contracts with 'em. Don't parade your soul around; live quiet and small and simple. Don't blame anybody for what happens, don't ask favors and, Esme, don't look for approval. There's joy at the middle, but you got to trust things enough to turn your back on the party and choose it."

"Ember," said Esme, "you're amazing."

On a sudden impulse, she got up from her stool, went round the table to Ember's corner, and hugged the old woman's small, plump body against her, bending down to kiss the top of her head. Ember close smelled of wood smoke and herbs and garlic—wood smoke principally; but a very pleasant, wholesome smell.

After a moment, slightly embarrassed at her own display of emotion, she released her and stepped back, and returned to sit on her stool again. Ember looked across at her, dark eyes kind and laughing and wise.

"Jabez'll be up the orchard, Esme," she said. "Always goes up the orchard when he's upset. And I've upset him good and proper this morning. Overstepped his boundaries by about fifteen mile." She spoke with perfect tranquillity, making no comment on Esme's gesture of affection and contemplating with peaceful detachment the distress she had caused Jabez.

"He'll come round," she added. "Needs a bit of a shove sometimes, does Jabez."

She got up from her chair and opened the stove door, fed

it with more firewood, and began to collect the breakfast crockery for washing up.

"You'll find him in the orchard," she repeated.

Esme hesitated. "Maybe he'd rather not be disturbed—maybe I should just go home," she ventured.

Ember paused with the pile of crocks in her hands and regarded her in a way that made Esme feel that she was pitied, better understood than she was quite comfortable with, and an unwilling source of amusement.

"What you get out of this life depends on what you put in, my lady," was all Ember offered, saying again, "You'll find him in the orchard," before busying herself with her tasks at the sink—this required turning her back on Esme: The conversation seemed to have terminated.

Esme drew breath to say one more thing, but, "In the orchard," said Ember firmly, and did not look round.

So Esme wandered up into the orchard, where she did indeed find Jabez in the furthest corner, sitting on a pile of firewood, smoking a cigarette, and looking upset.

"I'm on my way home, Jabez." Esme approached him, speaking in a cheerful, ordinary tone, choosing to ignore the look on his face. She had to wait a little while for his reply, and wondered if it would be better just to go, but eventually, "What must you think of us?" he said, bitterly.

"Think of you? You and Ember? I think I'm so, so lucky to have you as my friends. You feel like real friends, true friends, both of you. You always make me feel welcome and loved. And I love your honesty—I wish the world had more people in it as honest as you and Ember."

He shot her a glance of incredulity. "Ember! I dare swear the world could stand another one or two as honest as me, but if I thought there were any more like Ember I'd take to the woods or top myself!"

"Jabez, why are you so upset?" Esme was beginning to laugh; it all seemed a bit out of proportion. "She was only joking! She didn't mean it!"

"Joking? Ember doesn't make jokes. She sees what's inside you, and she got no mercy. And I hate it. It wasn't proper what she said—it wasn't decent. Bike shed! I'm not that kind of man!"

He looked at the end of his cigarette, saw it had gone out, and threw it with some force into the hedge. From under the silver eyebrows another fierce glance shot her way. "And, yes, you are welcome. And you are loved. But I'm not—I wouldn't—" He stopped, finding himself in difficult territory. "I'm not that kind of man," he said again. He bent his head, and Esme looked at him sitting with his shoulders hunched to his ears, his elbows resting on his knees, and his hands clasped tight together. She noted her own sense of hope that resulted from his being unable to go through with his insistence that he was not and that he wouldn't. *And what on earth am I doing?* she asked her heart. *What am I offering him anyway? Where does Jabez fit into my world? How can I be anything but a day-tripper in his?*

She watched him, not sure what to do. They seemed to have reached an impasse, it was time to go; and yet she felt certain that she would leave him unhappy all day if she couldn't bring something better out of this before she left. So, what to put in? For what after all did she want to get out of this life, this encounter? *There is only now*, Ember had said: "If you aren't living now, why then you're dead." What did she want now, then? Her head and her heart seemed to have met head-on in a Wiles Green lane too narrow for passing places. She just knew she didn't want him to look so upset.

"I know you aren't that kind of man," she said at last. "Bike sheds, I mean. For didn't you tell me once, making love should be done in a bed; because it's a thing of tenderness, and it should be warm and comfortable?"

Startled, he looked up at her. *So that*, she thought, *is what it takes to make this man look at me for more than two seconds at a time.* She raised her eyebrows, enquiring, smiling at him, deliberately keeping things light. Trying to, at least. He swallowed, blinked, continued to look at her. She had rather hoped he might laugh, but he looked absolutely transfixed.

"What must you think of me?" She echoed his words to him, but gently, offering him his own dignity back. "Jabez, I think I should go."

Now whatever have I got myself into? she asked herself, as she turned and left him, sitting motionless on the pile of logs.

Is this normal behavior? she wondered, exasperated, as she got on her bike and set off through the lanes. *Doesn't he know how to make light of a thing? Whatever next?* She pedaled furiously along the lanes back to Southarbour. *I'm neglecting my work. I should be in my study! Why am I wasting time on visiting people who will never come to chapel and on pottering round the countryside on a bicycle?*

Suddenly thrust closer to Jabez than she had quite expected to be, she felt flustered and defensive. She directed the energy of her confusion into cycling fast, quite impressed at the ease with which she could master the hills these days. Without allowing it to break into her conscious mind, she turned vigorously from the sense that there was something unfair about keeping from Jabez the plans for her future. She lumped them together in her mind, *Jabez and Ember*, and reflected that delightful as they both were, they were also undeniably eccentric, odd, and difficult. Tiresome of Jabez to make so much of Ember's mischievous joke; tasteless and provocative of Ember to say it in the first place. She avoided the memory of her own quick pleasure at what he had said—"nice to hold"—and of something more unsaid between them in the orchard: "For didn't you tell me, making love should be done in a bed?" Jabez looking at her, startled, hearing what she didn't say—shouldn't say, couldn't say, because she was leaving. And because—with an effort she suppressed the whole memory—there was nothing to be said.

When she reached the safety of the parsonage, Esme felt surprised and impressed with herself to see that she had made it out to Wiles Green and back, and had half an hour's conversation, and it still wasn't quite ten o'clock. She made a cup of coffee and retreated to her study with two biscuits. She switched on the computer and going online to check her inbox she found an e-mail from her superintendent minister. He had something to discuss with her, he said, and would she ring him, to make an appointment.

E-mail didn't come naturally or easily to Esme's superintendent, though he had recognized the necessity of electronic communications and mastered the basics required. He was of the old school and utterly predictable; in the study every morning, visiting in the afternoons, meetings in the evening. His wife, Sheila, had dedicated her life to being his mainstay and support, her unself-conscious sweetness of manner and warmhearted concern for others providing the backbone of the pastoral care he offered. On the occasions she had been in his parsonage, it amazed and intrigued Esme to see that, after thirty-seven years of ministry, when he heard the telephone ring, which he probably did about twenty times a day, her superintendent would still run from wherever he stood in the house to answer it.

She wondered why he had asked to see her. An inarticulate man with few social skills, he would never contact his colleagues unless he found it unavoidable to do so. A miner's son, brought up in a family of seven children, frugality was nearer than second nature to him; his phone calls were short, his letters came by second-class post, and he would calculate in advance whether he had to mail them at all, carefully consulting his diary to ascertain if he might rather take advantage of crossing paths with the recipient at a forthcoming church business meeting. He had worked out the shortest mileage from his parsonage to every destination his work regularly encompassed. He wasted no money of his own and none of the circuit's, though he was generous with both when called upon by others in need. His preaching was sound, safe, uninspiring, and conscientiously recycled over the thirty-seven years, each sermon annotated with the occasions and venues of all its outings.

Esme respected him; in his dealings with his colleagues, he erred from strict fairness only when he felt it necessary to be kind; he understood his administrative responsibilities clearly and undertook them with meticulous detail, remembered everything, and she trusted him to play his part in the circuit reconstruction with honesty, competence, kindness, discretion, and total lack of imagination.

She picked up the telephone and dialed his number. Nine thirty on a Tuesday morning in late November. He answered the telephone instantly, being seated, as she had visualized, in the padded office swivel chair provided by the circuit, at his desk in the study.

"Brian Robinson," he said, in his loud, unemotional way.

"Hello, it's Esme. You wanted to see me."

"Ah, yes, my dear. Some news from the chairman I'd like to discuss with you when you can spare a moment."

"I can come over today if you like," she replied.

"Today? Now let me see. I've got a funeral call later this morning, about eleven, and a Wesley guild in the afternoon. Tomorrow is my midweek communion, and then in the afternoon I'm running Sheila to the osteopath for her regular visit, taking in some pastoral calls on the way home. How about Thursday?"

"Can't do," said Esme. "I've got a school assembly early, a sick communion, then I'm the speaker for the ladies' fellowship at Brockhyrst Priory after lunch, and a wedding rehearsal in the evening. Friday's busy all day too—I mean, I can pop over right now, I can be with you in ten minutes; or even we could talk on the phone?"

"Oh no, I'd rather not discuss this on the telephone. Let me see...." He paused. She could hear him breathing. He already had a funeral call to take him away from his sermon preparation in the study. This would further eat into his time. It was Tuesday and he liked to type up and print his order of service and notices sheet on Thursday morning; the sermon would have to be finished before then. Esme could feel him weighing it up in his mind.

"Well, all right. My funeral call is no more than half a mile from you. I'll finish off this correspondence later, and come over to you now. See you shortly. Righto."

Puzzled and curious, a quarter of an hour later Esme opened the door to his ring on the loud electric bell and offered him coffee. He accepted the offer, but asked for a small cup. Since he passed his sixtieth birthday, large cups of coffee taken early had started to be a problem to him later in the morning.

He seated himself on her sofa, she gave him a coffee and sat in the armchair, and looked at him, his almost-bald head covered by a few thin strands combed carefully from above his left ear over the pink shining expanse of his scalp to meet the balancing growth of hair at his right ear. The elbows and cuffs of his battered tweed jacket had been reinforced with leather, probably by Sheila. His hand-knitted dark blue waistcoat concealed the fact that his clerical shirt was really only a stock, easily removed when it was time to do his half hour of gardening while Sheila washed up the dishes after their lunch.

"Well?" said Esme.

"It's about your appointment, my dear."

It transpired that a minister from a circuit in a wealthy suburb of London had rather precipitately abandoned his congregation in the company of his senior steward, who was the wife of his organist. The organist, heartbroken and embittered, had refused to have anything further to do with the Methodist church and offered his services to the Baptists (they had gratefully accepted, having been managing for years with a second-rate pianist who could neither sight-read nor play the pedals). The church community had been left shocked and distressed, without a minister, a senior steward, or an organist.

In the immediate emergency, the chairman himself had

plugged such gaps as he could, and the other staff of the circuit had arranged medium-term pastoral and preaching cover. But the chairman had promised to do what he could to secure a new minister without waiting for the usual slow wheels of stationing to begin to grind. Knowing that when Esme left she would not be replaced, it had occurred to him that though she should give her congregations ample time to make their parting, and the circuit ample time to adjust, nonetheless her move might be brought forward and considered before the usual time in May, if she were interested in investigating the possibility.

"It's a plum job," her superintendent stated frankly. "If you want to do well, this would set you on your way. They wouldn't tolerate just anybody in that part of Surrey. It's a compliment to your preaching and admin gifts. There's a rough patch in that circuit, but the section they're offering you is very smart indeed. Good parsonage—I've been in it. Compliment to your pastoral gifts too—it will take something to pull the congregation through this in one piece. Chairman thinks highly of you, my dear; he knows you won't let him down. What do you think? Take a look?"

Something in Esme's stomach gave a lurch as the reality of her move came alarmingly nearer. She hesitated. Then, reasoning that as she had committed herself to going, this could save protracted uncertainty, and prove a shrewd step on her inevitably nomadic chosen path, she agreed to pursue the matter. Her superintendent congratulated her; evidently he approved. It made little difference in this circuit except for accelerating the time-table of restructuring. It would help the chairman out of a hole, which would be regarded favorably. And he felt it would be a sound and positive step for Esme, which made him feel a lot better about her having been edged out of the team. Without real thought or discussion, she felt herself crossing another threshold.

When he left, promising to contact the chairman for her, who would initiate the necessary liaison, Esme closed the door behind him and leaned her back on it, feeling shaky and terribly weary.

This had been a sound decision for a minister. If she discussed it with her mother, or any of her family, they would be enthusiastic, Esme felt sure. Her colleagues would be impressed and think she had done well. The circuit stewards would feel relieved. Her own church stewards and members would feel as positive about this as about any move. It was only …

With a sigh, feeling slow and tired and inexplicably miserable, Esme made her way like a sleepwalker to the kitchen. She made herself another coffee and, being temporarily out of flapjacks, took half a packet of biscuits into her study with her. She sat down at her desk and opened the document folder on the computer to check her notes for the last school assembly she had done.

Until she had talked this through with Jabez, she wouldn't really know what she thought about it herself. What were the implications of that anyway, she asked herself? And why anyway did the deepest part of her say, *Not yet! Not yet!* whenever she thought about telling Jabez and Ember? Would it cause them so much of a problem? They had certainly been good friends, but she told herself it would be vanity to presume she figured that much in their lives, whatever had passed between them this morning.

She opened the file named Priory Street Infant School. She put Ember and Jabez and everything about the move out of her mind. Nothing had been decided. It would take ages anyway. Next week saw the beginning of Advent. She was unlikely to hear anything before the New Year.

Esme worked determinedly through what remained of the morning. She cycled out to see a blind and frail housebound church member on the outskirts of Brockhyrst Priory in the afternoon. On the way home she called in to the DVD library to choose a film, then stopped at the supermarket and did her shopping, wobbling rather precariously home with her bicycle basket full and three carrier bags dangling from the handlebars unevenly weighting the bike.

She spent three hours as afternoon crossed over into evening ransacking poetry anthologies and the Internet to put together a presentation for the Ladies Fellowship on *The Spirituality of Winter*. While her supper heated in the microwave, she printed out the poems she had downloaded. Then she took her meal on a tray with a cup of coffee into the sitting room to watch her film. She ate her supper from the plastic container it had come in, telling herself that this was simplicity interpreted by the twenty-first century. In another mood she might have found the film funny and touching: Tonight it seemed irritating and trite. She paused it four times to answer the telephone, without really minding the interruption.

At eleven o'clock that night, the film finished, and she took the tray through the dark passage into the kitchen, where she caught sight of her bicycle handlebars resting against the windowsill. She had forgotten to put it away in the shed.

She deposited her fork and mug in the sink. She looked at the encrusted remains of overmicrowaved lasagna on the walls of the empty plastic container, and guiltily threw it in the bin, trying not to think about Jabez's disapproval of excess packaging. Then she opened the kitchen door and went out into the back garden to put her bike away. The streets were quiet at this time of night, apart from the sound of a vehicle with a diesel engine climbing the hill toward the parsonage and then ceasing somewhere nearby. She took hold of the cold bike, and, as she wheeled it to the shed, stopped to look up at the night sky. Here in Southarbour the darkness was never profound enough for many stars to be seen. But tonight a sickle moon shone clear and bright in a sky mostly clear of cloud now, and the tingle of frost nipped the end of her nose.

In the shed she startled herself by treading on an empty

plastic flowerpot, which broke with a loud crack. It was difficult to stow the bike in the dark, especially as the shed was not large and already accommodated the lawnmower. Extricating herself, she shot home the bolt to fasten the door and snapped the padlock shut. As she did so, she half thought she heard someone speak her name; with a sudden fright as she turned, she realized she was not alone in the garden.

Her clutch of terror turned to simple astonishment as she recognized the figure standing on the frosty grass between the gate at the bottom of the garden and the shed where she stood herself.

"Jabez?"

Esme's breath as she spoke lingered in a cloud on the frigid air. She stared at him in amazement—for Jabez indeed it was.

She had not been mistaken in thinking she heard his voice quietly speak her name, half wanting her to hear, half afraid to reveal his presence.

The moonlight discerned him, but though he carried something, held something in his hand, she did not take in what he had there. Now seen, he stood there quite still, and across that distance of yards, and even in the dimness of night, there formed between Esme's eyes and his an electric corridor, such that she felt she might say for certain—and maybe for the first time ever—that looking into the eyes of Jabez Ferrall, her eyes had beheld an immortal soul.

He did not move. Just looked at her, with eyes as full of life, as vital, as a fox or deer or any wild thing that, first surprised, will hold your gaze in message and appraisal; total encounter, a momentary precursor to inevitable flight.

It occurred to Esme that he had expected to find her out in the garden as little as she had expected to find him. Her immediate surmise, that something was wrong, gave way to a sense that having not expected to be discovered, he was urgently contemplating retreat.

So it came about that Esme abandoned her first intention of speech—"Are you all right?"—the question framed in practical, conventional format in the bright, sociable mind that filled all the front stage of her habitual thinking. Instead, from somewhere else, perhaps from the twilight mind of her solar plexus reaching out to worlds beyond, came unbidden the words she actually said. "Don't run away. Please. Don't run away."

And she said it to the wildness and shyness in him, to his privacy and to the depths of half-healed pain in him that, for some reason she couldn't understand, suddenly stood before her. His face changed then. The uncertainty of the wild thing poised on the brink of involuntary flight crystallized into something more frightened, as will came in to control instinct and he knew he would stay. He came across the garden to her.

She understood when he spoke. The fear that had stolen across him like a shadow more somber than the darkness bewildered her until she heard him say, "I've brought you some flowers."

Flowers. In November. In the middle of the night.

And then she felt as scared as he did, because obviously he was offering her his heart. And where did that leave them?

Esme thought fast. She could see no way not to hurt him. To accept the implicit gift of his love would be a gross unfairness in view of her intention of moving away. To refuse it would wound and humiliate him. He saw her hesitation, and something changed. He did his own quick thinking.

"I been uneasy all day—about what was said this morning." His eyes met hers, and she saw the flicker of prevarication in them. "I hadn't thought to find you out and about at this hour. I thought you'd be in bed. It had been my intention to leave these here for you. For the morning. To apologize. Ember and me, we may overstep the mark sometimes. We're simple country folk. You mustn't expect we'll always get it right."

Esme had to admire the skill with which he turned his self-offering into the building of an unbridgeable chasm between them. It hurt, though.

"Ember and you?" she said, picking up the very deliberate discontinuity he had placed between them and her. "Simple country folk. Are you?" Her eyes met his gaze, level and direct.

"Yes," he replied quietly.

Oh, God, her soul sent its silent distress flare, *now don't let us turn this into a fight.* Troubled, anxious not to damage the friendship between them that had become such a source of strength to her, instinctively, without conscious formulation, the core of her spirit reached out for help and strength.

He looked down at the flowers in his hand, and held them out to her. In the garden at the front of his cottage, one yellow rose that climbed against the house bloomed gamely on into December. Mingled with ivy from the hedge, rosemary, and a feathery spray of blue juniper (filched from the garden of the Old Police House; she recognized it), the last of these roses were what he had brought her.

"Jabez, come inside," she said, as she put out her hand to take his flowers.

He rewarded her with a tense, shy smile.

"I think I'd best not stay."

She felt the splinting of his pride in the stillness of the way he spoke.

"Jabez—" but he shook his head.

"I'll see you soon," he said, gently. "Leave it now."

He left the roses in her hand, and in an understated gesture of finality, he turned and made his way across the moonlit garden, out through the gate, as quietly as he had come.

I'll see you soon. She examined this small token of hope. It was something, but she felt bereft.

It felt impossible, too difficult. Jabez's life had been built on a different foundation entirely from hers. His sense of self and his sense of belonging grew out of rootedness in the earth and the family, out of how he had loved, and out of the making of his hands. What Esme aspired to had been based on professional achievement and on membership of a body of people scattered across the world—some whom she had never met, some all too familiar. But they were bonded together by the traditions and doctrines they believed in—or in some cases accepted without analysis, for the comfort of a sense of belonging. She felt a sudden sharp misgiving about the wisdom of tying home and income to so structured an ideology. *What happens when a person changes?* she asked herself in sudden panic. To walk with God is an unfolding rhythm of life, a wild music of many moods and tempos, embracing the shadows of doubt and disillusionment and the black dark of despair as well as the sweet blue heavens of joy and affirmation, the glorious sunset colors of the soul moved by beauty, amazed by peace. To serve the church as an ordained minister is an altogether narrower, more prosaic thing.

As she stood there alone, holding her flowers and still looking along the empty garden at the gate Jabez had closed behind him, Esme became aware of herself shivering. She went indoors, finding a vase for her flowers, locking up for the night, making a hot-water bottle for her bed, the core of her congealed into a hard lump of wretchedness.

"I'm sorry, Jabez," she whispered in the darkness as she curled round her hot-water bottle in her cold bed. "I'll come out and see you in the morning."

And after awhile, she slept, but she woke early.

Is it too soon to go and see them again? Am I sending the wrong signals and making things worse by going to see them so often? As Esme bathed and dressed and cleaned her teeth, she felt completely at sea, alone in the complications of a situation that was pulling her relentlessly in conflicting directions. Then, seeing that the day promised fair again, and recalling that the next few days were filled with commitments already, bringing it to Sunday night before another opportunity presented itself, Esme decided to cycle out to Wiles Green again whether it was wise or not. The separation Jabez had made between them the night before had been sensible and redeemed an awkward situation, but the ache it left felt unbearable. She couldn't contemplate waiting a week to put it right.

She went, a little later than the morning before.

As she pushed her bike around into his yard, she could hear their voices in the kitchen. Through the window at the back of the house she saw Jabez standing, washing up at the sink. He glanced up and caught her eye as she passed. She heard him speak quietly and then the conversation ceased.

"Morning!" she called cheerfully as she propped her bike against the wall and came in through the door, which, despite the cold, stood open for the sunshine. Esme stepped over Jabez's boots, abandoned in the doorway.

Above the kitchen table, in the corner that held the warmth of the stove, the drying rack had been let down on its pulley system, and Ember was folding dry washing from it onto the kitchen table. "Talk of the Devil," she said amiably as Esme came in. She drew breath for further speech, but Jabez suddenly stopped what he was doing, gripped the edge of the sink, and, imploring, almost wailed, "Please! Ember—*please!*"

What on earth was she about to say? Esme wondered, but for once Ember forbore, continuing serenely with her task. Jabez left the sink, wiping his hands on the drying-up cloth, and said more calmly, with only a trace of desperation, and without looking at her, "I'll make a cup of tea, shall I?"

"That would be very nice," said Ember, with an elaborate civility designed to betray other matters below the surface.

"What?" asked Esme. "What is it?" She wondered if Jabez had told Ember of their meeting the night before.

"Have you fetched the milk in, Ember?" asked Jabez, ignoring Esme's question.

"Still on the front step, I imagine," Ember replied, turning her gaze on him in bland innocence. "You better go and fetch it."

"Ember, please," he entreated again, and hesitated a moment before going through the house to open the front door.

Ember moved like lightning, quicker than any woman of eighty-six should be able to move, to push the kitchen door closed with her foot.

Lower than Esme had imagined it was possible for a

person to speak and still make herself audible, Ember said as she passed Esme in returning to the table, "He been telling me how much he loves you. I never would have guessed he had that much passion about him. You better watch out."

And she was back folding clothes in silence when Jabez pushed through the door with a pint of milk in his hand, looking from one to the other of them in helpless suspicion.

These words dispelled all Esme's anxiety; she had not turned him away irretrievably then. She felt a wave of joy that it was as she had hoped, and not admitted that she hoped. An irrepressible desire to giggle began to bubble up inside her.

"You seem a bit low on firewood," she said, her words slightly unsteady as she tried to still the quaver of laughter that wanted to escape. "Shall I get some more in from outside?"

"That'd be kind," said Jabez doggedly, setting the milk down on the table. Where he stood obscured the way past the stove, and Esme had to come by him for the wood basket.

"Excuse me, then," she said sweetly, gently putting her hands on his waist as she brushed by. It was the first time she had ever touched him, except the moment long ago that her fingers had touched his on the bicycle handlebars and the brief inevitable meeting of their hands as he gave her the flowers last night. He turned and looked at her, searching, as she came back past him with the basket. She said nothing, but Ember's words had started something effervescing in her soul like sparkles of sunlight, and she couldn't help the grin that tugged at the corners of her mouth.

As she was two steps into the yard, she heard him say in quiet but vehement reproach, appalled, "Ember, how *could* you?"

When Esme returned to the kitchen, Jabez would not look at her. He made her a mug of tea, and set it before her without speaking as she sat down at his table. Ember had taken the pile of clean linen to put away, and Esme searched for a way into his self-conscious silence.

"Thank you for the flowers," she said gently, after awhile. "You shouldn't have picked the last of your roses for me."

He shrugged, embarrassed. "You're welcome. I—well, you're welcome." She sat, watching him. "Jabez, for goodness sake, look at me!" So he did, but only for a moment. "Leave it," he said, shaking his head. "Leave it, let it sort itself out. Let's just see how we go."

She sighed. "Okay. But—are we all right? Are you all right? I mean—is it all right between us?"

He stretched across the table and with his fingertips lightly stroked her hand.

"It's all right," he said, "but leave it for now. Esme, I got work to do. I'm expected in Brockhyrst Priory at half-past nine."

She drank her tea, and as she left the cottage, he came outside with her to collect the necessary tools for his morning's work from the shed.

He smiled at her, so hopelessly shy he made her feel shy too.

This is crazy, she told herself. *We're like teenagers! And whenever am I going to tell him about my job?*

❋

The days that followed plunged Esme into an unremitting round of pre-Christmas social gatherings and liturgies. She drove out to Wiles Green and called at the cottage after the Portland Street carol service on the second Sunday of Advent, but apart from that there seemed no time; even the Sunday evenings after worship had turned into special occasions celebrated with obligatory mince pies. Esme hated mince pies, but it would have been impolitic to confess it.

The busyness of the season drove from her mind all concerns about the impending move, apart from the occasional pang of wistfulness as she reflected that if things developed smoothly, this would be her last Christmas with her congregations here.

Neither could she give much time to worrying about her friendship with Jabez. With characteristic self-possession he had contained his mortification at having his confidences of love betrayed, and when she called after church in mid-Advent, he made her welcome, cooking her supper and hearing with quiet amusement her exasperation at all the excesses smothering the simple beauty of Christmas. Esme asked him if, in time to decorate Portland Street chapel for the junior school end-of-term carol service on Tuesday, she might have some of the ivy and the bright-berried holly that grew in his hedge at the top of the orchard. Jabez readily agreed, offering to cut her some and bring it over on Monday afternoon.

"If I don't find you home, I'll leave it somewhere in the yard," he said. "Unless—" he hesitated. "Would you rather I take it straight to the chapel?"

Esme's heart went out to him. She sensed that Jabez would rather do almost anything than involve himself with a party of church members arranging flowers. "My place will do fine," she said. "It's really kind of you to bring it over for me."

Ember had chuckled at the relief on his face.

About ten days before Christmas, Esme became conscious of how tired she felt. She looked at her packed diary, which had long overrun any hope of a day off before Boxing Day, turning the pages desperately in search of something she could cancel without causing offense. She found nothing.

Christmas day fell on a Saturday that year, and the preceding weekend held a Christmas Fayre at Portland Street on the Saturday morning (Esme had been written down to open it with a prayer and then help run the white elephant stall); a church concert at Brockhyrst Priory on the Saturday evening (Esme had been asked to say a blessing at the end); and on the Sunday the junior church nativity presentation at Portland Street in the morning, followed by two carol services one after another in the evening at Wiles Green and Brockhyrst Priory.

As she stood in the doorway of Brockhyrst Priory

Methodist Chapel in the bitter cold, shaking the hands of visitors leaving the Saturday-evening concert, Esme's head ached and her throat felt sore.

"Nice for you to have an evening off!" beamed the husband of one of the choir members, and Esme looked at him in amazed disbelief, unable for a moment to frame a reply.

"Yes," she said lamely then, seeing some response was required. She had no need to summon a smile. Her Christmas smile had become a permanent fixture. Her face ached when she let the smiling mask drop as she got into her car to go home.

On the Monday morning, when the ladies from Portland Street came for the annual "Parsonage Pies" event, erecting folding tables laden with bric-a-brac for sale in her front room, Esme was beginning to feel shivery and distant. Grateful that welcoming them into her kitchen with all the chapel crockery, coffee, and boxes of biscuits seemed to be all that was required of her, she subsided onto one of the chairs that she had ranged round the walls of her dining room, the table being pushed against the wall below the hatch to serve coffee.

Normally she felt encouraged and cheered by the jollity and good fellowship of these gatherings. The evident goodwill and friendliness of her church members was heartening to see, but through that morning, as people came and went in faithful support of the event, her head swam and her eyeballs hurt her. She felt faint and dizzy and slightly nauseous, but most of all, despite the air desiccated by the central heating, she felt so cold.

The ladies washed up, counted the takings from the bric-a-brac stall, asked Esme if she would mind if they left all the unsold bits and pieces with her at the parsonage, and made their cheerful departure at about one o'clock.

I must go to bed, Esme thought as she said thank you and smiled and waved in farewell to the last one. *I've got to go to bed. I can't be ill now, there's the junior school end-of-term concert tomorrow and all the Christmas services coming up. I can't be ill. I expect I'll be better if I just have a lie-down.*

Shivering uncontrollably, her teeth chattering, she began to climb the stairs. She wanted her hot-water bottle, but it seemed such a long way to go to fetch it. She thought she ought to lock the back door, which meant returning to the kitchen anyway, so she persevered in her journey to collect the hot-water bottle. She felt as though she would never reach her bedroom, and when she reached the top of the stairs, she crawled along the landing on her hands and knees. When she got to her bed, she collapsed onto it and lay there for a while, summoning the strength to make her way back down. Eventually, with an effort, she sat up on the bed, pulled off her clothes, and dropped them on the floor. Even the touch of her nightdress seemed to hurt her skin as she put it on, but she felt pathetically grateful for the snuggly softness of her dressing gown over it, a warm pink chosen to be comforting. She sat for a while, and then made herself begin the trip back to the kitchen; but halfway down the flight of stairs she crumpled and sank down, shaking, hunched into a heap of feverish misery. *Oh, God, I feel so ill,* she muttered. *Oh, help!*

She sat there for a few minutes, shivering violently. She felt as though she were spinning in the cold loneliness of black space, weak and drained and empty. *Oh, God, I need somebody. I feel so ill.* She gave up all hope of moving, and just sat in a state of collapse.

She vaguely heard a knock at the back door without taking in what it was. The knock was repeated, and the door opened. She heard Jabez's voice calling, "Esme?" and it felt like the most welcome sound in the world.

"Hello!" she called back, embarrassed at the feeble croak of her voice. *For heaven's sake!* she thought. *Half an hour ago I was on my feet saying good-bye to people, I can't be that bad.* She lifted her head and leaned it against the banisters, listening to the sound of him kicking his boots off just inside the kitchen door before he came through from the kitchen into the hall toward the sound of her voice.

He looked up and saw her. "Esme!"—and the next moment she was enfolded in his arms.

"I don't feel very well," she murmured, turning toward him, shivering, clinging to him pathetically for warmth and restoration.

"Come on, sweetheart, you shouldn't be here. Let me put you to bed."

Esme clutched at his sweater, longing for the friendly, woolly feeling of it, and nuzzled her face against him, smelling him; tobacco and machine oil and the warm, human smell of him.

He held her for a moment, and she felt him kiss her hair, felt herself enfolded in absolute tenderness.

"You're not well, my love, look at the state of you," he said. "Let me put you to bed. What are you doing sitting here?"

"I was going to fill my hot-water bottle," Esme said, reaching to pull it out from where it had wedged between her and the banisters. He took it from her and laid it down on the stairs.

"I'll do that," he said, "and get you a hot drink if you'd like one. Come on now."

He came upstairs with her, and she showed him which was her bedroom. He straightened the bedclothes and turned back the quilt, and Esme curled up on the bed, her dressing gown wrapped tightly around her, shivering convulsively, her teeth chattering.

He tucked the quilt round her, and she stayed there curled in a tight ball while he went down to the kitchen and boiled the kettle. He was back quickly with the hot-water bottle and a steaming cup of medicated lemon drink for colds and flu that he had found at the back of the cupboard where Esme kept her tea and coffee.

She took the hot-water bottle into the bed gratefully, and

gradually its warmth enabled her to relax. After a few minutes she sat up, and propped against the pillows she drank the hot mixture he had made her. She began to feel warmer and a little less desperate.

"Is there anything more I can do for you, my love?" Jabez asked her as he took the empty cup from her hands and put it on her dressing table ready to take downstairs.

"Yes," said Esme. Even as she spoke, a rational part of her mind was telling her, *Don't do this, Esme; don't drag him into this any deeper—be fair,* but she said, "I want you to lie on the bed with me and hold me. Oh, Jabez, I feel so ill."

For a moment he hesitated, looking down at her. Her eyes ached unbearably, and now she was beginning to feel hot. She lifted back the covers and immediately a wave of shivery cold returned. She closed her eyes. "I feel so ill," she said again. "Please, Jabez."

Diffidently, because she asked it, he lay down on the bed beside her, and took her into his arms. "Just for a little while," he said. "I think you need to go to sleep, my love." Esme snuggled against him, hungry for the comfort of his kindness and warmth. As he held her, breathing quietly, saying nothing, the softness of his beard against her forehead; as the tension smoothed out of her, she began to feel his heartbeat, and an unfamiliar sense of trust and peace welled up and suffused her whole being. She felt like a child again. She felt as though she'd come home.

"Esme," she heard him say gently as drowsiness

enveloped her, "will it be all right if I let someone like Mr. Griffiths know you aren't well? I guess this is a busy week, and it might be as well to sort out someone to step in for you."

"Oh … yes, please … whatever … thank you, Jabez.…" And she fell asleep in his arms.

For the next twenty-four hours Esme drifted in and out of feverish sleep. For two days after that she felt too weak to get out of bed. Each day Jabez called in twice to make sure she was all right, and he brought her simple, nourishing things to eat and left her with a hot drink in a Thermos flask by her bed. A message came from Marcus to say he had contacted the people in her diary, as passed on to him by Jabez, and she need have no concerns, just get well. He added that five other people from Brockhyrst Priory had flu, including the organist; but not to worry, he would deputize on the organ for the Christmas services if necessary.

On Christmas Eve, when Esme was on her feet and feeling like herself again, shaky but normal, she discovered with delight that in three days of illness she had lost five pounds, which made it all worthwhile. Jabez called in to see her in the morning and expressed doubt about her being sufficiently recovered for the Christmas services, but she reassured him she would be fine and thanked him, promising to call in to the cottage before she went away to visit her family.

She felt well enough to take the children's crib service at Portland Street, and their midnight communion, and despite feeling strangely insubstantial by Christmas morning, she managed the early service at Brockhyrst Priory, where Marcus played for her.

"Well done!" she said to him afterward. "I had no idea you could play!"

"Oh, well …" He shrugged his shoulders in deprecation. "I can fill in, my dear, but I'm not a patch on good old Clifford. When he plays, the spirit soars, but with me it's more a case of Toccata and Fudge in D minor, and that's if you're lucky on a good day. Glad to help out—but are you sure you're better? Should you be here?"

Esme smiled at him. "I feel a bit floaty, but I'm fine really. Thanks for all your help."

Marcus looked at her thoughtfully. "Just as well Jabez Ferrall was about; he explained he'd been calling in with the church greenery and found you unwell. Kind of him to help out with decorating the church for Christmas. Jabez is a good man."

"Ah! *There* you are, my dear!" Hilda's arm was suddenly around Esme's shoulders in a loving squeeze. "I was looking for you at the door and someone said, '*There* she is, look, Hilda, over by the organ!'—and here you are indeed. A teeny little Christmas gift, dear—just a small packet of fossilized ginger, very warming, good for the circulation. Merry Christmas!"

"Crystallized," murmured Marcus, as he turned to assemble his sheets of music and lock up the organ console.

"Merry Christmas," he added, looking at Esme over the top of his glasses. "And make sure you get some rest."

Esme went straight from Brockhyrst Priory to the morning service at Wiles Green, where one by one as they left the chapel, her congregation expressed their love and concern— "Are you all right?" "Take it easy, now!" "Have a nice rest with your family after tomorrow."

She thought of the Christmas cards mingled with "Get well" cards crammed on every ledge and surface at the parsonage, the greetings and affection of her church members.

As she walked away from the chapel toward her car, Esme felt warmed and encouraged by their friendship and support, and privileged that she should be its focus.

"Esme."

When she reached her car, Esme looked around to see who had spoken her name. In the shadow of the yew tree, well out of the sight of worshippers leaving the chapel, stood Jabez.

"Would you like to come to us for lunch, or have you got other plans?" he asked.

Esme smiled, grateful.

"Happy Christmas," she said. "I'd love to be with you."

EIGHT

In the days between Christmas and New Year's, Esme spent time with her parents and with her brother and his family who lived near them.

Over dinner one evening she told them about the changes agreed for the Southarbour circuit, and the suggested possibility of a move to Surrey. They listened with interest and saw it overall as a positive move—"Provided no one's doing you down or trying to push you out of where you are at present," her brother said.

"Is the rectory in the Surrey parish nice?" asked her mother, and Esme explained that everything had still to be discussed, letters written, meetings arranged. Looking at the Surrey parsonage belonged to a later stage of negotiation.

She wondered whether to talk to them about Jabez but decided there was nothing really to tell. He had never referred again to the moment of intimacy they had shared when she was ill, and on Christmas Day she saw in his manner no hint of an invitation offered to move their relationship onto a deeper level. He was his usual self; quiet, friendly, and kind. Nothing more. Yet she felt so much had passed between them that to refrain from mentioning him to her family seemed wrong.

"I have made some very dear friends in Southarbour," she said to her family, as her mother brought in the glass and silver-plate French press steaming from the kitchen at the end of their meal. Unsure how much to say, or how to describe Jabez and Ember, Esme hesitated. It seemed odd that, though they had become so important to her, in all the discussions with her colleagues and now with her family, there never seemed an appropriate point to mention them, to bring them into the equation. She supposed it was that there was no more to be said than that she loved them; and love had little place in decision-making about house moves and career opportunities.

"It's my one misgiving about going," she went on; "I don't want to leave them."

"That's the way of the world, young Esme," her father said sagely, as her mother handed him the jug of cream to pour into his coffee. "Life was ever thus. You're a professional woman with a living to earn; you must put your career first. Friends are all very well, but I'm afraid what you must do is just move on and forget them. It's sad, but that's how it has to be. The job has to come first. Just forget them. Welcome to the real world."

Her mother nodded thoughtfully in agreement, and her brother added, "Besides, Es, if you play your cards right and stay good friends with them, you'll have seaside holidays for life, which can't be bad."

It sounded so sensible. *Perhaps that's what's wrong with me,* thought Esme; *maybe I just haven't got my feet on the ground. After all, I have got my living to earn. No one's offering me an alternative. And there's nothing to be gained by feeling miserable about what's inevitable.*

She did not pursue the matter, and her family had no questions to ask about Jabez and Ember, seeing nothing of influence or significance in the relationship.

By the beginning of February, the negotiations for Esme's move had begun in earnest. The chairman had spoken to the circuit stewards in Surrey, and representatives from that circuit had discreetly attended one of her services to hear her preach. She had broken the news to the stewards of each of her three chapels and found it oddly gratifying to see them so stunned and upset at losing her (with the single exception of Miss Trigg, who made little comment, but whose face shone with holy triumph).

By March, the Southarbour circuit church councils had begun their arguments about how the circuit chapels should be redistributed between the remaining staff; and Esme had received a letter inviting her to Surrey to meet the stewards and some of the officeholders of the churches she would serve.

Only at this stage did Esme finally make herself talk to

Jabez about the changes that were by now far more than a proposal.

She sat on an upturned wooden crate by the fire in his workshop on a cold day in early March, absentmindedly stroking the ears of the purring cat rolling in the warm ashes.

"There are to be changes in the circuit, Jabez."

Jabez said nothing. She looked up at him, standing at his workbench in the light from the window, methodically cleaning the parts of a bicycle headset in a biodegradable solvent. Sometimes when Barton's Bikes at Southarbour had more bicycles than they could handle, they subcontracted work out to him. This was one of their customer's bikes.

"It means a move for me earlier than normal. I'm being asked to look at two churches in Surrey."

He paused for a moment, suddenly still, and then glanced across at her. "Oh, yes?" he said. "Excuse me a moment, I must wash my hands before I grease these ball bearings, I think I'm dirtier than they are."

While he was gone, Esme reflected that he seemed to have minimal reaction to her news. She thought of the distress among her Brockhyrst Priory stewards when she broke it to them, and the disappointment of her Wiles Green stewards. By comparison, Jabez appeared little disturbed. *What does he feel for me?* she wondered. *Anything?*

When he returned, he opened the grease pot and began to position the ball bearings in the cup, carefully coating them with the right amount of grease.

"Is it what you want?" he said at last, without looking at her.

Esme explained how the decision had come about, emphasizing that she had in reality not much choice.

"Here, they need me to move, so I need a church; there they need a minister. I ought at least to go and look."

With precise attention, Jabez put back the forks and all the parts he had dismantled and looked around for his headset spanners. "I had them a minute ago," he remarked, exasperated; adding, "and you don't mind leaving?"

"All ministers have to leave," said Esme. "Well, not ministers in local appointment, they just stay local, but they get paid only if they're lucky. Those of us in the full-time work have to move on. That's why it's called itinerant ministry. That's the setup."

"Yes," said Jabez, tightening the top cup gently with his fingers, until he had it tight enough for there to be no play in the headset, "I do know."

He seemed distant, unconcerned. *I was worrying about nothing,* Esme said to herself; *I could have told him ages ago.*

"So they've invited me to go and see—not till April, because one of the circuit stewards is away on a cruise and their superintendent is recovering from open-heart surgery."

Jabez nodded, holding the cup in place with one of the headset spanners (found hidden beneath his cleaning rag) while he locked it in place with the other.

"What if you don't like it?"

"I'm not sure really. Back to the drawing board I suppose. Anyway, it's worth a try."

Again he nodded, and he asked no more questions.

Esme had expected something more from the conversation. She wished he might at least have said something to reassure her of their continuing friendship after her move. In some deep place she refused to look at, it hurt that he said nothing to try to persuade her to stay. His remoteness felt like a rebuff, a denial of the warmth and closeness between them. It confirmed the decision for her; her father was right, she had nothing to stay for—in the real world people move on. She remembered as a child hearing him remark heavily on more than one occasion, "You can't eat hope. Love doesn't pay the bills." She thought he was probably right, but somehow it made her feel so sad.

The time that followed felt strange, a limbo. The weeks of Lent pursued their usual pattern, culminating in the intensity of Holy Week and Easter, late this year again.

When, on the second week of Eastertide, the date for her interview in Surrey finally came around, Esme felt intrigued and excited, her misgivings now mingled with curiosity.

Lent had been busy, and though she had continued to call in to the cottage, she had found Jabez quiet and withdrawn, expressing little interest in the information she had gleaned so far about the Surrey congregation. Disappointed, rather hurt by his disinclination to discuss all that the changes meant, Esme wondered if she had imagined or at least misjudged the quality of their relationship. She wondered if it was simply that the daily round of his own world occupied his thoughts, and he was too insular to look past that into the concerns of her life. Chilled by his response, she felt discouraged from mentioning her plans to Ember—and nothing in Ember's conversation led Esme to believe that Jabez had talked to her either.

Alone in her study after evening worship on the Sunday before she was due to make her visit to Surrey, Esme felt suddenly swamped by loneliness. The people she had met in her congregations were to be left behind, forgotten, no looking back. Ministers who hung on to old friends were a nuisance to pastors who succeeded them. Her family lived by principles that sounded sensible and practical but left her feeling cold and empty. Her colleagues simply felt relieved and grateful that it was Esme going and not one of them. Jabez appeared to have closed his heart to her. She quite desperately hungered for someone to want her, to say nice things to her, to offer her a place to belong. Surrey began to look like a beacon of hope.

On the day of the interview, she dressed with care, took the new map books she had bought from the supermarket service station, and set out with a sense of adventure.

She returned from that day more than anything else flattered to have been considered: The experience had brought the sense of a career taking off. Glancing into the windows of the estate agents as she had stopped to investigate the high street, she had been astonished by the house prices for that area. Surrey seemed to be one vast green suburb populated with sleek cars drawn up in ones and twos on the brick-laid driveways of massive houses. Esme had never seen so much evidence of money in her life. The leather suites on which she was invited to sit, the up-to-the-minute fitted kitchens she glimpsed through doorways, the quality of the music centers she saw in the living rooms whose size was accentuated by the flawless yardage of immaculately steam-cleaned carpets; the groomed gardens with their azalea beds and judiciously selected conifers and huge pots spilling with begonias, and the large, confident voice of the steward who led her interview—a retired barrister—had impressed upon her the significance of this appointment. It meant she was on the way up. If she took this chance she might no longer be poor Esme out in the sticks while she recovered from her husband leaving her. Her colleagues and her family would stop feeling sorry for her at last. When she stepped through the arched porch and over the threshold of that solid 1930s parsonage set back in its huge leafy garden, she would have made it.

The stewards asked Esme what her response would be if they invited her to come. She found herself caught in a final indecision, as though she were waiting for a reason to change her mind.

"This seems like a wonderful appointment," she said honestly. "I like the chapels and all the people I've met. There are no problems at all. Just because I'm a cautious person, can

I say I should need to think it over carefully before I say 'yes'?"

This prudent response was favorably received, and Esme drove home feeling exultant that such an opportunity had been held out to her, and that they so clearly liked her. She turned impatiently from the tug of sadness for Jabez and Ember, for the cottage with its apple trees and quietness, its wood smoke and lavender and hens. *After all*, she told herself, *with a garden that size I could plant my own apple tree: I could grow lavender and keep hens myself. What would be the difference?* There was an answer to that, and she refused to acknowledge it.

In the days that followed, a letter came with gratifying speed from the senior circuit steward of the Surrey chapel, offering her the appointment if she felt inclined to take it up.

Excited, with the letter still in her hand, Esme left the envelope lying on her study desk, and hastily locking the back door she got in her car, threw the letter onto the passenger seat, and drove out to Wiles Green. She had to share her news with somebody whether Jabez was interested or not.

As she made her way through the lanes darkened by the unfurling leaf canopy and narrowed by the wild herbs and grasses sprouting in the verges, enjoying the spreading green of spring, Esme admitted to herself how much she had grown to love this hidden, beautiful place, and how much she would miss it. She smiled at the recollection of a chance remark overheard the previous Sunday.

Greeting her congregation as they made their way out of the chapel, she had heard the door steward say amiably to Hilda Griffiths, "Hasn't it been lovely and warm! Such a change from all the damp, chilly days we've had. It's brought the flowers on so, the garden looks beautiful."

"My dear!" Hilda had nodded with enthusiasm. "Marcus and I have been out in the woods and fields with the Ramblers, and it's delightful, quite delightful. And I don't care what they say, I know people frown on it and complain about it, but I think rape is *lovely*. I'd hardly know the spring had come without it."

Esme laughed aloud as she remembered the momentary shocked bewilderment on her door steward's face; but as she looked along the lane and saw through the cool green tunnel of trees the blazing glory of yellow rape in dazzling blossom, she had to concede that Hilda was right. *Poor old Marcus*—she grinned—*he'll be getting an undeserved reputation!*

She brought her car to rest on the roadside by the Old Police House, and snatched the letter up from the passenger seat, too impatient to negotiate in the car the potholed track leading to the yard.

Her intention focused on Jabez's whereabouts, Esme walked with the swiftness of purpose up the rutted lane and around the cottage, but the loveliness of the orchard in spring blossom flooded her consciousness with its glory, and she smiled at it as if to a person, in spontaneous happiness at its beauty, which shone into her soul so vividly although her footsteps hardly paused.

She found Jabez sitting on the ground outside in the yard, in the sunshine, evidently taking a break from giving Marcus's lawnmower its spring service, the dismantled parts spread about him. He sat with his back against the cottage wall, smoking a roll-up, a mug of tea steaming on the flags beside him. She paused for a moment, the ineffable aura of peace that hung about him affecting her almost physically. And from that came a rush of love from the middle of her, a gratitude to have known this man and this place; to have learned so much, and have been loved so much, to have been allowed into his refuge-place and known his wisdom, and his gentleness.

That he had heard her step and was aware of her she knew with no doubt. She never really understood why he kept this stillness, allowed her to approach without acknowledgement, not speaking or looking at her until their togetherness in the space was a self-established fact. Yet this was so much a part of him, and she found it had the effect of holding a momentary mirror to her soul, show-ing her the quality of self that she brought to today's encounter, before the dubious currency of conversation opened its own negotiations.

"Jabez, I've had a letter from the church in Surrey!" Esme felt too excited at the importance of her news to let the time of coming into the presence of another soul unfold. She expected him to turn his head then, and look up at her with the familiar warmth of welcome: It surprised her when, instead, his habitual quietness fell into an almost total stillness, as though every rhythm of his being had temporarily stopped dead.

"Jabez?" she said, unsure.

And then he did turn his head to look at her. He smiled, her excitement requiring a response, but he asked her nothing.

"Sit down a minute while I get you a cup of tea," he said, getting to his feet. "Then you can tell me all about it."

The kitchen door stood open, and he took only a moment to return with her tea, but in that time she felt the inside of her fidgeting with eagerness to tell him.

She took her mug—"Thanks"—and perched on the edge of the wooden chair that stood in the yard among the bits of Marcus's lawnmower. Jabez slid his back down the wall to resume his earlier position. Part of the peace in Jabez's company was that having brick dust all down his jacket was no more a consideration than the oil-black that usually smudged his hands and had extended its grubby influence to every garment he wore. The exacting social requirements of etiquette and cleanliness were waived.

"They've invited me!" she said, pride and delight spilling into her voice. It felt like such an achievement, in spite of which Esme had a sense that it would be utterly impossible to communicate the consequence of any of this to Jabez.

So, "It's a big opportunity," was all she said, rather

lamely, watching him inspect the end of his cigarette, which had gone out, and then take a drink of his tea.

Advancement and career openings meant less than nothing to Jabez, that Esme understood, but she could not repress a sense of disappointment that he said not a word, only patted his pockets to locate his matches, relit the flimsy cigarette, drew on it, and contemplated the drift of smoke he breathed out into the spring sunshine. At last, his voice level, steady, he asked her, "Then how long have we got?"

Esme could never analyze, though on occasion she had given it a lot of thought, how Jabez could both create an aura of stillness even when he was working, or walking down the street, and equally impart a sense of movement when, as now, he sat entirely still yet in some way she could not define, seemed to be vanishing, withdrawing into himself, before her eyes.

"Stationing normally takes about eighteen months," she said. "But because of the particular situation both here and in Surrey, they're going to curtail my appointment here. It might be as early as this autumn. More likely in the beginning of the winter. We just want to give ourselves time to do everything properly." She waited for him to speak again, eventually saying into the silence, "Aren't you pleased for me?"

He took a drink of his tea.

"I shall miss you," he said finally. "If it's what you want, of course, I'm pleased for you." He glanced up at her, squinting into the sunlight. "I'm sorry, I'm not meaning to be a wet blanket. I can't quite imagine life without you now."

Esme smiled. "You can always come and visit me at the parsonage in Surrey! It's huge. You could stay overnight."

Jabez stubbed his cigarette out thoughtfully on the stone flags of the yard. "Can I?" he said. "Thank you."

He picked up his mug, drank most of the tea, and tossed the dregs down the nearby drain. "Better get on," he remarked. "Well done, Esme; that's great news."

Esme watched him work until she finished her cup of tea. Deflated by the flatness and anticlimax of his reaction, she decided against trying to show him the letter. He was evidently determined not to discuss it. It was hard to think of anyone who would be pleased to read it among her church members either. So after a little while of further desultory conversation, she took the letter home and telephoned her mother, who was comfortingly congratulatory.

As she sat down at her desk with a cup of coffee that afternoon, and switched on her computer to draft her order of service for Sunday in time for the organist phoning through for the hymns, Esme felt exulted in her success. *I've made it!* she said to herself. Then, as she waited for the computer to be ready, unexpectedly her mood changed to reveal an inexplicable underlying weariness, as though the whole Surrey thing amounted to no more than a balloon brought home by a child from a party. She had a sudden sense of her professional life as a flimsy house built to impress; instead of a solid foundation, an empty reservoir of loneliness.

Don't be silly, you're just tired, she told herself firmly. She turned from the thought, reminding herself that staying was no longer an option, and she opened a new file and set up the page as she wanted it.

In the yard of his cottage at Wiles Green, carefully, meticulously, Jabez completed the servicing of the lawnmower. He loaded it in the back of his truck, returned it to Marcus's garage, and received his payment politely. He wanted to ask Marcus how much he knew about Esme's move but thought better of it in case she preferred anything kept private.

Through the afternoon he occupied himself, working doggedly, systematically, sorting and tidying things in his workshop, listing spare parts to be ordered. He took some old oil to be recycled and called for some bread at the bakers on the way home. His face was still and remote as he worked, like reflections on dark water. In some locked recess of his being, he felt the terrifying music of grief begin again, and he held his being as still as he could to quiet its broken, discordant cacophony. His hands shook. He had been this way before. He felt it approaching.

Ember, coming through to feed the hens toward evening, found him standing in the middle of the living room, his face in his hands, the convulsing muscles of his belly bending him almost double, his silver waterfall of hair shaking with the storm of sobbing that racked his body, the muffled groan of his voice in despair, "Oh, Jesus; oh, Jesus."

Ember went swiftly to him, and with firm hands guided him to the battered old sofa, sat him down, and seated herself beside him, very close, one hand on his back and one on his knee, feeling his body hard and tense with his anguish.

"What?" she asked him. "Who has done this to you?"

Long ago, Jabez, having wondered if when a heart breaks it snaps like a dry twig or more raggedly like a green branch, or rends reluctantly like the tearing of strong linen, discovered that in fact the human heart never breaks at all. Its tragedy is that it belongs to our flesh, and however lacerated and swollen and bruised, it goes on loving, it cannot let go, being offered neither the respite nor the welcome end of breaking.

"She's leaving me. Oh, it's so painful! So painful! So painful! She's going." He sobbed out the words incoherently. "Oh, God, it just hurts so much, so much, so much!"

He collapsed into a paroxysm of weeping, and Ember waited, quite still, while the tempest shook and racked and wrenched the frame of him.

Eventually the choking sobs that tore him abated, until he sat trembling, his breath shuddering and catching, his hands covering his face.

Then Ember lifted the corner of her apron and, removing his hands one after the other from his face, wiped away the tears without speaking. He did not look at her, but shook his head, hopelessly, deep tremors of grief running through his whole body.

"Oh dear," he said at last. "Oh, dear, dear me; what am I going to do? Whatever am I going to do? Oh, dear …" In utter misery he wrung his hands together, and then his face twisted as he collapsed again into helpless weeping.

"I can't!" he cried out through the tears. "I can't go through it again! I can't lose her! Oh, God, help me. Oh, God, what can I do?"

Ember held him, rocked him gently, talked soothing nonsense to him, stroked his hands. She sat by him until, empty and wrecked, he was still. Then, "Lie down, Jabez," she said, "while I make up the fire."

She put a cushion to pillow his head and made him lie down on the couch, stood in pity watching his body involuntarily contracting into a tight ball as the torture of grief started again, and his features distorted once more into a mask of agony. He turned his face away into the privacy of the cushion.

Ember frowned, in a small, densely concentrated space of thought. Then her habitual expression of clarity and determination returned. She left him, went to her room, and pulled the blanket from her bed, brought it downstairs and tucked it around him. She knelt at the hearth to light the fire, then got to her feet and stood by the sofa again to look at him, curled up in desolation, his eyes open but gazing without hope at nothing. Ember bent and stroked the silver hair, tenderly molding her hand to the contours of his head and neck.

"You just rest now, my lamb," she said. "Get you some sleep. It'll be all right. You'll not lose her. 'Tis entirely of God that lies between you and she. 'Tis not a passing fancy, 'tis eternal. Take comfort now and rest. It will be well, Jabez, I promise you."

She regarded him a moment longer, then treading quietly she left the room, found her coat and scarf, fed the hens and locked them in against the visits of the fox, shut up the garden shed and the workshop, fetched her hat and stick, and set off to walk to Southarbour.

It had turned midnight when Esme, finishing off the updating of her pastoral lists on her computer, was startled by a determined knocking at her door. She switched on the porch light and drew back the bolt.

"Good gracious, Ember, whatever is it?" she asked, astonished as she opened the door and beheld the small and furious bundle of rage wrapped in winter woollies on her doorstep. "Come in!"

"Thank you, I will," snapped Ember, continuing as she stepped into the hall. "What do they teach you in these Christian chapels? Anything? Nothing? Have you no shame? Have you no pity? Have you no wisdom? No understanding? No insight? Do they not teach you that *love brings responsibility?*"

She stood, bristling, glaring at Esme, her obsidian eyes bright with anger.

Esme experienced the familiar quailing in her abdomen, the urge to run, lie, get help. She wondered if there was any place in the world safe from old ladies.

"What are you talking about, Ember?" she asked when the gunfire of questions had stopped. "Come into the kitchen. Let me make you some coffee. How did you get here? It's awfully late. Come on."

She let Ember follow her into the kitchen, filled the electric kettle, and switched it on to boil.

"I walked."

Esme turned and looked at her in amazement. "Walked? Why, Ember, you're eighty-six! It's seven miles to Wiles Green from here! It must have taken you forever!"

Esme often felt that Ember's eyes might almost as well have had sound effects. Just now they looked as though they should be spitting and crackling like faulty electricals.

"Yes," said Ember, as Esme set a mug of coffee down in front of her. "But it'll be a lot quicker getting back, because you'll be taking me in that car of yours when you come over to sort out the mess you've made of Jabez."

Esme looked completely taken aback. "Jabez? I have?" She stared at Ember, and then, slowly, comprehension dawned on her face. "Because of the appointment in Surrey?" she asked, horrified.

"Surrey? Where's that? What's the place like? Is it far away?"

Sitting down opposite Ember at the table, Esme told her about the appointment, the opportunity, the letter. She explained all that it meant, able somehow to put into words to Ember what Jabez would never understand—the desire to make something of herself, to do well, to get past the humiliation of other people's pity.

"I hadn't really thought through what it might mean to Jabez," she confessed. "I honestly don't know where things are going with him and me. I feel as though I've known him forever, although it hasn't really been very long, and I can see he loves me dearly, but—well—he's not a very demonstrative man, is he? In any case, just suppose Jabez and I were together—and that still is presuming something beyond where we seem to be right now—could he not come with me? There must be bicycles and lawnmowers to fix in Surrey, mustn't there? Women move to go with their men. These days the men are learning to move with the women."

Ember considered this, frowning ferociously at the table.

"I believe," she said then, thoughtfully, "in the freedom of living beings. Not only human beings, mind you, but all beings. I believe we should live in ways that respect the freedom of all beings. And protect it from those that have no such respect. Protection brings limiting of course. Locking things in at night from the fox, maybe. It's a complicated thing. Be that as it may, among human beings, I believe in the freedom of women as well as the freedom of men. I was married but a year or two, and I never missed him when he was gone. I didn't want a man cluttering up my life. Mistaking me for his mother and clamoring for the needs of his belly and his bed. Confounded nuisances are men. Meeting Jabez Ferrall was quite a surprise to me. He don't flirt with anyone, he can think, he lives by his principles, he expects to do his own cooking, and he don't expect either of us to clean his house—had I a-been twenty years younger he might have caused me to revise my habits of mind. I'm not sending you to sleep with my chuntering on, am I?"

Esme smiled at her. "Go on."

"So I believe in your freedom, Esme. I can see you're an ambitious woman. You have an urge to get on in life. But I think I see also in the woman you are, something that understands simplicity; how precious it is—how you have to work for it and struggle for it and defend it in this day and age. And then again, you're a spiritual woman; so am I. And if you'll forgive the tedious hearken-to-me of an old woman to a young one, I believe I got to remind you that simplicity is the gateway to spiritual living. You can't have one without the other. That's why you love Jabez—because love him you do, my dear; and I think you'd find yourself in a pretty pickle lost in the barren desert of all they streets and cars without Jabez Ferrall's bicycle shed for a refuge. You was hungry enough in your soul when you first found him. Am I not right?"

"Yes, I suppose so." Esme sighed. She stirred. "I suppose so."

"You got to see, there's something you are overlooking in Jabez. He won't transplant. You might as well try to put a sixty-eight-year-old tree in a clay pot, take it with you to this Surrey, stick it in the flower bed, and hope it'll be all right. Jabez is not just passing through Wiles Green. He was born there. His parents were born there. It's his home. His father was born in the bedroom where Jabez sleeps of a night. Jabez brought his bride to bed in that cottage, and she bore his children there, three of them—two of them grown and gone into the world, and his baby girl buried under the apple tree in his orchard there. He nursed his wife in that cottage when she was sick and 'twas from there that they carried out her body. You might as well take a fancy to tag the moon along with you on the end of a string as try to uproot Jabez from his cottage. The kind of men you mean that move about the world, and the professional women who keep them moving— some of them are sophisticated, some of them are unhappy, some of them are like air plants that thrive on any rock where they perch. But they've forgotten, the whole modern world has forgotten, the meaning of home. And maybe your Jesus was much to blame. Itchy feet, that man. What can you expect, born in a stable, dropped like a bit of baggage at the journey's end. Hardly knew where he belonged, I should think."

"Well, not in this world, anyway," said Esme. "But, thank you, Ember. If I'm honest I hadn't liked to look at it too closely, really. I can't see that I've got many options. I have tried to talk to Jabez about the new job, but he just blanks me out."

She cupped her hands around the warm mug of coffee, gazing thoughtfully into space. "You're right. I do love him. We must surely be able to sort something out."

"Then it may be all down to you, my dear. I told you before, Jabez needs a bit of a shove sometimes. Doesn't like to push himself forward or intrude where he's not wanted."

"Not that kind of man," said Esme, with a smile, downing the rest of her coffee. "Now, what about tonight? Are you staying here? Am I taking you home?"

"Taking me home," replied Ember firmly. "He's not fit to be left alone at present. Almost made hisself sick sobbing this night."

"*What?*" Esme stared at Ember in horror. "For goodness sake! Okay, let's go. I'm ready, I'll just get my coat."

Ember looked at her speculatively.

"What?" Esme asked her.

"I'll just use your lavatory if I may," Ember said, coyly. It rang a little odd, but it passed Esme by—"Oh, I'm sorry, I should have asked you before," she said. "There's one downstairs and one upstairs."

"Upstairs, please," Ember replied decidedly and headed purposefully for the stairs.

While Ember was in the bathroom, Esme went back into her study to tidy away confidential files and shut down her computer. Then she went out to put her bike away in the garage, returned to lock the back door, and find her car keys, after which Ember appeared on the stairs, clutching her coat about her, ready for the outdoors.

"'Tis cold tonight," she remarked conversationally. "I hope the blossom don't get frosted."

Esme felt concerned about Jabez, but she enjoyed the drive to Wiles Green, the stars shining down from a clear sky until she lost sight of them as the road dipped down between the trees and hedges, and the moonlight flicked barred on her car through the branches overhead. There coming up from the ditch her headlights picked out a fox sliding silently into the undergrowth, and alongside the field gate the striped face of a badger watching them go by.

When they reached Wiles Green and turned off the road, Ember suggested they park the car in the lane—there might be too little space to turn around in the yard with the way Jabez had left the truck parked, not expecting Esme to come tonight, she explained—and reassured Esme they would be in nobody's way. This seemed sensible enough, so they left the car in the lane and walked together along the path around to the kitchen door.

"Freezing in here, stove's out," muttered Ember as she stepped into the house. "I left him in the living room," she added.

Esme looked toward the door that led into the house. No lights had been turned on, but in the living room maybe there was a glow of firelight she could see. With a sudden feeling of apprehension, guilty at the unhappiness she had caused, she went hesitantly through from the kitchen into the room beyond.

Bright moonlight shone into the room and found the silver lights of his hair. He was sitting with Ember's blanket pulled around his shoulders, gazing at the glowing remains of the fire, very still. Even in the kindness of shadow and firelight, his face looked haggard and lost and old.

"Jabez?"

He looked up in amazement. "Esme!" He stared at her. "What time is it?" he asked, bewildered.

"Nearly two o'clock, I think. Ember came to find me. She said you were really upset."

He moved his hand in a vague gesture of deprecation. "I'm all right. What do you mean she came to find you? *Walked*, you mean?"

Esme nodded. "Yes. It's taken her hours. Jabez, can I put the lamp on? I can hardly see you."

"Of course," he said. As she turned back to him from the light switch, he was blinking from the comparative brightness, and then as he adjusted to it, she looked at him more closely, his eyes baggy and bloodshot, his face ravaged from weeping.

"Jabez, you look exhausted! You look absolutely done in. Oh, I'm so sorry about what I said; I didn't mean to hurt you so. It'll be all right, we can work something out."

Ember appeared in the door behind her.

"Exhausted? He's not the only one. And if he's tired, then it's time he was in bed. I'm going that way myself. You, too, my love. I've brought your night things."

"I beg your pardon?" Esme was beginning to feel out of her depth.

"I brought your night things from your bed at the parsonage. Have some sense, Esme. Look at the state of him. I'm tired, you're tired, *he* looks like he died last week. What did you hope to do? Try and have a conversation with him? You'll have to save that till the morning."

"But where will I sleep?" said Esme.

Ember looked at her very hard. "Well, not in my bed, for that's where I shall be in five minutes. You can work something out between you, I should imagine."

Jabez pushed his hand, trembling with weariness, across his face and through his hair. "I'll sleep on the sofa," he murmured.

"I don't think so," retorted Ember, shortly. "You've let the kitchen stove go out, and you don't look like you're about to spring to your feet and build up the fire beside you. I certainly am not planning to forage for firewood at such an hour of the night. And I'll want my blanket for my own bed, thank you. Seven miles I've walked for you this night, Jabez Ferrall. I've fetched her back for you. I've filched her night things out of her bedroom to satisfy your modesty. Pull yourself together! Think of a better way to keep warm."

With that she unbuttoned her coat and produced from

within its folds Esme's nightdress, which she tossed onto the floor at his feet, dragged the blanket off his shoulders, and trailed it behind her as she clumped up the stairs. They heard the decisive closing of her door.

Jabez dropped his face into his hands. "Oh, my God," Esme heard his groan, muffled.

She couldn't help laughing. "Oh, for goodness sake, Jabez, it's not so bad! We're grown-up people. I'm forty-five, you're sixty-eight, I don't suppose it will wreak havoc with our innocence to share a bed together, will it? For one night?"

He didn't move.

She stepped closer to him to pick up her nightdress, and as she stooped she put her hand on his knee. "Please, Jabez. Let's go to bed."

He rubbed his face and his eyes, then put his hand down to squeeze hers gently where it lay on his knee. He looking entirely dazed, bewildered with weariness and emotional exhaustion.

"Jabez?" she said.

Jabez sighed, a long, deep, shuddering sigh. He turned his head to look at her, and Esme had a sense of him drawing upon resources deep within, summoning the last dregs of energy to face this thing properly, say what he wanted to say. She knelt down on the floor beside him, waiting for him to frame what was inside him. His eyes dark and deep held hers, serious—all his soul looking out at her there.

"Esme, I understand the common sense of it. 'Tis late,

I'm worn out, here are you, there's one bed. But it isn't as simple as that, is it? What's held out here is a possibility to be one. What Ember has in mind, and what you and me are not saying, is this isn't about sleeping, not one bit. It's about you and me making love."

He smiled then, and lifted his hand to her face, his fingertips delicately tracing the outlines of her cheek. "Tired I may be, but if I let my mind dwell on that, I don't feel very sleepy, and I think you may know by now, I wouldn't need much persuading."

He hesitated a moment, then continued, finding the courage to be honest:

"I been so lonely, Esme. At night in bed sometimes I could have wept for loneliness. Just for a cuddle, to feel someone warm beside me. Some nights I been lying here hugging the pillow for some comfort. I been so terribly lonely. And I love you so much. It seems like forever I've longed for you and loved you. Only I never dared offer myself, because I've got nothing to give you, and I couldn't see how I could fit in with your life. What we're talking about now is what I've dreamed for, yearned for, wanted more than I can find the words to say. Don't you know that? Surely you could see?

"But for all that, I got to say, I can't really approve of this. Love is something faithful, something that endures. If what you're planning is to move away from Wiles Green and leave me, then I think we'd do wrong to look for any kind of union more than the friendship we already have—and always will have. Oh, my dearest! You *must* know, my body's yours, and my love, and all that's mine to give, if you'll have me; but I just think it should be not at all or forever. We got to sort ourselves out first, before we get into this. We got to have an understanding. Esme, I can't reach out for something that's only a mirage, a union for only one night. It's too important to me. I love you too much for that. It would be unbearable. It would break my heart."

Watching him, listening to him, Esme discerned the intensity of his soul unconcealed in his eyes searching hers and the vulnerable uncertainty of his mouth.

"Am I too old-fashioned?" he said, anxious. "Did you want us to—do you mind?"

Esme smiled. "Don't worry, I think it'll be all right," she said gently. "We can talk about it in the morning. We've got each other. We've got time. It'll be okay."

Remembering her first swift instinct that here was a man who would never cheat her, gratitude and trust quickened in the very roots of her soul for the honorable patience of his love.

"Then, are we—" he hesitated. "I mean—do you want to be … Esme, what are we to one another?"

Esme did not reply. She lifted herself to kneel up, close against him as he sat on the couch, taking him into her arms. She held him to her, her heart opening to a flood of protective love, moved to compassion for his defenseless longing for her and the humility of his self-offering. She stroked him gently, brushing her lips against his face, until with a small, half-suppressed groan of yearning, his mouth found hers and he kissed her—hungrily, urgently—very thoroughly, she thought, for a man with so many reservations. Held close in the ardor of his embrace, she felt his heart beating against hers. It was answer enough. As he kissed her again, every trace of reserve in her melted. She closed her eyes and let her whole being open to his passion and tenderness, the exquisite gentleness of his love.

He kissed her brow, her cheeks, her throat, lost in his wanting her, the irresistible hunger of his love.

And then he just cradled her, his love enfolding her; for each of them homecoming, heart's desire, completion.

"That's all right, then," he said eventually, and he sat back on the sofa, looking at her in the lamplight, his eyes shining with the joy of finding himself loved.

"For tonight, sleep in my bed, my lady. I'll make up the fire down here. No doubt I've a bit of kindling in the kitchen; and I believe I may have another blanket if I look.

"Come on, then," he said, as Esme stood up and he pushed himself up onto his feet. He stood a moment, letting his body adjust, cramped from sitting so long, then took her hand and led her toward the stairs.

"We got no electricity upstairs," commented Jabez as she followed him up, "but there's a candle in the bedroom."

Esme felt the same sense of curiosity and excitement as

she had on the first day he welcomed her into his cottage as he opened his bedroom door and lit the candle that stood by a box of matches on the windowsill just within the doorway.

The head of his bed, a big bed—his marriage bed, Esme thought—stood against the breast of the chimney that passed through on its way up from the living room below. A wardrobe with a simple door of boards had been built into the recess on one side of the chimney and shelves crammed with books into the other alcove. In front of the bookshelves stood a small table with a glass of water.

He turned back the covers of the bed. "Here 'tis, then. I hope you'll be comfortable," and with gentle and humble simplicity he took her into his arms and drew her to him one more time. He closed his eyes and pressed his lips against her forehead, moving his face tenderly against hers.

"Good night, my dearest, my darling, my love," he whispered. "Sleep well. God bless you."

She settled her head against the curve of his shoulder, and Jabez pressed his lips against her hair. Here in his cottage, held in his arms, Esme felt a sense of homecoming and peace.

"Time for bed," he said eventually, and smiled at her, leaving one last kiss upon her brow.

Jabez closed the door quietly behind him as he left her in his bedroom in the candlelight, and Esme listened to his footsteps on the stairs. She shivered as she changed into her nightdress and climbed into the cold, unfamiliar bed. It felt strange, and she missed him, wanting him there beside her.

Downstairs, Jabez, who had lied about both the blanket and the kindling, turned out the light and curled up as best he could under such warmth as his coat offered for a covering on the couch. He didn't mind but closed his eyes in peace.

"Thank you," he whispered into the grateful dark, "thank you, thank you. Oh, please let me have this. Please don't let her leave me. Please don't let her go."

When Esme awoke from a deep and peaceful sleep, she felt completely disoriented for a minute to find herself in an unfamiliar bed. The room had filled with the clear light of day, and through the window, which Jabez kept ajar, poured the glory of a blackbird's song.

As the night's events reassembled themselves in her consciousness, Esme wondered about what lay ahead. She supposed that a properly responsible woman would have viewed the future with misgiving. But any such qualms were lost in the beautiful peace she felt, lying in the homely simplicity of Jabez's bedroom washed in spring sunshine, aware of the distant household sounds of someone riddling the ashes in the kitchen stove, and of the absolute security of the cocoon of love she felt around her.

She stretched her body luxuriously in the bed and yawned. Then presently she got up and picked up her clothes discarded on the floor, dressed herself, and went down to find Jabez and Ember.

"Slept well?" asked Ember innocently. "Jabez has gone out to the shed for some kindling. We'll have the kettle on anytime soon."

"Where's your car, Esme?" asked Jabez as he came in with his arms full of wood.

"I left it just off the road in the lane," Esme explained—"Ember thought it would be tricky to turn around again in the yard."

Jabez didn't answer her at once. He slipped the logs into the basket and dropped the kindling wood in his hand onto the floor in front of the stove. Ember busied herself with getting together breakfast crockery.

"Atmosphere!" exclaimed Esme. "*Now* what's wrong?"

Jabez squatted before the stove and poked in various twists of paper and torn card, striking a match to set light to these before slowly adding the kindling as the flames took hold.

"Two things," he said. "Two things that Ember knows. First is that every car has a reverse gear and is well able to get out the same way it got in. Second is that Wiles Green gets up early, and if your car was in my lane at first light this morning, all the village will know it by midday, not sparing the chapel. Ember, you really have surpassed yourself, I hardly know what to say to you."

Ember took the jar of oats and the saltcellar off the shelf in readiness for making porridge.

"You'll just have to make an honest woman of her then, won't you?" she replied, undented.

"Yes, I see what your intention was." Jabez glared at her over his shoulder, really annoyed. "But I just think you should mind your own business for five minutes!"

Ember ignored this remark, but Esme smiled happily.

"I think it'll be all right, Jabez. Diplomacy and subterfuge come easily to ministers. It's the only way to come through the job alive. Let's say a pastoral visit—you know; you weren't well. Didn't Ember walk all the way to Southarbour to find me? Surely that must have been a pastoral emergency? Anyway, I thought you wanted to marry me. That seemed to be what you were saying last night."

Ember leaned past him to get the kettle from the hot plate and took it to the sink to fill, all without a word, but Esme could see the mischievous grin on her face as she carried the water back and set it on the top of the stove.

Jabez continued slowly to feed the firebox with wood, blowing gently on its contents.

"I did hear you," he said after awhile, "but I expect you'll be wanting a cup of tea as well as an answer."

Having satisfied himself it was well alight, he fitted in a small log and closed the door, adjusting the draft to get it burning briskly.

He stood up and wiped the soot and wood ash from his hands onto his trousers.

He turned around in the small kitchen and contemplated her. The evasion, the quick glances, the wild creature hiding had all gone. His eyes looking down at her were purely happy.

"I can't think why you would want me," he said. "I am nothing and I got nothing and that's how it's likely to stay. But I do like to go about things properly. If you and me are going to be together, then it's going to be for real."

And he went down on one knee before her and took her hand in his. "Esme, I'm yours if you want me. Will you marry me?"

"Oh, yes," said Esme, wondering how much joy the human spirit could contain. "Oh, yes! The details we can work out later on."

On both knees then, he drew her close to him and touched his lips to hers. "I'd like to kiss you properly too," he said, "but not while we've got an audience. That's private."

"Private! Ha!" Ember opened the tea caddy and ladled two spoons of tea leaves into the pot. "If you'd been let to keep your private life private, you wouldn't have one at all, Jabez Ferrall! I reckon I *deserved* to be a witness to that."

She regarded them with shining, inscrutable eyes.

"And I'm very happy for you both, except I think you took a devil of a long time about it. Hang back? I've never seen a man like it, so help me I have not. I'll get the milk in then, for I don't suppose you have."

On the shingle beach at Southarbour, Esme found a spot where the banked pebbles and the wooden groyne, green with weed, made a shelter against the sharp spring wind that cut so cold.

Sitting there, no one and nothing between herself and the meeting of the supple ocean with the wide grey sky, she allowed the thoughts to come.

There would be no future, then, such as she had planned. No career. There would be the satisfaction neither of success nor of admiration. Her friends and acquaintances—most of all, her family—would have come to see the solid, respectable, unimaginative amplitude of the suburban parsonage, unwitting temple of complacency; and they would have been impressed. Should she against her better judgment allow them to see her in the setting of Jabez Ferrall's cottage, they would most likely think she had taken leave of her senses. And then—how could they visit her there without meeting Jabez and (even more to the point) Ember? Esme brooded on this. She couldn't get as far as visualizing her family's reaction—it was impossible to imagine introducing Ember to them at all. Her movement from full-time itinerant ministry to the precarious territory of local appointment—an honorarium or a half stipend at best; filling gaps in colleagues' absences, gleaning unwanted funerals and helping out with weddings—it would draw puzzled pity, questions, along with the inevitable inability of modern people to understand Jabez and his sense of home. It would be impossible to explain that he would expect to live with his wife—and live with her in his own cottage, and that was just how it was; a way of being that had no dialogue with contemporary employment structures. In today's world, a professional woman with savvy tended her career, watched her back, and saw to her pension. If Esme chose Jabez, she would grow old into grinding poverty, torn at times no doubt between the necessity to earn a living and being there to care for Ember and Jabez as the frailties of old age began to make themselves felt.

She wondered, "What have I done?" but at the same time registered with mild surprise her lack of dread or regret or apprehension. Her place in the institution of the church with its bureaucracy and liturgy and petty feuds failed to fix her attention. Without noticing the shift, as she looked out over the patient tides of the ocean waves, her mind drifted, and she began to think about silver. Silver had been tarnished in the narrow world of tradition that shuts out life, reduced to thirty coins that betrayed a man to death. But even silver, the currency of human greed, had kept its beauty if she remembered to open her vision to the living earth.

The silver of the clouds in this overcast day, underlit by a barred wash of rose as afternoon drew toward evening. The muscular rippling of the sea, reflecting the brightness of the sky like pewter, silvery bright along the paths of the light. The silver, clear light of day; not the squinting glare of cloudless midsummer, but this cool and lucid dove-light. She thought of Jabez's hair, as the sunlight caught it, the faintest suggestion of auburn warming its stranded silver fall—youth's last allusion.

Jabez ... the look in his eyes. Observant. Perceptive. Shy

sometimes, bright glances other times. Fleetingly, in the midnight garden, the utter longing of his love. Warm in laughter. The downward gaze of controlled annoyance when Ember needled him to exasperation. Quiet gaze, intelligent, focused on a piece of machinery. Shafts she had glimpsed, steep drops to remembered pain; dizzy, acute, frightening. Jabez, his eyes dark and deep in the shadow and moonlight, drawing her to himself, gentle.

She had made her choice, and there were no regrets.

Jabez had little or nothing to offer her but himself and the willingness to share with her everything he had. To take this path, considered prosaically, was to embrace poverty and insecurity.

But Jabez, with his humble trust in the power of simplicity, gave her an obscure sense of safety; as though his cottage, hedged about with its fragrant herbs and ancient apple trees, was a sanctuary where she could be absolutely safe; the place, she realized, where she had at last found peace.

And she knew that she wanted to be there with him more than anything. Having found her way there, if she could believe the goodness in life enough to stay, it would be a shelter and a resting place. Friendship, honesty, belonging; a fireside, a home, simplicity, and space. Having found her way there, it was too precious to let go. She had made her choice as, in the unfolding months of deepening friendship, she had let all that it meant lodge inside her and become a deep, upwelling, crystal source of hope. It was like a church to her;

like the little church she had glimpsed in a field from the train so long ago. A place of refuge, a way of life offering space to be and time to think, a chance to feel with her fingers the dusty hem of Christ's homespun robe, and find the daily walking meditation of the barefoot way of prayer.

... a little more ...

When a delightful concert comes to an end,

the orchestra might offer an encore.

When a fine meal comes to an end,

it's always nice to savor a bit of dessert.

When a great story comes to an end,

we think you may want to linger.

And so, we offer ...

AfterWords—just a little something more after you

have finished a David C. Cook novel.

We invite you to stay awhile in the story.

Thanks for reading!

Turn the page for ...

• **Discussion Questions**

• **A Conversation with Penelope Wilcock**

Discussion Questions

At the beginning of the novel, Esme reads words she had written years ago about a country church she saw through a train window. What do you think this church represents to her?

What contributes to Esme's restlessness at the beginning of the novel? How does she begin to move past this feeling?

After Esme's first husband leaves, she throws herself into her work. How do you see this affecting her emotionally and spiritually?

Esme is immediately fascinated by Jabez. Why do you think she finds him so intriguing?

Esme fears what people will think of her if they find out that she feels unable to pray. Do you think pretense is more or less apparent in ministry than other vocations? Why or why not?

Jabez feels the church's prayers for his wife, Maeve, were filled with unreality. What do you think he means by this?

Esme faces the dilemma of choosing fulfillment through professional success or through relationship. Why do you think she chooses not to move?

A Conversation with Penelope Wilcock

The book opens with a quotation from *Grey Owl:* "Down the avenue of trees I can see a spot of sunlight. I'm trying so hard to get there." How does this image relate to Jabez and Esme's spiritual journey?

At the point at which the story opens, Esme is living with an unacknowledged numbness, damage from the loneliness of her role as a minister, from the bereavement of her failed marriage, and from her sense of unfulfillment in terms of personal faith. Jabez is frozen at a place of loneliness and grief after the death of his wife, and is coping, but only just. Though he has a deep personal faith, he finds the answers and attitudes he meets in church unsatisfactory. Yet each of them has an instinct to reach for something that makes sense of life; that brings wholeness, healing, and fulfillment. To reach the place of openly admitted love and need of each other that they are at by the end of the book is a matter of struggle for each of them, permitting vulnerability, risking much. It is the end of one journey toward warmth and light but, as always in life, will be the beginning of another.

The Clear Light of Day is about insight. How do you see this theme illustrated in the teachings of Jesus?

Of the four evangelists, Mark and John focus particularly on this theme. Mark's gospel has a particular teaching structure, seeking to awaken the minds of his readers to the foundational role of suffering in the call of the Messiah. Mark, in his tiny prologue states, "Here begins the gospel of Jesus Christ the Son of God," and what unfolds in the following chapters is an invitation to insight, to understand who Jesus is and what he came to do.

The first chapters are full of questions: "Who is this that even the wind and sea obey him? Who is this who can forgive sins? Who is this who can heal the sick and cast out demons?" etc. Then Jesus asks his disciples, "And you—who do you say I am?" ("I am" of course is the name of God.) This question, and Peter's consequent confession of faith, follows on the heels of the healing of the blind man. And Peter is commended by Jesus for his faith, but then sharply rebuked ("Get behind me, Satan") for remonstrating with Jesus about the necessity of Christ's suffering and death.

There then follows a block of teaching about the crucial necessity for Jesus to suffer and die, and in the middle of this block of teaching, at the midpoint of the gospel, comes the Mount of Transfiguration where Jesus is revealed in glory for who he is. At the end of the teaching on suffering comes the healing of blind Bartimaeus, one whose sight is instantly restored—and then the Passion narrative begins to roll, culminating in the declaration of faith by the unnamed outsider, the Roman centurion—"Surely this man was the Son of God" (bringing us back full circle to the prologue). Thus one can see, the whole gospel is about attaining insight into who Jesus is (the Son of God) and what that means (accepting the role of Suffering Servant). The central teaching block about suffering, in the middle of which Jesus blazes forth in transfigured glory, flanked as it is by the two healings of blind men, the first representing Peter who saw but not properly, the second representing the disciple who follows in the way of the cross (Bartimaeus is described as following Jesus "in the Way" after his healing), is all about revelation and insight; hence the healing of blindness being the miracle chosen.

In John's gospel, the presence of Christ is portrayed as light moving through a dark world. From the prologue, which speaks of light present but not recognized, not understood, but never extinguished, through the miracles that John calls "signs" (pointing the way to us or helping us understand), and through the teachings that speak of Jesus as light and exhorting the faithful to work while the light is with them for the dark times will come, light and vision are central themes. This culminates in the story of the resurrection morning (John 20:1–10), where Peter and the beloved disciple run to the garden tomb. The English word "saw" occurs three times in this story, but each time it means something different in the Greek. First, the beloved disciple "sees" (glimpses, catches sight of) the grave clothes, but does not go in. Then Peter goes in, and he "sees" (examines, scrutinizes) the grave clothes and the head-cloth, then the beloved disciple also goes in, and he "sees" (catches on, gets it, understands) and believes. So it's about entering in, and about the movement of light and dark: In the darkness of the tomb, the light of faith and insight awaits them; as they enter the darkness, the light enters them.

The Gospels are wonderful documents, and insight is a central theme in the Gospels: The teaching of Jesus fits into that overall communication, teaching who he was, what he came for, and the cosmic spiritual shift effected by his redeeming death on the cross.

The Clear Light of Day follows the quest of an ordained minister's personal search for inner peace. How does Esme begin to find her way out of formality and into a natural expression of her faith?

The Clear Light of Day is intended as the first book of a trilogy. In this book, Jabez and Ember each have quite a clear and settled outlook on life, but Esme is reaching for something that feels more real to her than what she currently has. Right at the end of the book, because of the healing that comes about in her through being loved, and because of the glimpses she is reaching of a vision of simplicity, Esme comes to a position of hope that her uncertainties and restlessness may begin to resolve. I am working at present on the second book of the trilogy, *The Light Returning,* which will explore the relationship between the spiritual and the physical, and the natural rhythms of the seasons with the teaching of the Christian faith.

Like Esme you have served as a minister in the Methodist church. Is *The Clear Light of Day* in any way autobiographical?

I think maybe all novels must be a little autobiographical. I have been pleased to find that readers of *The Clear Light of Day* who are Methodist members, in the different Methodist circuits where I had worked, all thought it was their circuit I was writing about. So I guess there must be something true to life there. But Esme is not me, though I am familiar with the dilemmas and stresses of her working week.

after words

The novel seems to suggest that spirituality is expressed in the daily rhythm of life. How does this view of spirituality differ from one that creates a false dichotomy between the secular and the sacred?

On British television recently, we saw a program called *God Is Green*, which threw a challenge to all the mainstream religions, especially to those in leadership, regarding their silence about the serious issues of climate change and global warming that face us all. The problem for church leaders, of course, is they are so busy doing all that must be done in service of the organization, there is no way they have the leisure for the detailed thinking and transformation that such challenges as climate change and global warming require. In order to discover and exercise vision, we have to disentangle from the treadmill of maintaining the status quo, and take time and space to be with the silence of what is real, like Jesus going into the desert. I believe that spirituality is holistic and expresses itself essentially in attitude and in choice. However holy we feel, however fervently we praise God, if the small daily choices we make don't celebrate the Creator in his creation, or serve the Redeemer in loving his lost sheep, or reverence the mystery and wonder that encounters us in the ordinary moments of life, then we haven't grasped the meaning of righteousness.

As a pastor, I found this especially challenging. I once heard a member of one of my congregations say with appreciation and approval, regarding an act of worship led by a visiting preacher, "We told her what we wanted, and that's exactly what she did." My difficulty was always that fulfilling the expectations and established traditions of my congregations never allowed me to demonstrate and develop my own sense of call and vision, which saw things differently.

At the present time, I am working out a new form of expression for my ministry and am not currently the pastor of a congregation. I believe that the threshold of all spiritual practice is simplicity. Without simplicity, the spiritual path can't even get started. I am establishing a spiritual daily path that practices the presence of God in the detail of everyday life. I preach and teach about faith, life, spirituality, and practice healing, craft liturgy and ceremony, conduct retreats, and write about the way of faith. Other than that I live very, very quietly, eating simple food mindfully prepared, chosen with thought to honor the Creator in his creation. I consciously create beauty, and do not engage in fast and worldly pursuits. I focus on modesty and reverence, on quietness and prayerfulness. I think about the links and consequences that my actions and choices set in motion—the journey that will be made by the coins I spend in purchases I make: Who will they enrich? Will they bless my neighborhood community by becoming part of the trade network of family businesses, or impoverish it by being taken away for the pockets of corporate giants and their shareholders? The food I eat: Will it make me calm and peaceable, healthy and alert for service and positive relationship—or will it make me nervy, tired, aggressive, and ill, one who has to be served rather than serving?

I believe, along with so many other people of faith, that God speaks through the joy and immediacy of creation. So I touch the presence of God in the birds in my garden and in the ancient stone of the pillars in the parish church and in the flowing of rivers, clouds driven by the wind, the currents of the sea.

And most of all, the light—ordinary light; sunlight, firelight, starlight, the light that shines out of all living beings—light is a carrier of mystery, and acts as a parable for me, of the Christlight, of the light that betokens the presence of the living God, of the light that is shining in a person when they wake up, when faith is born.